Goodness Mercy

Book Two, Mercy Me Mysteries

By Tracy L. Ward

Willow Hill House

Ontario, Canada

GOODNESS MERCY

First Edition
ISBN: 978-0-9958914-8-7

Cover Art Copyright © 2019 by Jessica Allain

Edited by Lourdes Venard, Comma Sense Editing

For the girl in the library
who already has a pile of books
waiting to be read at home.

TRACY L. WARD

Chapter 1

Toronto, 1890—Mercy Eaton hadn't set foot in a graveyard in nearly two decades. The dead never rested, not while she was around. Their souls would perk up, take notice, and come forth demanding to be acknowledged. Their energy would attack her, wave after wave of twisted and oft-deformed existence. She never saw them, only felt them, like blocks of hardened air every which way she turned. A maze of spiderwebs, unseen and only felt, tangling Mercy up, wrapping around her as she moved, encasing her, making it nearly impossible for her to truly break free.

She would have rather done anything else than follow Detective Jeremiah Walker into the Necropolis in the dead of night and yet, not unlike the souls of the departed, she was tangled up in him, lured by his energy, drawn to be as close to him as possible. She was falling in love with him and she was beginning to hate herself for it.

"She said the body was over here," he said, unaware of Mercy's struggles. He was already ahead of her by a number of paces, his lantern giving very little light compared to the blackness of night. She could forgive his neglect. Their macabre task had been sprung at them among a fit of wails and lamentations from his recently returned wife, who remained holed up at his house hiding from the gallows. Walker's mind was obviously elsewhere. Mercy could not fault him for that.

She resisted the urge to call out to him as her space was flooded with the dead. She felt swarmed, the spiderwebs having morphed into pinpoints which encircled her, gaining momentum as they funnelled around her entire body. Were they fighting for her attention or merely fighting among themselves?

If there was a body she could quench their incessant needling by touching it. Skin-to-skin contact worked best.

She could use the skills she had discovered when she was seven years old and learn of the deceased's life in a matter of seconds. In a graveyard there were no bodies, no easily accessible ones in any case, and so there was no way for her to end their needling of her, no way to appease their frustration.

She leaned on a nearby grave marker to catch her breath and recalibrate her equilibrium. Not completely recovered from her last escapade with Detective Walker, she felt light-headed and short of breath. She closed her eyes against the mob. "Please," she whispered into the night, "not now."

When she opened her eyes again Walker was standing right in front of her, his lantern aloft. "Are you all right, Ms. Eaton?"

Mercy looked about them. The spectres were gone, their essence evaporated.

"I knew this was a bad idea," Walker said. "You're too weak. I'm escorting you home." He moved closer as if to pull her from the stone, to guide her away.

"No," Mercy said, wriggling from his grasp. She met his gaze. "I can do this." She could not move far, however, and was forced to remain where she was. He was not a large man, but he certainly had the air of one, a commanding presence that at first intimidated her but now endeared her to him. She suppressed a smile at the thought of it. Now was not the time.

An hour before, she had professed her love for him and for a moment it appeared he might have been prepared to profess the same until his wife showed up, ruining everything. It was all well and good to love a man who had been abandoned by his wife, but to love a man who was now searching for a dead body in order to protect her? Mercy should really draw the line somewhere.

There was an intimacy in their standoff, a genuine concern on Detective Walker's part. Whatever may have existed between them hours before needed to end, and the sooner the better, for both their sakes.

"Please," she said, breaking their silent stare. "I want to help."

Relenting, Walker took a step back but remained close, unsure how steady Mercy was on her feet. To her surprise,

Mercy could walk without the weighted feeling that had greeted her when they first entered the gates.

The open space was darker than she had expected. The lantern only gave enough light to reveal the closest grave markers but little else beyond. The dead body Ruth had spoken of seemed more a needle in the proverbial haystack. The details of its exact or even general location were sketchy, her panic overriding her directional aptitude.

"She said it was nearer Amelia Street," Walker said, once again leading the way, however much slower this time.

"She also said something about Winchester." Mercy looked back toward the entrance to the cemetery. Both streets were at opposite sides of the burial ground. Mercy stumbled over a tree root and fell forward, bumping into Walker. Instinctively, he turned and wrapped his arm around her to keep her from falling. Had he done this a few weeks ago, Mercy would have pushed him off and made some curt remark about his forward manner, but that night, with the world turned black around them and the noise of the city streets turned to silence, she welcomed his assistance. Perhaps even relished in it.

"Careful there," he said, loosening his grip around her but not pulling his arm away.

Seconds passed before Mercy lowered her gaze and stepped back, signalling her return to balanced footing. She managed a quick thank you before releasing a steadying breath. Her heart thundered beneath her chest as her stomach fluttered. Why did he have to smell so delicious? Had she not stepped back how long would he have held onto her?

She forged ahead in an effort to forget the intimacy between them. Within two steps she saw the outline of something ahead of them. "Bring the lantern," she said, reaching behind her and waving Jeremiah forward. The light was dim but it was enough. Slumped at the base of a large monument lay the body of a man, blood staining the front of his white, tailored shirt and dark grey suit.

"It's true," Mercy said as Walker drew closer to the body. "She wasn't embellishing."

Part of Mercy had hoped Ruth was merely overwrought, that her proclamations of doom and gloom were more indicative of her penchant for melodrama and not actual fact. Faced with a real body, a slain man dressed and abandoned where Ruth had told them to search, Mercy now realized the severity of trouble Ruth was in. And not only Ruth but Walker as well, for he had the misfortune of being married to the woman.

Mercy kept her distance and watched as Walker surveyed the man's condition. He was indeed no longer for this world and nothing could be done at that point to save him. Ever the detective, Walker placed the lantern nearby and began a search of the body.

"He's been shot," Walker said. "Two bullets... to the stomach."

Mercy winced. He'd have lived on for a few minutes after such an injury. Stomach wounds did not equal instantaneous death. The victim lingered, aware, in pain, praying for it all to end.

"I can read him," Mercy said, stepping forward.

"Don't touch him!" Walker's hand shot up, stopping her from coming any closer. His words were a command, loud and clear. Mercy dared not move. "You are still too weak," Walker explained, his tone softening. "I cannot risk it."

Mercy did not protest.

"Look for a weapon," he said. "It's most likely small... a handgun."

Mercy hadn't the faintest clue what to look for exactly. She'd only ever seen such a weapon once, perhaps twice, and each time she'd never gotten a good look of it. In the darkness, it could be anywhere and she hadn't the advantage to direct the light.

Walker pulled back the man's overcoat and searched his inside breast pockets before moving on to the pockets of the trousers. There was money, change mostly, a spring knife, and a small collection of business cards wrapped with a rubber band.

A flicker of light to their right caught Mercy's attention. Nearer the gate Mercy could see the outline of a person, a lantern held out in front of them. "Walker, someone's coming!"

As soon as she spoke, their own lantern light was extinguished. She heard a sound of metal, as if Walker had snatched up their light from the ground, and seconds later he was grabbing her waist and guiding her behind a large monument not ten feet away. In the darkness she felt him pressing against her, gently leaning her back into the tall stone. He stood in front of her, a single finger pressed into her lips to keep her quiet.

They waited as the seconds passed and her eyes adjusted to the absence of light. Walker was directly before her, his face inches from her own, his breath warming the skin of her collarbone. She felt herself weakening with the smell of him. She could kiss him. She very much wanted to. And he would kiss her in return. She knew he would. The appropriateness of such an action remained in question, given his current marital status, and the fact that they were about to be caught trespassing in the cemetery at night, but such details were minor when passion was involved.

Walker slowly leaned to the side to peer around the corner of their hiding place and quickly snapped back.

"I saw something," came a voice from the darkness. "Over here!" The voice was only feet from them. Past Walker's shoulder, Mercy could see weak shadows playing on the ground and gravestone as whoever held the lantern walked around. Straining to hear, Mercy could detect another set of footfalls quickly catching up to the man who had called out.

"Lovers?"

A laugh escaped the first man and the movement of the shadows came to a stop. "Not unless she finally grew tired of him."

"Holy— Geez!"

The first man laughed. "Get a hold of yourself, will ya? Looks like our report of trespassers just turned into a murder," he said.

"Who should we get? Walker?"

Mercy felt Walker stiffen.

"Nah, we can handle it, can't we? What can he do that we can't do, huh?"

Mercy couldn't help but smile at this. Oh, how they underestimated him. Since childhood, Mercy had held a natural distrust of the profession, Walker included. She had only recently taken a liking to him after working a case together. Best described as a bloodhound, Walker would follow the trail relentlessly until it caught him his quarry. He didn't abuse the authority bestowed upon him, but he wasn't against roughing up someone deserving. He was fair, that was the only way to describe it. In truth, he was unlike any police officer she had ever known.

And it had been so very easy for her to fall in love with him.

She felt him tugging at her arm. "We have to go," he whispered. "They'll be back and we can't be discovered here."

Mercy looked back in the direction of the body. "Let me read it," she said. "It can tell us things."

"No, not after what happened last time."

He pulled her away, weaving deftly between tombstones, heading for the gate opposite than the one they had entered.

"Walker, please!" She tugged back on his arm, forcing him to stop. "Why did you bring me here with you if you weren't going to use my gift?"

In the dim light she could see him looking directly at her, the shine of his eye moving about as if searching for the answer to her question.

"I don't know," he said at last. "I don't know why I brought you. It was a mistake." He pulled her away.

She thought about defying him and running back. If she got a good enough start, and reached the body a few seconds before he did, he'd not be able to stop the images. She could get a few things at least, perhaps enough to tell them who he was and how he'd come to be shot. She looked back and saw the officers' lights returning. She heard voices in the distance. There wasn't enough time to evade them if she went back. They'd be discovered. She cared little about her own reputation but she had to consider the impact on Walker and his career.

ɚ ꙅ

The hansom cab ride home was a silent one. When they pulled up to the curb outside Mercy's bay and gable home in the heart of St. Andrew's Ward, Walker slipped out the door first and then offered Mercy a stable hand as she traversed down the rickety carriage steps.

"Thank you, Detective Walker," she said sheepishly At that point Mercy just wanted to get inside. The night had been a near-complete charade. It began with her professing her love and would end with him taking the carriage back to his wife. His undeserving wife, but wife nonetheless.

Walker did not release her hand straightaway. The lamplight they stood under betrayed his need to say something that he obviously found difficult to bring to his lips.

He slipped some coins to the driver and motioned for him to move on.

"What is it, Walker?" Mercy asked, taking a half step toward him. Was it now his turn to profess love and adoration? He felt it. She knew it. While she convalesced in the bed the last few weeks she had had plenty of time to think about their interactions. She had replayed every conversation, every stare, every smile exchanged. Prior to that evening she had no doubt that he returned her affection. He had all but confessed her suspicions to be true. She realized he was not free to act upon any of their desires but she thought having heard the truth of his heart would mitigate at least some of the pain she felt for never being able to have him as her own.

"I..." His words came out unsure. "I just wanted to make sure you understood that the events this evening are to be held in confidence."

Mercy raised an eyebrow. "Confidence?"

Walker released a breath. "I imagine it goes without saying but"—he pulled back his shoulders—"I am saying it nonetheless."

Mercy tried to keep her facial features steady. She could not have him seeing her disappointment or guessing at her broken heart. "Yes, of course," she said, so evenly she surprised herself. She forced a closed-mouth smile. 'You have my assurance. Nothing said or done this evening will pass my lips."

He smiled at this and suddenly looked twenty pounds lighter. "Thank you, Ms. Eaton. We will talk soon," he said, as he walked away, heading down the sidewalk. "In the meantime, get some rest. You look tired."

Mercy's mood soured further. It was after midnight and she would have been in bed for hours had it not been for Detective Walker's escapade to save his wife from the gallows. She muttered to herself as she put the key into the lock of her front door. She needn't have bothered. The door sprung open and Edith appeared.

"Mama!" She looked her mother over. "We were just about to go out and look for you."

"No need," Mercy said, slipping inside. "I am perfectly well."

Constance, Mercy's sister, charged from the parlour. "Where have you been at this hour of night?"

"She was with that scoundrel detective, no doubt."

Mercy spied Alexander, Constance's husband, farther in the room. Her reading room, where she met clients, a room that was strictly off limits.

"What are you doing in my parlour?" Mercy asked. She went inside to push in the drawers of her large armoire and straighten the fabric of the table covering.

"We were only looking for clues to where you may have gone," Edith said. She stayed back closer to Constance.

"You were not permitted to leave your bed," Constance said. "You aren't strong enough."

"Forgive me, Connie. There was something I needed to do."

Alexander threw a hand up. "For Pete's sake, you could have at least told your daughter where you were headed. It would have saved us all from being dragged over here in the middle of the night. We were but a few minutes from summoning a constable."

"Am I expected to stand here to be scolded in my own home?" Mercy asked.

"We are only worried for you," Constance said. "Had we known you were with Detective Walker, we wouldn't have been so concerned."

"Speak for yourself, wife." Everyone looked to Alexander. "Nothing good will come of this family's association with him, mark my words." He raised a finger in warning but refused to look toward Mercy at all.

"Well, you needn't bother working yourself into a tizzy on

my account," Mercy said, pushing in one of the chairs to her table. "Tonight was the last of it. Whatever Walker chooses to do from here on out is no concern of mine," she said unconvincingly.

Constance and Edith exchanged knowing glances.

"It's true. Whether you chose to believe it or not," Mercy insisted. "Now, if you'll excuse me, I am very tired and don't entirely appreciate this newly discovered interest into my personal life." She raised her chin an inch and brushed back a strand of hair from her forehead.

Constance looked reluctant to go but she was ushered into the hall by Alexander. "If it were just your personal life you wouldn't hear a peep from me," he said, "but your shenanigans have given my wife the crazy notion that we can raise a child not our own."

At the door he turned in place and looked down his nose at Mercy, as she followed them to the hall. "Should that child ever be left in my care you'll find it right back here on your doorstep, Mercy. And I won't feel a bit of shame about it."

"I imagine not. One must have pride to ever feel an ounce of shame."

"Mercy!" Constance quickly put herself between her husband and Mercy.

"You little trollop!" His voice grew muffled as Constance pushed him out the door.

"Calm yourself, Alex," she said. "Remember what the doctor said."

Mercy secretly wished the man would have a heart attack and die. She'd not feel a smidgen of remorse for having precipitated it.

The door closed a second later and the house fell silent. "Let this be your warning, Edith, marry a man like that and you shall find yourself without a mother."

"Is that why you never married?" Edith asked. "Uncle Alexander scared you away from matrimony."

Mercy chuckled. "Hardly." She turned and headed for the base of the stairs. "I appreciate your concern, darling daughter, but you truly shouldn't have." She put her hand on the bannister. "If I ever go missing again you may console yourself that your dear mama is making a fool of herself yet again and nothing more."

"But what if you are truly in danger next time?" Edith called out as Mercy climbed the stairs.

"There isn't much likelihood of that, Edith dear. Lightning rarely strikes the same place twice." Mercy smiled down to her daughter and then slipped off to her room.

Chapter 2

By morning Mercy had a headache and a pronounced sinking feeling in the pit of her stomach. She must have borne her troubles on her face because Edith's expression fell when she saw her. "Would you like me to stay home from school?" she asked, almost eagerly.

"You'd like that, wouldn't you? Tending your frail and misguided mama, who only has herself to blame for her current state."

Edith shrugged. "Better than another day of ballroom dancing." She pulled a face as she slid a stack of books from the hall table and hugged them to her chest.

"Ballroom dancing? Since when have the sisters of the abbey started teaching you girls ballroom dancing?"

"Since Sister Mary came back from New England. She says it's the epitome of refinement and expects us to use the skills she teaches us to snag ourselves a worthwhile husband."

Mercy raised an eyebrow. "What does Sister Mary know about snagging a husband, a worthwhile one to boot?" Mercy nearly laughed at the thought. "The last thing you need is a husband at fourteen years old."

"Almost fifteen," Edith corrected.

"Your age isn't my concern. I pay a pretty penny to see that you are educated properly and this is the material they deem worthy of attention?" Mercy could feel her blood rising and Edith shrank back at her words, perhaps feeling sorry for ever having brought it up.

"I could stay home," she offered. "You can see I won't be missing much."

"No, Edith," Mercy said, pulling the door open and guiding her daughter to it. "You are going. I'll see you when you get home."

Raven, their black cat, scooted in almost as soon the door was opened wide enough, another night of galivanting to his credit.

"Could you stay out of trouble, at least until I get back?" Edith asked, watching her feet carefully as she stepped outside so she wouldn't tread on their family pet.

"What is that supposed to mean?"

"I miss out on everything."

Mercy found the statement amusing as Edith herself had caused a fair amount of trouble of her own. Thankfully, though, Edith had not been present for the most troubling of events. "Edith dear, there is a reason for that, now off you go before you miss the morning bell."

Mercy closed the door before Edith had the opportunity to say anything else. She may have still been recovering from her mishap but she had bills to pay and that meant there was work to be done, headache or no headache.

Within the hour, however, Mercy regretted her decision not to cancel her clients. The headache had tripled its intensity and it was all she could do to listen to Mrs. Marybelle drone on about her deceased cat, Cinder, who had departed the world nearly ten years before.

"He hadn't a clue what hit him," she said, while she and Mercy stood in front of the door. "The beet cart came out of nowhere and that's why I think he's confused. He follows me around. He doesn't know he's dead."

"He knows he's dead," Mercy said without thinking. She pulled open the door and tried to usher Mrs. Marybelle out.

"Is that what he told you? Just now?" Mrs. Marybelle pointed to the floor.

Mercy followed where she pointed and wondered if the woman believed the cat spirit was rubbing against her legs as she spoke. "In a manner of speaking... yes," Mercy agreed. At that point she'd agree to anything to have the woman go.

"He's choosing to spend eternity with me? Oh, how lovely." Mrs. Marybelle looked to the floor and tapped the side of her skirt. "Let's go, Cinder," she said, as if calling the cat to follow her. "I'll give you a nice saucer of milk when we get home."

Mercy smiled at the image of Mrs. Marybelle's home dotted with untouched saucers of milk. It would be quite the conversation starter she was sure.

A young man was standing on the porch when Mercy opened the door for Mrs. Marybelle. Mercy smiled at the sight of Maxwell London, whom she had known since he was an infant. Now at sixteen years old he was taller than Mercy and sweeter than ever.

"Good morning, young man," Mrs. Marybelle said, nearly pushing him to the side as she manoeuvred her cane. "Careful not to step on my cat."

Maxwell leaned into Mercy as they watched the woman leave to a waiting carriage. "Something must be wrong with my eyesight, Ms. Eaton," he said quietly so only Mercy could hear. "I don't see any cat."

Mercy shook her head. "Because there isn't one." She waved him inside, smiling at the thought of having a sane person to speak with for a while. "Best come inside, Maxwell. I can make us some tea."

Maxwell removed his cap as soon as he entered the foyer and followed Mercy down the hall to the kitchen at the back of the house. "Is Miss Edith around?" he asked hopefully.

"No, darling. Edith has school." She turned the tap at the sink to fill the kettle.

"Oh yes, of course. I just haven't seen either of you in so long... I suppose I was just eager to say hello."

Mercy smiled. It seemed Maxwell had always had a soft spot for Edith. As early as four years old Maxwell had been protecting her from the other children, those who would tease her for her looks or the dark tone of her skin, a legacy passed down from her negro father. And Mercy couldn't have loved Maxwell more for that.

"I'll be sure to tell her you stopped by."

Maxwell tried to suppress a smile and nodded. "I haven't been around all that much. I got a job, you see."

"A job, is it? And here I thought you'd found yourself a girl."

"No, ma'am, there ain't no girl for me but one—" He stopped himself, nearly choking back the word, and then looked up suddenly, hoping Mercy hadn't heard his slip. Mercy had heard it, and added it to the all the other times he had let it known he fancied Edith. She pretended she hadn't heard it, though, as she had done many times before, and moved about the kitchen to prepare their tea.

"I'm working for my uncle," he continued, running his hand through his blond hair. "He said it weren't right what happened to Mama. How she died an' all."

More than a year had passed since Maxwell's mother, Hazel, died from pneumonia, but the pain of it was still fresh on the young man's face. Mercy herself couldn't quite believe such a dear friend was gone. For fourteen years they had depended upon each other, both single mothers raising small children in a world that would rather see the children in orphanages than be reminded that women out of wedlock were capable of having sexual intercourse. Despite the shame the world would have them feel, Mercy and Hazel thrived, raising their children alone yet together. They both made it out of Mercer Reformatory with strength enough to withstand the pressure to give up their children. They were fierce and determined women and Hazel deserved to be there still.

"She was a good woman, your mother," Mercy said, placing a teacup and saucer in front of him. She took a seat opposite him at the table and offered him a cookie from a plate between them. "She's very proud of you, you know."

"Does she tell you that?" Maxwell asked, his mood perking up at the thought of his mother communicating from beyond the grave.

"Oh yes," Mercy lied. "All the time. She loves you dearly and is watching over you. Keeping you on the straight and narrow." Mercy clasped her hand over his and gave a gentle squeeze. "But there's only so much she can do, you know, from the other side. You have to make sure you make good choices, Maxwell, choices that your mother would approve of."

Maxwell nodded eagerly. "I'm trying. Tell her, I'm trying."

"Tell her yourself," Mercy said, lifting her cup to her mouth. "She can hear you."

He smiled.

It wasn't easy lying so often, and to people Mercy cared about. In truth, she hadn't had any contact with Hazel, not since her passing, no matter how hard Mercy concentrated. Her gift with the dead wasn't so much of a gift when it only came under certain circumstances, and it wasn't entirely useful when she still felt as clueless about the afterlife as everyone else.

When Hazel died Mercy did not read her body. The soul's call, the one that beckons for their story to be told, was muted by Mercy's profound grief. She could not have brought herself to read her friend's body. Close friends and relatives had become strictly off limits. Mercy had learned as much the day she accidently read her father. A child of seven couldn't have known such a curse existed. She'd reached out to touch her father's dead hand as he lay in the casket, something she'd always done while he lived. The images that followed were brief but explicit, enough to make the seven-year-old Mercy retch on her mother's prized rug.

"Well, I was hoping maybe you could tell her about my job, so that she doesn't have to worry about me anymore."

Mercy smiled. "She never worried for a minute and neither have I. You are a very capable young man..." Mercy hesitated. "But are you sure you want to be working for your uncle?" She'd never be comfortable enough to tell him the reason for her caution. Hazel herself had told Mercy a story or two about her brother, Ezekiel London, stories that had made Mercy's blood run cold. She wasn't entirely sure Maxwell should be working for such a man.

"I've looked everywhere else," Maxwell said. "He's the only one who'll take me on."

She doubted he had looked *everywhere*, but he certainly wouldn't have been the only young man in the city who had found it difficult to secure a place. Good positions required expertise, something of which a young man of sixteen was surely lacking.

"Then you be sure to do a good job. Perhaps in a year or two you can secure an apprenticeship."

"My mother told you to tell me this?" he asked.

"No," Mercy said honestly. "I'm telling you this. It's best you don't think of yourself as stuck in place. If things don't work out with your uncle you are capable of other types of work, yes?"

Maxwell beamed. "Yes."

Mercy smiled over her cup of tea.

"Ah geez, Ms. Eaton." Maxwell blushed slightly. "You have to let me pay you for your time." He stood and started fishing around in his pocket for payment.

"Certainly not," Mercy said. "I would not accept a dime from Hazel's son. Not now and not ever."

"I can pay my way. I'm a working man now."

"I don't need your money, Maxwell London. I promised your mother I'd look after you, Now, seeing as you're a working man, you aught to get to it or your uncle will be wondering what happened to you."

"Will you tell Miss Edith I stopped by and asked about her?"

"Of course. She'll be sad to have missed you but will be happy to hear you came by."

"May I come again, to see Edith?"

"Of course. Now, go."

Just before he left Maxwell bent in and kissed Mercy on her cheek. "Thank you, Ms. Eaton," he said, beaming in a way only self-assured and enthused young men can.

Chapter 3

"Stay away from the window!" Jeremiah crossed the room quickly to where Ruth stood looking out over the street at the front of the house. He pulled the drapes closed and held them together with clenched fists. "No one can see you. That's part of our agreement."

Jeremiah's wife shrugged with nonchalance and stepped toward the middle of the room. "Tell me, husband, why are there so many crates and boxes all over this place?"

"If you must know, I had decided to move until you decided to show your face again." With the drapes closed, he went back to the mirror above the mantel and finished securing his tie.

"Move where?" Her face came into view in the mirror behind him.

"I was going to move in with MacNeal."

Ruth let out a bemused laughed. "Oh, honey, we both know you are a bit of a cold fish, but there's no reason to turn to the company of men." She placed a hand over her mouth as if to hide her laughter.

"I have not turned to the company of men." Jeremiah eyed her, annoyed by the very suggestion. A comment like that, if made in public, could have been enough to have him arrested. "I am merely interested in saving the cost and, considering you no longer saw need to grace this house with your presence, things were getting somewhat lonely here all by myself."

Jeremiah found it difficult to look at her. Her very presence was disrupting everything he had come to accept about his life. It had taken him six months to realize she was not coming back and a fair amount of that time realizing he didn't want her back. "And I most certainly am *not* a cold fish."

This only incited more laughter. From the other side of the room, she looked at him playfully, as she did when he first began to court her. She was trying to entice him, lure him in with her natural charm. She was accustomed to getting her way, and had been quite successful when it came to Jeremiah. There was a time he would have done anything for her, anything short of committing a crime, and that is where their connection departed. Ruth wasn't above such things, not when the inducement was strong enough.

"I've asked my mother to come by at midday to check on you."

Ruth scoffed. "That old hag."

Jeremiah blanched. His mother may have been a lot of things but she was not a hag and did not deserve such slander, and certainly not at the hands of one the likes of Ruth.

"What about that pretty little thing from last night? Couldn't she come check on me? I'd much rather prefer her company than that of Mrs. Audulay." Ruth was pouting now, another one of her manoeuvres she used to bend others to her will.

"I am aware of this tactic," he said.

"What tactic?"

"You know my mother is unrelenting. She will not give in to you, so instead you aim your sights on a supposedly easier target."

"Boy, you certainly seem to have me *all* figured out." Ruth was being facetious, of course. Even if Walker were close to the mark, she'd never admit it. "Your supposition couldn't be further from the truth. That pretty woman appears far more agreeable than your mother, that's all. If I'm going to be shut up here, I'd like to be with someone at least closer to my age."

Jeremiah scowled. "You will leave Ms. Eaton out of this."

"Oh, Ms. Eaton, is that her name? I should have known she was an Eaton. She has the look of false royalty."

"She is of no relation to Timothy Eaton, so you can get that right out of your head. There is no money there for you to exploit."

"Very well." Ruth was not fazed by this. She was hardly fazed by anything. She'd manoeuvre and scheme and fraud her way through life exploiting any and every avenue presented to her and that is exactly how she'd ended up the wife of Jeremiah Walker in the first place. "She seems a lovely little thing, maybe a bit plain. Her wardrobe could use a bit of sprucing up."

"She does not require any *sprucing up*, not by you in any case. She is a lovely woman and I implore you to leave her be."

"You implore me? Strong words from a married man." Ruth smiled and started taking half steps toward him. "Tell me, husband, is anything going on between you and Ms. Eaton? Anything your unsuspecting wife should know about?"

"Unsuspecting!" Jeremiah scoffed. "The last time we saw each other I told you I was filing for divorce and suddenly you are back in my life, in my home, acting as if you never left and expecting fidelity, something you never seemed to be able to manage, might I add."

"Really, Jeremy, sometimes you can be so harsh."

Jeremiah came toward her, leaning close and showing his frustration. "Harsh? Harsh? I am investigating the death of your lover, or at least whom I suspect was your lover, all in an effort to save you from the gallows. Lord knows why I bother, as I have a sneaking suspicion that even if you didn't pull the trigger that killed the man you must be involved in his death in some manner."

Ruth couldn't look at him, despite his nose inches from her face.

"Tell me then, was he your lover?" Jeremiah pressed. "Your only lover or one in a series of lovers?"

Ruth raised her chin a notch when she turned to face him. Her jaw was tight, her gaze indignant. "What does it matter to you how many lovers I've had?"

"I am your husband," Jeremiah growled. "Maybe that means nothing to you but it certainly means something to me." He turned from her and paced the room. "Maybe this was a mistake. I should take you down to the station and force you to give a statement."

"No, please!" She came to him and grabbed his shirt, forcing him to look at her. "I didn't do it, I swear. I had nothing to do with Edward's death. If I go to the station it won't matter what I say. They won't believe me and you know they won't."

Jeremiah searched her features, looking for signs of sincerity. Somewhere hidden beneath all the emotional games, the manipulation, the tumult was a scared woman trying to make her way in the world. For a time Jeremiah thought he could bring that woman to the forefront, change her life in such a way she no longer saw a need to manipulate her way through life. He had been wrong, of course. Ruth was a woman who knew no other means of getting what she wanted.

"If you want me to help you, you have to do exactly as I say. No arguing. If you want to be saved from the gallows, you are going to do things my way for once."

Ruth nodded eagerly. "Yes," she said. "Yes, of course. I'll do anything. Just tell me what to do."

"Stay away from that window."

"All right."

"Do not leave this house. Don't go out to the back garden, don't walk to the park. Nothing. If you need something, you tell me and I will get it for you."

"Yes. I can do that."

"And you have to be honest with me. If I ask you a question throughout the process of this investigation, any question, you will give me the answer I need, yes?"

Ruth nodded, her enthusiasm for this stipulation markedly subdued. "Yes," she said meekly. "I'll try."

Jeremiah grabbed her under the arm and pulled her closer to him. "No, no I'll try. You will answer my questions honestly or you'll be marching to the station in handcuffs."

Ruth swallowed nervously. "Yes, all right. I understand."

He released her. "All right. His name is Edward. What's his last name then?"

"Dubois."

"French?"

"Quebecois." Ruth emphasized her accent, most likely to show off how cultured she was.

"Where does he live?"

"He has a place in St. David's."

"Where?"

Ruth hesitated.

"Where?" he repeated more forcefully.

"Winchester Street. I don't remember the number." She

smiled. "I was never sober enough—you aren't going to go over there, are you?"

"Of course—"

"You can't."

Jeremiah stared at her blankly, a silent challenge.

She hugged herself as if preferring to slink away. He would most definitely head there after such a response.

"Who do you think did this to him?" he asked. He was approaching her like he would any other witness who was slightly hostile and somewhat untrustworthy.

She shrugged.

"You were there?"

"No."

"But you must have seen his body?"

"Well, yeah. We arranged to meet there at nine. He was dead when I found him. I was scared for my life so I ran here."

Jeremiah eyed her. "You said last night 'they want to see me hang'. Who is 'they'?"

"Them that would do such a thing."

"Ruth—"

"I don't know, Jeremy."

"You do know. You know a heck of a lot more than you're telling me!"

"Only what I told you. We were supposed to meet, but by the time I got there he was bleeding all over, so I came here."

"Could he have still been alive when you discovered him?"

"I didn't check. I just got out of there, 'fraid it would be me next."

Jeremiah chuckled internally at this. So like Ruth. He glanced to the clock above the mantel. "I have to go. I'm already late. Like I said, Mother will be checking up on you around midday. If you aren't here, she will tell me and I will no longer be able to guarantee your safety."

Her mood lightened. She looked almost hopeful. "I'll be here."

"Good. I'll be back as soon as I can." He pulled his jacket from the hook at the back of the door. Before he left, he gave her a look of warning. As he closed the door behind him, he cursed himself for allowing her to weasel her way back into his life.

Chapter 4

Mercy was having a difficult time concentrating for much of the morning. She saw three clients back to back, each one engrossed in their own troubles and questions while her mind was awash with the events of the evening before. She wished she could go back in time and read the body of the man. She was convinced that had she done so they'd know more about the man himself without having to rely on Ruth's own account.

Around mid-morning Mercy made herself another tea and walked it back to her parlour. She passed the hallway table and spied a folded piece of paper with one corner tucked under the vase. 'Ms. Eaton' was written on the outside of the fold.

If you have some time this morning,
please come find me at the station house.
~Walker

She looked to the clock in her parlour. If she left right then she'd have three hours before her next scheduled client. She looked to the note again, wondering why she was even thinking of dropping everything to answer his beck and call. Hadn't she said she was done with him the night before? She had gone to his place to say her piece, to part as friends, and somehow ended up in the middle of a graveyard at midnight stumbling over dead bodies.

Mercy closed her eyes against the absurdity and would have liked to banish the entire episode from her memory. He was a married man. His wife had returned home. He should not be involving her in any more escapades.

She took in the note again and turned it over, looking for any indication of when it may have been written. It could have been any time: that morning, the week prior. There was no way to tell. She couldn't even remember if she had seen it there earlier that day. It looked recent but there was no way of telling for sure.

No, she told herself. Absolutely not. Leave the police work for the policemen.

She stood at her parlour window, which overlooked the front garden, and took a sip of tea. She desperately tried to ignore the itch that told her to go, just to see what it was he wanted. Maybe it was minor, something unrelated to the murder completely. Perhaps she had forgotten something and he needed to return it to her. If that were the case, wouldn't he have just left it on the table instead?

Her mood soured further the more she thought about it. *Damn him.* She put down her tea and marched to the hallway for her hat.

&ewline

Mercy felt more than a little apprehensive as she approached the station house. She was making a fool of herself. Everyone would think she was chasing after him, more than they already suspected. If she cared anything about her reputation, she should keep her distance and let Walker do the chasing. She should not be so willing to abandon her plans for the day because of a simple note.

Would he chase her, though? Certainly not with his wife recently returned home. Perhaps before he might have. There was something there, wasn't there? Something kindling between them. That was before, she reminded herself. And nothing can be done for it now.

The busy hum of the station lowered considerably as soon as Mercy was through the doors. She could feel numerous eyes on her as she approached the desk sergeant. They knew, all of them. They knew she had been taken. They knew Walker had been incensed when he heard the news. They knew it had been Walker who tracked her down and saved her life. Lord knows what else they knew.

"How are you feeling, Ms. Eaton?" the desk sergeant asked, turning his attention from a fellow officer and approaching Mercy from the opposite side of the desk.

"Well enough," she said, hoping he hadn't heard the

quiver in her voice. She could feel the looks behind her, could feel them as if they burned heat onto her neck.

"When we heard you were recovering in the hospital... well, we were all glad for it," he said. His gaze bounced over her shoulder and then back again. He as well could see the attention her presence had garnered.

"Thank you," Mercy managed to say. "Your well wishes were much appreciated."

She felt someone come alongside her and touch her elbow. "Ms. Eaton." MacNeal smiled when she turned to face him. "It's good to see you about. On the mend, are we?"

"Yes, somewhat."

"That's good to hear. We were all very anxious for your recovery, Walker especially."

"Oh." The word escaped her as if merely a breath. She was not entirely surprised but she was surprised by how pleased such a revelation made her feel.

"I apologize, I can't speak for long. I have been assigned a big case, a murder."

"Has Detective Walker been assigned to it as well?" She looked to the hall, half expecting him to waltz out at any moment.

"No, actually. This is to be my first time leading an investigative team," he said. He leaned in and lowered his voice. "A body was found last night shot at the Necropolis. I'm quite tickled by it actually, not the murder of course, but the... the—"

"Opportunity."

He smiled. "Exactly."

"I'm positive you'll do a stellar job, Sergeant MacNeal," she said.

"I appreciate the confidence, Ms. Eaton, but I imagine I'll be looking to Walker for assistance along the way."

Mercy hid her trepidation behind a pasted smile. "I'm sure he will be glad to assist in whatever way you require."

"Ms. Eaton!"

Mercy looked up and saw Walker had just entered the room. Any noise that remained from her entrance was silenced by his sudden appearance. Mercy resisted the urge to run from the building. Why must everything she do be such a spectacle?

Walker approached the desk. "MacNeal, heard you got the Necropolis case," he said.

Mercy sensed a strain in Walker's voice, disinterest to hide his actual interest, but MacNeal didn't seem to notice.

MacNeal's chest puffed out slightly at Walker's remark. "Why, yes. I'm headed there now to observe the scene."

"Leave no stone unturned."

Mercy winced at Walker's words, an accusation hidden among them that implied MacNeal would be anything less than thorough.

MacNeal nodded and turned to Mercy before leaving. "Enjoy the rest of your day, Ms. Eaton."

Walker slid the gate open at the side of the desk, inviting her back into the restricted area of the station. "Care to join me?" he said.

Mercy hesitated, as many eyes in the room were on them.

He must have recognized the attention they were being given. "Thank you for agreeing to come down to the station. I have those papers for you to sign," he said, his voice elevated slightly above his normal volume.

"Thank you, Detective," Mercy said. She gave one final glance to the room before entering the hall. Indeed, by that time, every set of eyes were upon them, concluding any number of things about their connection to each other. Yes, she realized, coming to the station had been a big mistake.

She presented him with the note. "I couldn't determine if you'd written it today or some other time," she said.

He surveyed the paper and smiled. "I left this for you over a week ago," he said.

"Oh..." She should have known. "Edith wasn't at home for me to ask. I shouldn't have come." She turned to leave, not wanting to drag out the embarrassment any further. He stopped her.

"Not at all. I'm glad to see you."

She felt him touch her arm just below the shoulder. It was brief, but intimate. Enough to send a thrill of heat straight to her stomach.

She lifted her eyes just in time to see him take half a step back. She realized someone was coming down the hall. They parted, allowing the officer to pass. When Mercy looked up she saw strain on Jeremiah's face. Was he truly glad to see her?

"Now that you're here, I think I could use you. A woman came into the station earlier this morning," he said, gesturing for her to accompany him down the hall. "She is distraught. Apparently, her husband didn't return home last night and she thinks something may have happened to him."

"Could he be the man we found?" Mercy checked the hall to make sure they were alone but wouldn't say anymore.

"Ruth told me his name was Edward. Mrs. Carver's husband is named James."

Mercy was unfazed by this. "Wouldn't be the first man to lie to his mistress," Mercy offered. "Or his wife, for that matter."

"I suppose it could be a double life," Walker conceded. "I'm trying to figure it all out but... she seems reluctant to say much."

"I don't see how I could be of much help exactly."

"Women trust other women," Walker explained. "Perhaps having you in the room will help her feel more at ease."

Mercy raised an eyebrow. "You want me to sit in with you during an interview?"

"Well, yes, if you are willing."

Jeremiah led the way and opened a door at the end of the hall. Mercy could see the woman through the windowed walls of the room before she turned into the doorway. She was a small, young thing with unruly blond hair and a discoloured blue dress. When she looked up from her handkerchief Mercy saw her red-rimmed eyes and ruddy cheeks. She had been crying for a considerable amount of time, it seemed.

"Mrs. Carver, may I introduce you to Ms. Mercy Eaton. She's going to sit in with us while I ask a few more questions."

"A woman police officer," the woman said, looking Mercy up and down. "Who would have thought?"

"Oh, I'm not"—Mercy looked to Walker, who gave a quick shake of his head—"surprised to hear you say that."

Walker indicated the chair opposite Mrs. Carver for Mercy to sit in and then sat at the very end of the table

Once they were all settled, he opened a dossier folder and revealed a few pages of notes.

"Mrs. Carver, you said your husband, Mr. James Carver, was expected home sometime before ten last night, is that correct?"

After a quick glance to Mercy, Mrs. Carver nodded and then released a sniffle.

"You woke this morning and realized he hadn't been in."

"Yes, it's very unusual. He was on a business trip for a few days."

"Where was his business trip?"

"Boston."

"Does he go there on business often?" Mercy asked before she could stop herself. She avoided Walker's gaze.

"Why, yes," Mrs. Carver answered. "He goes once a month at least, sometimes more frequently."

"He takes the train then?" Walker asked.

Mrs. Carver nodded.

"How long have you and Mr. Carver been married?" Mercy asked.

"Ms. Eaton, that isn't relevant," Walker said.

"Mrs. Carver?" Mercy trained her gaze on the woman opposite her.

"Nearly five years."

Mercy nodded. "And his absence makes you afraid?"

Mrs. Carver struggled to answer. She closed her eyes and made a face as if meaning to hold back her tears. "Yes. This is so unlike him," she said, her voice betraying her desperation.

Mercy reached over the table and clasped a hand over Mrs. Carver's. Immediately, Mercy felt a rush of heat up her arm. The woman's distress radiated throughout Mercy's body. She turned to look at Detective Walker. "It's not him," Mercy said without hesitation.

Walker pulled back his shoulders in surprise. He looked to where Mercy and Mrs. Carver held hands. "Are you sure?"

Mercy nodded. "Yes."

"I don't understand," Mrs. Carver said, hiding half her face with her handkerchief.

Mercy offered a closed-mouth smile. "Mrs. Carver, we

don't know where your husband is," she said as gently as she could, "and trust me when I say that, at this moment, that is a good thing."

Mrs. Carver swallowed nervously and nodded.

æ   ❦

It took Mercy and Detective Walker nearly half an hour to escort Mrs. Carver to her home near the lakeshore. The route that would return Walker to the station house took them down Front Street but it did not take long for Mercy to realize he was in no particular hurry to get back to the office. They walked in silence for two blocks before Mercy decided to come out with it.

"How did you know I would be able to tell if Mrs. Carver's husband was the man from the cemetery?"

"I didn't know," Walker said. "You could have told me you could do that. Would have saved me countless hours, and not just in this case."

"I didn't know either."

Walker stopped and turned to face her directly. "Are you telling me you made up that bit about it not being her husband?"

"No, nothing like that. It's most definitely not him. I could feel it when I touched her. That's never happened before," Mercy said. "At least not that I can remember."

There had been times when Mercy had made assumptions about people; she had known what they did for a living or perhaps the type of home they lived in from a single handshake, maybe even how many children a person had. She had always reasoned it as a lucky guess at the time, and never imagined it was part of her gift of reading people. Reading living people beyond parlour tricks was nothing Mercy had ever been terribly good at. Were she good at it, it would not have taken her weeks to discover Walker was married.

"How was Ruth this morning?" Mercy asked.

"Same old Ruth," Walker said, resuming their slow pace down the sidewalk. "I imagine it would take longer than six months to change a person completely."

Mercy chuckled. "And only if they want to change."

Walker eyed her but said nothing.

"Did you tell her what we found?"

"Yes, some."

"Is she upset?" The woman had been certain she would be hanged for the man's murder. It must have been upsetting to know the body was now in possession of the Toronto Police.

"She hasn't said much," he said with a short release of breath.

"Oh." Mercy found this surprising.

Walker pulled back on Mercy's arm, forcing her to turn to him. "Ms. Eaton—"

Three pops rang out from farther down Station Street, followed by the high-pitched scream of a woman. When Mercy looked, she saw a handful of people running from the Station Street doors of Union Station and more pouring out from the track side.

"Stay here," Walker commanded before charging through the intersection of Front and York Streets, narrowly escaping the crush of carriage wheels. Never good at doing what she was told, Mercy followed him across the street, less than ten paces from him.

Mercy watched as he bounded over the many sets of tracks on the north side before reaching the building. She was forced to walk slower from fear the heels of her boots would be caught between the wood planks and the metal of the tracks.

Walker turned his back into the wall just outside the front doors of the train station and pulled his gun from his inside pocket. At the sight of the weapon, Mercy froze. She wasn't sure what she had just heard but now, with a pistol in front of her, she knew it had been gunshots.

"Ms. Eaton!" Walker waved for her to come closer to the wall, beneath the protection of the overhang.

Fear propelled her forward, slamming her into the stone wall alongside Detective Walker. "What's going on, Walker?" she asked. Inside the building they could hear yelling and a few muffled screams.

"I don't know." Walker turned in place, never leaving the safety of the wall, and peered through the window opening of the train station doors. Mercy grabbed his arm in an attempt to pull him back. Walker didn't seem to notice.

"I want you to stay close to the wall and walk to that corner." Walker's voice was calm and reassuring. "You must do this, you understand. You must hide around that corner until this is over. Promise me you will do this."

She felt Walker's hands guiding her away from the doors. She couldn't leave him there but she knew he'd never come with her. He had to go in.

Mercy walked backward, keeping one hand on the wall as she went, and kept her gaze on Walker as he waited for the right moment to head inside. Another gunshot rang out from inside the building, followed by the sound of shattering glass. A second later, just as Walker moved to head inside, the front doors burst open and a man carrying a satchel in one hand ran from the building. He charged through Walker, sending him back into the wall, and then raced down the walkway at breakneck speed.

From her place at the corner of the building Mercy saw the look of confusion on Walker's face as the man ran from him. For a brief moment it looked as if he were an unfortunate traveller who had broken free from the violence inside. But then Mercy saw the gun in his other hand, still smoking slightly from having been recently fired.

"Gun!" Mercy said, jumping out from behind the corner. She looked to Walker. "GUN!"

Walker looked up and ran after him. The man with the gun was only a few feet from Mercy, charging straight for her. Without a moment to contemplate the wisdom of her decision, Mercy readied herself for impact. She widened her stance and put her hands out in front of her, thinking nothing of the gun in his hand. In the end she was no match for his speed and determination. He plowed through her, pushing her aside and sending her to the cement of the sidewalk.

She fought back, trying to grab whatever she could to prevent his escape. Her fist circled around his shirt, sending buttons into the air, but the man was still able to wriggle free. She was thrown to the ground in the tussle. Just when she thought he would run he turned to her, towering over her, gun drawn. He stared at her unblinkingly, his finger on the trigger, his mouth twitching as if to smile.

Click.

Mercy flinched.

Nothing happened. His eyes went to Walker, now racing for them. Another step brought the gunman to the curb, then up on a horse, which had been saddled and stood waiting, its reins tied loosely to a nearby post.

"Are you hurt? Are you hurt?"

Mercy felt Walker kneel in the ground beside her. She tried to wave him off. He needed to follow in pursuit. "Go, Walker," she managed to say through the pain that radiated from her wrists and knees. "Go after him."

When she looked up she saw the horse and rider charging up York Street, nearly colliding with an unsuspecting cart and driver as he made a right on Front.

"I'll never catch up to him now," Walker said breathlessly.

Mercy gave a quick exhale and slumped slightly. She would have fallen back into the sidewalk from exhaustion had she not seen two more men, running toward them. One appeared to be coaxing the other.

"Let's go. Let's go!"

The men were coming toward them, looking behind them in panic. They seemed ready to dodge Mercy and Walker, one going one way, the other the opposite. Walker sprung up and pounced, bringing the man who yelled to the ground.

With a quick turn on her hip, Mercy put her leg out in the other man's way. With great force his leg collided with hers and he fumbled. He nearly rolled from the sidewalk out into the tracks. A handbag he had been carrying skidded from his grasp and opened, spilling some of the contents about him.

Mercy recoiled from the pain of the impact, closing her eyes, and prayed Walker would pick up the man before he too had the chance to get to his horse.

"Arrest him, Walker!" she yelled, as she clutched her leg. "For God's sake, arrest him."

When the pain had subsided enough, Mercy opened her eyes to see Walker had placed both men in handcuffs, securing to a nearby train car. It took half a second for her to realize one of them wasn't a man at all, but rather a boy around the age of sixteen, who went by the name of Maxwell.

Chapter 5

Shards of glass littered the floor where Jeremiah walked. The soles of his boots ground the pieces down even more and made the surface treacherous to walk on. Ms. Eaton approached the door sheepishly and stopped when Jeremiah raised his hand.

"It's best you stay to the side, Ms. Eaton," he said.

Thankfully, she nodded and remained at the door.

There was a man's body not far from the exit. Blood pooled around him, mixing with the glass. A group of people, clearly shaken and in a state of shock, were gathered together not too far from the dead man. In front of them was a haphazard pile of luggage, trunks and handbags, valises and briefcases.

"They came at us with guns," one man said, stepping toward Jeremiah. A woman at his side, most likely his wife, clung to him in fright.

Jeremiah glanced to the others. Some began reaching for their bags among the pile as if they intended to leave. "No one is to go anywhere," he said. He snapped his fingers at a man pulling a bag from the pile.

"This is my bag," he said, in a French-Canadian accent. "You cannot detain us."

"I can and I will," Jeremiah said. "Return the bag where you found it."

The man stared as if to challenge Jeremiah's authority.

"My name is Detective Inspector Jeremiah Walker. I'm with the Toronto Police. Others are on their way," he said to the gathered people. A conductor came out slowly from behind the ticket counter, and other travellers began to spill out from their hiding places. "I will need to speak to everyone in turn," he continued. "I need you all to remain calm. This horrid event will be over soon enough."

He looked back to the front doors and saw Ms. Eaton looking on. She did not look well. Her face was flushed white. "Ms. Eaton, would you be so kind as to help fetch some water? I believe some of these ladies are in need of it." He looked to the conductor, who nodded and then motioned for Ms. Eaton to follow him.

As Ms. Eaton passed, Jeremiah noticed she was limping. "Are you all right?" he asked, reaching for her hand as if to hold her up.

"I'm fine," she answered, moving his hand away.

He could not help but watch as she followed the conductor into the back room.

"I have a train to catch," a woman said from the crowd.

"I'm sorry to say that no trains will be leaving the station for some time," Jeremiah said, turning his attention back to his group of witnesses, "not until we've gathered evidence and determine what killed this man."

"A gunshot killed him, that's what," the French-Canadian man said gruffly.

"I know this has been a great shock to you all, but things would proceed much more easily if you agree to work with us, and not against us." As Jeremiah spoke all the front doors opened and police officers entered the building in a steady stream with their guns drawn.

"And where were any of you moments ago, huh?" a man asked.

The officers fanned out into the perimeter of the room. They followed Jeremiah's directions, some heading to the train platforms, others securing all entrances and exits. MacNeal entered, a uniformed constable beside him. Together they guided the two handcuffed suspects through the doors and held fast to their arms so they couldn't make a getaway. "Found the presents you left us," MacNeal said.

Jeremiah looked to the one man's wrists, cuffed in front of him. They were a deep colour of red, worn out from trying to pry his hands loose. "Like a bird, are you?" Jeremiah asked. "Can't be caged."

"I'll bring them back to the station," MacNeal said. "Chief Johnson's on his way."

Jeremiah nodded.

"Is that Ms. Eaton?"

Ms. Eaton and the conductor had returned with a trolley cart of glasses and a crystal pitcher of water. Her limp was even more pronounced.

"What on earth is she doing here?" MacNeal asked.

Jeremiah licked his lips. "She's had quite a fright and injured her leg, I'm afraid. I would be much obliged, when you leave, if you took Ms. Eaton with you to seek medical attention."

MacNeal eyed his partner. Before anyone else, MacNeal had guessed at Jeremiah's fondness for Ms. Eaton, and wasn't above poking fun at his superior officer for it. MacNeal was an ally, however; Jeremiah knew he could trust him.

"Yes, of course," MacNeal said, a sly smile touching the edges of his mouth. "But if she offers me a kiss of gratitude, I'll not turn her away."

Jeremiah chuckled. "I wouldn't expect any less." When he thought MacNeal was no longer looking at him Jeremiah's gaze drifted to Ms. Eaton. He'd never be able to describe the panic he felt when he saw the first gunman turn on her. His heart stopped the second the gunman pulled the trigger.

He wished she had run, or ducked behind the safety of the building, but in truth he knew there had been no time. The collision was inevitable. She had taken the hit and still had enough wherewithal to help him apprehend the second gunman. She truly was a remarkable woman.

Jeremiah turned his attention back to the body. The man wore a beige suit with brown patches at his elbows. His bowler hat had rolled from his head, landing a few feet away. The wound to his chest was large, the bullet having ripped through the thin fabric of his shirt. When Jeremiah crouched down he could see wisps of black staining the white of the shirt, even beneath the blotch of blood. He'd been shot with the gun right up against his chest.

"Sir, may we go now?" a gentleman called from the crowd of witnesses. "My wife is very shaken by what just happened. We'd like to go home."

Jeremiah decided he would interview that couple first. Over the course of nearly twenty interviews, segregating the witnesses as best as possible, Jeremiah discovered the gunmen had entered the station from the York Street doors, possibly arriving in Toronto via a train. But given the availability of their horses, Jeremiah believed this was unlikely. After the arrival and disembarking of the train from Niagara, one man blocked off the front doors, preventing anyone from leaving, while the others ordered everyone to put their baggage in a pile.

"The scoundrels," one woman said, hugging herself and then accepting a reassuring embrace from her husband.

"My wife took off her necklace and ring and prepared to give it to them but they didn't want it," one man said.

"What did they take?" Jeremiah asked.

"The one man chose that man's bag, that's it. Poor bloke wouldn't let it go. And he paid dearly for his choice. The other man, the youngest one, it's like he didn't know what to do. The third man, he had to force him to take a bag," the man said.

"Who fired their gun first?"

"The older man. Nearly straightaway," the woman huffed. "The sound of it gave me such a fright."

"There were three shots, I think, in the beginning. To get our attention," the man explained, pointing to the shattered glass skylight above them. "And then the other one, the younger one, his gun went off when he fumbled the bag."

"Fumbled the bag?"

The witness nodded. "His partner threw it at him. I think it took him by surprise." The man pointed to a spot on the floor a few feet from where they stood.

When Jeremiah stepped closer he saw the marble tile had splintered where the bullet hole had hit. "He was careless," the man said. "I grew up with guns. He hardly seemed to know how to hold it."

"Which man are we talking about?" Jeremiah asked.

"The young one."

"They both looked young to me," Jeremiah pointed out.

"The one who shaved this morning," the woman said at last. "He didn't look like he belonged with them. Too clean."

"He weren't gruff like the other two men neither," her husband said.

"Please tell me you apprehended the third man, the one who instigated all this," the woman said, placing her gloved hand over her chest.

Unable to lie, Jeremiah shook his head.

"I didn't see him in restraints, dear," her husband said.

"Oh, how am I to sleep tonight?" the woman asked.

"May we go now? You have our names and address," the man said, holding his wife upright. "You are welcome to ask more questions later. My wife really needs to rest."

Jeremiah nodded. "Thank you, both," he said, sorry to have to let them go. "You've been most helpful."

The details from the other witnesses were all similar, but still Jeremiah continued to interview them in turn.

"Detective Inspector Walker."

Jeremiah turned to a constable heading toward him.

"This man says he recognizes the victim." The constable pointed to a conductor just a few paces behind him.

Jeremiah nodded, excused the witness he was speaking with, and headed over to the ticket counter. The conductor's face glistened with sweat despite having removed his hat and jacket, both of which were draped over a chair farther into the ticket booth. He was a smaller man, with not much bulk to him. He leaned into the ticket counter as if that were the only thing keeping him upright. It was clear the man had been through quite an ordeal.

"You knew this man?" Jeremiah asked, cocking his head toward the body that was now covered with a blanket.

The conductor nodded.

"I recognized him straightaway. He's been coming here for years."

"Do you have a name for him?"

"He's Mr. Carver, sir. Mr. James Carver."

Jeremiah's heart sank. "Which train would Mr. Carver have arrived in?"

"My guess would be the Niagara train."

Jeremiah quickly wrote down the details as the conductor spoke. His notes were sparse, sometimes only single words. Just enough to jog his memory. He'd take better care later to relay all that was said, writing out long detailed reports. Meticulous records that no one else could match at the station.

"Was the Niagara train due last night, by any chance?" Jeremiah asked.

"Why, yes... It was delayed in St. Catherine's last night when the train hit a deer on the tracks. Gummed up the works. Had to have all travellers disembark for the night. How did you know?"

Jeremiah waved off his question.

"Does he travel with bags?"

The conductor shook his head. "Just a satchel, same one he had today."

"It was a fairly large satchel," Jeremiah said.

"Larger than usual, I suppose," he said.

Jeremiah nodded, his mind already heading down pathways of supposition, finding dead ends, diverting course, before finally coming back to the conversation at hand.

"Thank you, sir," he said. "You've been most helpful. If you think of anything else, be sure to contact me at the station."

The conductor took the card Jeremiah presented to him and gave a look of relief once the constable told him he was free to go.

Chapter 6

Mercy shifted on the bench in the carriage, trying to avoid looking up at Maxwell, who sat across from her. His hands were still cuffed and MacNeal sat directly beside him. She had done well to keep her shock and fury hidden but now with Maxwell so close she wasn't sure she'd be able to keep her composure. She would have liked to pounce on him, smacking him relentlessly as his mother would have done, but she also was unsure if she wanted MacNeal to know she knew him, and knew him well enough to consider him like her own son.

"You have quite a limp there, Ms. Eaton," MacNeal said, breaking the silence.

Mercy was forced to look up. Her eyes went immediately to Maxwell. "It was hardly avoidable," she said, her gaze steady despite the churning of her insides at the sight of him. "I couldn't just let him get away."

It did not hurt much, only when she walked or put pressure on the leg that took the brunt of the impact. She imagined she'd have a sizable bruise by day's end, but as she hinted to MacNeal, she'd have done it all again in a heartbeat, just to teach Maxwell that stealing luggage was hardly worth the risk.

"Judging by your fall, I imagine you have some injuries of your own," Mercy said to Maxwell.

He seemed shocked that she had spoken to him and adjusted in his seat. After a moment of silence, he turned to the window. This act of nonchalance did tug at Mercy's sense of decency. If she weren't careful she could end up lunging across the carriage and wrapping both hands around Maxwell's neck. Instead, she too turned to the window and steadied her breathing.

"Walker will not be happy when he finds out I took you home and not the hospital as he asked," MacNeal said.

"Walker can be as unhappy as he likes. I don't need a

hospital," Mercy said. "Maybe just a hot compress and a warm cup of tea." Mercy smoothed out the folds in her dress. "Walker would do much better once he stops trying to order me about."

MacNeal smiled warmly. "How's Edith?" he asked. "Recovered from the events of last week I hope."

Maxwell blanched at the mention of Edith and Mercy could have sworn she saw his chin tremble as he tried to suppress tears.

"Surprisingly, yes. Young people always have such resilience," Mercy answered.

"And you?"

Mercy turned her head to look at MacNeal but words failed her. How could she explain her own turmoil after being kidnapped and nearly killed?

"How are you feeling?" MacNeal's prodding was ill-timed. Mercy was no more in the mood to speak of her recovery than she was prepared to admit that Maxwell had been involved in a murder.

"I'm well, I suppose," she said. "Well enough, in any case."

"It seemed to affect Walker deeply."

Mercy's attention perked up at this. "Really?"

"Oh yes, he was quite concerned. Checked in on you at the hospital multiple times a day. He was beside himself."

Mercy struggled to suppress her smile. She was delighted at the thought of Walker caring for her in such a way.

"I can't imagine how badly it would have turned out for him if you'd been permanently injured or died. He would have lost his job."

"His job?"

Is that why Walker had been so concerned? He worried how it would reflect on him? Mercy felt her jaw tighten involuntarily.

"Oh yes, no way he could have recovered should that have happened." MacNeal infused a bit of laughter into his words, easy enough done now that the danger had passed.

"Of course." Mercy wasn't in control of her words. Inside, she seethed. She had mistaken his daily visits for genuine concern, perhaps even fledgling love.

"I think perhaps he thought the worst would happen and

that's why he arranged to move in with me," MacNeal continued, oblivious to Mercy's internal plight. "He said this morning he was reconsidering the arrangement."

"You mean, he won't be moving in with you after all?" Mercy asked.

"Appears not. I can't fathom what may have changed his mind. He seemed so determined when he first spoke about it a week ago."

Mercy knew why. Ruth had returned. She had been gone six months, leading Jeremiah to believe their marriage was as good as ended. But now she was back and he was thinking of his future again. A future with Ruth, not Mercy.

"Have you any idea why he may have changed his mind?" MacNeal asked.

Mercy feigned surprise. "As if Walker tells me anything." She stole a glance to the prisoner. "You should save your inquisitiveness for when you get to question him," she said, as the police carriage finally pulled up to the curb in front of her home. "The secrets he holds are far more crucial, don't you think?"

Maxwell lowered his gaze to the floor, sheepish and remorseful.

Mercy shooed away MacNeal's efforts to help her disembark. She paused at the carriage door to take one last look at Maxwell, who would most likely end up at Don Jail among the other murderers and thieves. It was a fate she'd never have suspected for such a sweet, well-spoken young man and yet she'd seen it with her own eyes and there was no denying it. He'd have to answer for his crime.

"Go easy on this one, MacNeal," she said at last, indicating Maxwell. "He's just a kid."

She snapped the carriage door shut and hurried for her house. Once the heavy wooden door was closed, Mercy leaned into it, thankful for her little hideaway from the noise of the city. She could have cried openly, weeping not only for the pain in her leg but the pain in her heart. Maxwell had been caught red-handed with a gun and a woman's bag. He was involved in a murder and she wasn't sure she could ever forgive him.

"You're home."

Mercy jumped at the sound of her daughter's voice

behind her. "Oh God! You scared me."

Edith laughed from the bottom of the stairs. "Doesn't take much these days."

Mercy passed her and went for the kitchen at the back of the house.

"You're limping!"

Mercy waved off her concern. "It's minor," she said. In the kitchen she set the copper kettle on the stove and stoked the fire, adding two more pieces of wood to get a proper boil. "Just a little gift to remember Detective Walker by."

"Detective Walker did that?" Edith slid into a chair at the table.

Mercy smiled. "No, it just seems whenever I am with that man something calamitous happens."

"And?"

When Mercy turned, she found her daughter's elbow on the table, her chin propped up by an upturned palm. She had already become accustomed to salacious stories involving her mother and a certain Toronto police detective.

"Oh, Edith, it's not like that," Mercy said as convincingly as she could muster. "It could never be like that."

Raven slept on one of the kitchen chairs, curled up in a ball, his slumber unaffected by the movement that took place all around him. Mercy gave him one long stroke starting from between his ears down the curve of his spine before she limped toward the larder. Seconds later she returned with a pat of butter and some bread left over from her trip to the bakery the day before.

"I saw Maxwell today," Edith said excitedly.

Mercy blanched, unsure how to approach the subject.

"He came to my school at lunchtime. Made all the other girls jealous. They wanted to know why he had come to see little ol' me." She laughed at the memory of it, most likely pleased as punch to have the envy of all the other girls at her private school. "He said he came by the house."

"Yes, I saw him. He came by this morning."

"He told me he got a job and I told him I was very proud of him and that he should take this job very seriously if he wanted to become a..." Edith's voice blended behind a background of Mercy's pounding heart. She hadn't the strength to tell Edith what she had seen that day and that Maxwell himself at been at the heart of it.

"His uncle must be a man of great means to have so many people working for him," Edith said. "What a great opportunity this is for Maxwell."

Mercy could not bring herself to agree.

"He's meeting me at school tomorrow in the park—"

Mercy dropped the butter knife to the table. "Edith, stop!"

Edith retreated from the table. Mercy felt instantly ashamed but was too angry, not at Edith but at Maxwell for having betrayed their trust.

"Your schoolwork is too important," she said, retrieving her knife. "I don't want you wasting your time, especially with a boy... or worrying about boys, or teasing me about a friendship I may have with a boy." Mercy nearly growled at this point, all her annoyances boiling over at the same time. She buttered the bread with determined purpose, ripping the soft slices in the process.

Opposite her, Edith cowered, unsure what to say or how to respond. "I'm sor—"

"Don't be sorry," Mercy snapped. "Be smart. Now I don't want to hear another word about Maxwell," she said. "Not tonight."

Edith gave a weak nod and accepted the piece of bread offered to her. "I'm going to eat this in my room."

For a moment Mercy was glad for the peace and quiet but shortly after she fell into one of the kitchen chairs and cried with her head in her hands. Hazel would be crying alongside her as well were she still alive. Never in a thousand lifetimes would Mercy have pegged Maxwell for such a person. She cursed his uncle, who no doubt had put him up to it, but she also cursed herself for not having been more forceful when Maxwell first told her he was to work for him.

Ezekiel London was the worst person Mercy had ever met outside the walls of Mercer Reformatory. He was arrogant, ruthless, and very cunning. He was always calculating, watching and studying others for ways to cheat them so he could line his own pockets. He cared nothing for others, only himself, and never confined himself to the constraints of the law. These were the conclusions Mercy had come to after a few brief interactions with him and many late-night conversations with Hazel, who had bore the brunt of the man's worst attributes.

She should have been more protective of Maxwell. She should have known Ezekiel would look to profit from his gullibility and naivety. She should have taken her task of watching out for Maxwell more seriously. Had she done so he'd not be heading to Don Jail at that very moment.

Worst of all, she hadn't the faintest idea how she was going to tell Edith, who adored him even more than Mercy did. The two had a special bond almost from the moment Edith was born.

A half hour passed before the worst of Mercy's tears dried up. She pushed herself up from the table, wiping the dampness from under her eyes, intent on cleaning herself up. She had a client due any moment and she knew she must look a fright.

Raven was awake now, sitting up right and eying her from the opposite chair. She could only see his face, the rest of him hidden by the bulk of the tabletop. He never liked her. He merely tolerated her. That moment was no different. He offered no solace, no commiseration. Just a blank stare before jumping from his perch and sauntering away.

Mercy checked her reflection in the mirror in the hallway and started when she saw a shadow just beyond the curtained window of her front door. The bell rang, a sound that normally excited her but now filled her with trepidation. How would she be able to work in her usual fashion when her intimate world had just been torn apart? How could she smile and offer trite advice when her entire body wanted to convulse in a fit of crying?

Pull yourself together, she said. It's only one more client and then the rest of the day you can do as you please. She patted her cheeks one last time and straightened her shoulders as she went for the door.

Mercy swung open the door with a marked determination. "Good day, Mr. McAllister—"

Walker raised an eyebrow. "Were you expecting someone else?"

Mercy didn't bother hiding her disappointment. "A client," she said, placing a hand on her hip.

"Then I won't waste much of your time," he said, sliding past her and removing his hat.

"Why are you here, Walker?" Mercy asked, careful to keep herself a few paces from him. She needed to distance herself, mentally and physically. He was a married man and nothing could be done for that.

"I came to see about your leg," he said, gesturing slightly with the hat in his hand. "MacNeal told me he didn't take you to have it looked at."

"It's fine," Mercy said curtly. "I didn't need to go to the hospital." She turned toward her parlour but as soon as she took a step she felt pain shoot up her leg. She couldn't help but cry out. Within seconds Walker was at her side. She tried to push him away but he did not listen, as per usual.

He led her to a nearby armchair and set her down. Then he brought over one of the chairs from her séance table and set a cushion on top.

"Truly, I don't need all this fuss." She tried to wave him away but couldn't bring herself to stop him when he picked up her ankle and placed it on top of the cushion. The feeling of his hand on her leg sent a sensation up through her body. The touch was only a second but it was long enough to have Mercy craving more.

"Mother, what's wrong?" Edith appeared at the bottom of the stairs. "I heard you call out."

"I'm fine." Oh, how Mercy wished everyone would stop fussing over her. "It's just sore. Don't worry about me. Go do your homework."

Reluctantly Edith left, but not before giving a quick glance to Walker and offering a smile. Walker paced to the hallway door and looked down to the kitchen where Edith had gone.

"Have you told her about what happened today?" he asked in a low voice.

Mercy shook her head and felt another shot of pain up her leg. "Not entirely," she said, wincing against the pain.

He looked displeased, torn between frustration and exasperation.

"Look, Walker, if you've come to admonish me for not doing as I was told at the train station, I agree. I should have hid behind the corner like you told me. It's no one's fault but my own, I acknowledge that."

"I wasn't going to admonish you," he said, plainly.

Mercy was silenced by this. "But... the man... he would have shot me... He did shoot me. My only good fortune is he hadn't... anymore... you know." She would have cried again had all her tears not been shed for Maxwell. She took a steadying breath and when she looked back to Walker she found him on the verge of tears as well. "I'm fine, Walker," she said, unconvincingly.

"You are a very strong woman," he said softly. "I know."

They locked eyes. Mercy could tell he wished he had the freedom to confess more.

Mercy felt silly. She stood up and hobbled to the door, ignoring the look of consternation from Walker. "I appreciate the concern you have for me," she said, resisting the urge to grit her teeth against the pain. "But I am expecting a client any moment now." Somehow the pain had gotten worse and she was really beginning to think she should sit down for rest.

"You aught to sit down," Walker said.

His words mirroring her own thoughts angered her enough to keep walking away.

"Mercy, please."

She stopped at the doorframe opposite him. He never called her Mercy. It was always Ms. Eaton this or Ms. Eaton that. He was never so informal. Except once. One time he had allowed her Christian name to slip from his lips before they were so rudely interrupted by his wife. But that was all water under the bridge. She was not going to be someone's mistress, not now, not ever.

He was one step from her at the other side of the doorframe. She didn't want to look at him but she could hardly stop herself. Tall, handsome. His expression had always been somewhat hardened but now he looked scared, of what, she had no idea.

"You haven't offended me," she said, in a manner she hoped would allay his fears.

His eyes brightened at her words.

"You just don't have to worry about me anymore," she clarified.

"Anymore?"

She returned his gaze, determined to meet this inevitable end with dignity. There was no hope for them, no future in which they could be together, not as she had once hoped. But she would not fall apart from it. She would return to her life as it was, as if she'd never met Jeremiah Walker, as if the last few weeks had never taken place. She and Edith could return to their everyday lives with a modicum of predictability and without Jeremiah Walker.

"I don't worry about you because I have to," he said. "I worry about you because I want to."

Mercy found herself leaning her back into the doorframe, using the strength of the house to hold her upright. A week ago, nay, two days ago, she had wanted to hear such an intimate confession. She'd have relished it and been delighted the words had crossed his lips, but she now knew this back and forth, this creation of excuses to see each other, was all wrong.

He took a step forward, breaking the space between them. Mercy stood taller, both afraid and anticipating what he might do. Her mouth grew dry and her heart raced with him just inches from her. This is how it had been in the cemetery, only it was dark then and she couldn't see much. Now she saw everything. She saw the way his gaze danced over her face. The way the corners of his mouth twitched, tickled by words he couldn't bring himself to say. She could even feel the heat of his breath on the outer fringes of her skin. She wanted to close her eyes, or look away, anything but live in this moment that could never be fully realized.

"Truth is, I can't stop thinking about you," he confessed. "Not since I heard that click and saw that you were unharmed."

He reached for her hand, and Mercy did nothing to stop him. Another half step closer and he was close enough to brush his nose against her cheek. Mercy swallowed and drank in the scent of him. She felt his fingers curl around her palm, holding her gently, as if just desiring skin-to-skin contact. Mercy closed her eyes in anticipation. He'd kiss her, he had no other option and Mercy hadn't the fortitude to stop him.

There was a knock at the door.

"I'll get it," Edith called out as she walked from the kitchen down the hall.

Walker dropped Mercy's hand and stepped back. Mercy raised a shaky hand to her chest and played with her necklace, an effort to hide the rapid heart beats and quickened breaths.

She was thankful for the doorframe that held her up.

Mr. McAllister came in with a boisterous air, greeting Edith warmly and happily shaking Mercy's hand. Walker ducked out of the way of the door so Mr. McAllister had room to walk into the parlour.

"So delightful to see you, Mr. McAllister," Mercy said, gesturing for the chairs around her séance table. "I will be with you momentarily." She pulled the parlour pocket door closed slightly and went into the hall to say her final goodbyes to Walker.

"Thank you, Edith."

Edith retreated to the kitchen, leaving Walker and Mercy alone once again.

A few seconds passed before Mercy realized the moment was gone, their intimacy replaced with awkward embarrassment. The spell was broken, the magic dispersed into the outer reaches of the room.

"I'll leave you to it," he said at last.

Mercy found herself nodding as she opened the front door for him.

"You should really rest that leg," he said from the porch.

"I will," she said, less angered by his concern and more saddened by it. As a married man his actions were dangerous, at the very least embarrassing. Mercy doubted he'd ever feel the confidence to do such a thing again, which in the end would be better for them all—Mercy, Jeremiah, and also his wife, Ruth.

"Goodbye, Walker," she said. The sound of the door latching shut made her wish she had such a latch for her heart.

Chapter 7

Jeremiah was carried back to the station house on thoughts of what had just happened. His regret grew stronger with every step and his heart grew heavy the more distance was put between him and Mercy. She was willing to let him kiss her. She made no attempt to move or stop him. She wanted the kiss as much as he did. But there was something else in the room, something other than Edith that stopped them. It prevented them from finding that place of intimacy they both so obviously craved.

He was a married man, married to a woman who no more deserved his love and devotion than she deserved the crown of England. Ruth was in hiding at their marital home, the home she had left months earlier to pursue another man, or perhaps men. She feared the gallows more than she feared domesticity.

Jeremiah was not so naive to think she had plans to return for good. She required his assistance, nothing more. When this latest episode was finally over, he'd seek his divorce, as scandalous as it would be, as emasculating as well. Nothing had changed in that regard. He had told her how he'd felt about their sham of a marriage. Ruth was aware of his intentions and yet she still came to him, begging, pleading for assistance. Just another instance of manipulation on her part, the overarching theme of a relationship doomed from the start.

No one noticed him when he slipped past the desk sergeant heading for his office. On his desk waited the satchel dropped by the second suspect.

Still in a haze, he circled his desk and practically fell back in his chair. He was in no mood to conduct inquiries, not after making such a fool of himself in front of Ms. Eaton. He willed himself back to the task at hand.

The bag was a medium brown colour with brass fittings, though tarnished from use. Inside, Jeremiah found men's clothing, a shaving kit in a wooden box, some silk handkerchiefs, and a notebook. What was absent was anything of real value. It defied reason that this bag would be chosen over all the other bags. And the jewellery that was offered, why hadn't any of the gunmen accepted any of the pieces?

He flipped through the pages of the notebook and found most pages blank, except a few in the very middle. On them were pencil drawings, rough sketches of animals: a pigeon, a goose, a squirrel. There were also a few pages of landscapes, simple scenes with only a few lines depicting vast images of trees, water, and a far-off building or structure. At the bottom of the last drawing were words printed in capital letters: "NOT GOOD ENOUGH." Enough was underlined three times, the pencil marks indenting heavily into the soft paper of the book.

Jeremiah made a list of the items and returned them neatly to the satchel. Just as he closed the clasp, MacNeal walked in.

"Where were you?" he asked.

"Interviewing witnesses," Jeremiah lied. He'd rather MacNeal not know he was at Ms. Eaton's house.

"I just took our suspects to Don," MacNeal said, pulling out his notebook. "Maxwell London, he's not known to us, and Wendall Simpson, who is very well known to us."

"London? Is he new to town?"

MacNeal shook his head. "He says he's born and raised in Toronto. He's had no prior run-ins with the law." MacNeal shrugged and closed his notebook.

"London's the young one, yes? Clean-shaven?"

MacNeal nodded.

"Witnesses say he was out of place and didn't pull the trigger that killed the man. The most we can get him for is theft."

"He's tight-lipped, I can tell you that much. Both of them are. Neither uttered a word the entire ride from the station to D'arcy Street and—"

"You took them to Ms. Eaton's house?"

MacNeal froze. "I had to, to escort Ms. Eaton home."

Jeremiah didn't even try to hide his agitation. "Ms. Eaton is a civilian whose only mistake was walking with me on

Front Street when it all happened."

"What was she doing walking with you?"

Jeremiah wasn't sure if MacNeal was teasing or questioning, but Jeremiah felt the sting either way. "She was helping me with a witness," Jeremiah answered coolly.

"Oh, I see, and this witness just forced you and Ms. Eaton to have a mid-morning stroll."

"Believe what you will, MacNeal, but you were wrong to show our suspects where she lives. It puts her and her daughter in danger." Jeremiah was not fooling around. He had never spoken to his partner so harshly. He'd regret it later. Not because he didn't think MacNeal deserved it, but more because he'd worry he gave the impression that he had deeper feelings for Ms. Eaton than he was willing to admit.

"Yes, all right, duly noted." MacNeal put his hands up in surrender. "I won't do it again." He pointed to the case on Jeremiah's desk. "Are you all right to investigate this on your own? I've got my own case I need to work on."

Jeremiah's stomach lurched. "How's your investigation going?" he asked, feigning nonchalance.

"Spent the morning at the scene. Only got back to the station house when we were alerted to something happening at the train station."

"Has the body been removed?"

"Yes, sir. He was deposited at the city morgue this morning. Funny thing... the man has nothing identifying on him. No money, no cards, nothing."

"Truthfully?"

"Not a single thing."

"Interesting, MacNeal. This may be a difficult case. If you need any assistance, let me know."

"You have you hands full now. Besides, Green's been assigned my second."

Jeremiah waved him off. "Green's too green," he said with a laugh. "I mean it, MacNeal. I'd be happy to help. Anytime."

MacNeal perked up at Jeremiah's offer. "I appreciate that, Walker. I really do."

He tapped the doorframe as he left. Immediately, Jeremiah drove his hand down into his trouser pocket and pulled out the items he had found on Edward Dubois's body the night before. He dumped the change and spring knife in the top drawer of his desk and then removed the rubber band from the business cards. They were weathered and worn; most likely having been in Mr. Dubois's possession for some time. Jeremiah flipped through them quickly, aware that MacNeal, or anyone else, could pop their head around his door at any second. There were about eight all together—Jeremiah stopped and pulled one of the cards from all the others. Prominently typed in the middle of the card was a name now very familiar to him.

James Carver.

Edward Dubois's flat was on the second floor above a meat market. The smell of bloody, raw muscle wafted up from the yard where butchers were busily hacking chunks of meat from hung carcasses. Jeremiah was forced to the very edge of the laneway, the only section of gravel not permeated with blood and discarded offal. Once inside the narrow passage that would lead him upstairs, Jeremiah was able to breathe.

In any normal investigation, he'd have identified himself to the landlord as an officer of the law and asked for admittance, but Jeremiah knew if he did that MacNeal would undoubtedly discover he had been there. Such a find would raise questions, questions Jeremiah wasn't too keen to answer.

Instead, Jeremiah went straight to Dubios's door and shouldered his way in. Two hard rams and the flimsy lock gave way with little fuss or noise.

The room was small with grey walls and caked plaster that was peeling and splitting in every direction. There was a single metal bed, its white paint also peeling. The bedclothes were not neat but rather splayed out, as if the last occupant had left for but a moment and would return any second. Other than the bed, there was a single dresser, with a footed mirror perched on top. A porcelain bowl for shaving sat in front of the mirror, still frothy from Mr.

Dubois's last shave.

In the corner behind the door was a small belly stove, its venting pipe disappearing up and into the ceiling. Behind it lay some thin pieces of wood, remnants most likely from the previous winter's supply.

Jeremiah circled the bed, the only path in the room that allowed for foot traffic, and went to the window. Pulling the thin and ragged lace curtains back, he looked out onto the rear yard, where meat spoiled in the late summer sun. The butchers better work fast, Jeremiah thought. The day was set to be a lot warmer than it had been yesterday.

When he turned to the bedside table, he found a gold-encased compact mirror. He knew exactly how to open it because it was he himself who had given it to Ruth while they courted. When he spied the silk scarf tied to the headboard, he slipped the compact mirror into his pocket and reached for the scarf. Within a matter of minutes, he found multiple items belonging to Ruth, clothing mostly. Some items he recognized, others he did not. Regardless, he gathered them all and laid them out on the neatest corner of the bed. There was too much for him to carry home himself without arising suspicion.

He looked about for a suitcase or bag of some sort but found nothing.

Out of the corner of his eyes he spied the belly stove. He released the latch and opened the groaning door. Inside he built a mound from the leftover wood. They were small, rough pieces but enough to set a flame. He used matches he found in the top drawer of the dresser. The room warmed almost immediately as the flames took hold. Quickly he gathered up Ruth's things and stood before the stove.

A part of him, deep inside, screamed for him not to do it. He knew he was burning something of interest to MacNeal and yet Ruth had sworn her innocence. Nothing good could come of MacNeal connecting Dubois to his wife. As much as he wished to walk away, Jeremiah knew he couldn't. One by one, he fed the clothing to the flames and then closed the stove door once his hands were empty. He waited long enough for the items to burn and then a few more moments to make sure the fire had died down.

By the time Jeremiah left, the temperature in the room had doubled. He could not stay a moment longer. He had no doubt Ruth's clothing was nothing but ash. He left by the same stairway he entered and casually made his way to the street.

❧　❧

Jeremiah was two houses from his front door when he heard the yelling. Without having to hear all that was said, he knew the voices belonged to Ruth and his mother. The shouting came at him even louder when he opened the front door.

"Why is it so impossible for you to do what you are told?" his mother asked, her voice cracking slightly as she spoke.

"Because I'll not have an old crone like you telling me what to do!" Ruth fired back.

"Who the hell are you calling an old crone?"

Ruth laughed at her adversary's words. "Oh, isn't it obvious?" she snarled.

Jeremiah rounded the doorframe and found his wife and his mother at opposite ends of the parlour, squaring off like elk gearing up to lock antlers. Ruth was still in her dressing gown, her curly hair cascading down over her shoulders. His mother was the polar opposite. Displaying her penchant to overdress, Vivian Audulay was in a full blue taffeta gown. Pearls and feathers adorned a hat she hadn't yet removed from her head. She could have been the picture of high-class refinement were it not for the bottle of liquor she held in a tightly closed fist in front of her.

His mother puffed out her cheeks and then stopped when she saw her son at the door. "Jeremy."

"What's this?" Jeremiah stood stunned, dividing his gaze between the two of them before Ruth rushed toward him, circling her arms about his torso.

"Thank goodness you are home," she said, her tone dramatically changed from derangement to soothing innocence. "I couldn't stomach another minute alone in this house and that woman...oh, she's just awful."

Over his wife's head Jeremiah saw his mother cross her

arms over her chest, her face souring even further at her daughter-in-law's words. "I'm afraid she's terrified your housekeeper," she said.

"Mrs. Landry?" Jeremiah closed his eyes at his stupidity. He'd forgotten about her near daily visits since Ruth left.

His mother walked to a side table and plunked down the nearly empty bottle in her hands. "She left the house shrieking to high heaven because of that gem of a wife you have," she said.

Jeremiah felt Ruth's grasp tighten around his middle lessen. "That woman has no right to enter this house," she proclaimed. "She's just nosey, like always." She raised her chin and looked to Jeremiah, who could not bring himself to touch her willingly nor could he drum up the strength to peel her off him.

"She had every right. I've asked her here."

"But why?" Ruth bristled and took a step back. "Please, darling, do not tell me that since my absence you have struck up a relationship with a married woman from down the street. Especially not one twenty years your senior." A laugh escaped her as she adjusted her dressing gown at her middle.

Jeremiah was determined to not let her comment affect him. "She cleans for me," he said, "and cooks sometimes. And she accomplishes twenty times more in the three hours here than you ever did the entire two years you lived here."

Ruth raised an eyebrow. "Oh really?"

Her offence surprised Jeremiah. Ruth had never once taken interest in the needs of the household and she certainly didn't derive any satisfaction from it, not as Jeremiah had heard of other women.

"She discovered your wife, naked as a jaybird, on the settee with nearly three bottles drank," his mother explained. "I came in to find Ruth chasing Mrs. Landry around the main floor of the house in her drawers and this bottle in her hands."

Jeremiah looked to his wife, who seemed content to look everywhere else but at him. Her expression remained indignant. "I need my morning tipple," she said. "Everyone does."

"Not everyone," Jeremiah said, walking toward his

mother at the side table. Numerous glasses were set about, all with various concoctions inside.

"What are you going to do with her?" Vivian asked quietly so Ruth wouldn't hear.

"I don't know," he answered honestly, gathering up the glasses.

Behind them Ruth grew preoccupied with the sofa cushions and a blanket left over from when Jeremiah had slept in the parlour the night before.

With the glasses in hand, Jeremiah led his mother into the kitchen.

"Well," she said, reaching up to pull the hatpin from her hat, "if it were up to me, I'd have put her out of her misery years ago."

"Mother."

"She's no good to anybody, not when she's always three sheets to the wind."

"She's going through a difficult time—"

"We're all going through a difficult time," his mother snapped. "When will you start to realize you are not responsible for her or her antics?"

Jeremiah gingerly placed the tumblers in the enamel sink and set about to pour the remaining liquor down the drain. "She is my wife."

"For how much longer? Because I cannot take much more of this. I cannot watch my only child pour his heart and soul into a woman who was never deserving."

"Yes, I understand, Mother. You told me and I should have listened." Jeremiah's words were sincere. He wished he'd had more sense to listen before he'd rushed to the church to sign the registry.

"And so you need to start listening now." Vivian squared her shoulders to him, pulling at his arms to return her gaze. "You need to take her to the station and get her to tell them what she knows. You need to do it now before this turns out very badly for you."

"It's already turned out very badly for me. My partner is the one investigating the murder."

"All the more reason to tell him what you know. To force her to make a statement."

"You know I can't do that."

"Why? Why can't you?... Unless you think she had more to do with that man's death than she is saying. That's it, isn't it? You think she's guilty." A panic rose into her face as spoke. "Jeremy, this could end very badly for you. Think of your career."

"I am thinking of my career! How do you think things will reflect on me, the husband of a woman who killed her lover?"

"Her lover, is it then?" Vivian gave a slight nod, the entirety of their situation becoming clearer. "How long was it going to be before you decided to explain to me that little nugget, then? You can't convince me you are all right with this."

"This has nothing to do with my feelings about my wife's lack of fidelity."

He saw his mother smile. "Oh, I think it does. I think that is all it's ever been about, her lack of loyalty to you. And you feeling this deep-seated desire to save her from herself, even at the expense of your own manhood."

Jeremiah refused to answer.

"She'll not be caged, you know," she continued. "How long before she breaks out of this prison you've created for her? She'll not stay, not long enough for you to officially clear her name, if such a thing is even possible."

"I have to try," Jeremiah answered.

"Yes, of course," she said, her tone almost mocking. "You try, but the rest of us know when to cut our losses and move on." She replaced her hat and stepped toward the foyer. "Like I did with your father."

"Mother, please—"

Jeremiah followed her into the hallway but he was too late. She slipped out and slammed the door behind her. By the time he returned to the parlour, Ruth was lounging on the sofa, her feet tucked up beside her, her hand gripped around the neck of a bottle of gin. Jeremiah snatched up the bottle as he walked by.

"Hey!"

Without a word he gathered up all the bottles with remaining liquid and went through the kitchen to the back door. He dumped out each bottle in the space beside the back steps and left the empty bottles on the landing.

"I wasn't finished with those," Ruth whined from behind him in the kitchen.

"No one has ever died from lack of liquor," he said, slapping the door shut. He ignored her pouting and reached into his pocket for her compact mirror.

"Here," he said, holding it out for her.

She grabbed it gleefully. "You found it," she said, conveniently forgetting she had begged him not to go to Dubois's house.

Walker sidestepped past her and poured himself a drink of water from the faucet.

"Is that all of it?" Ruth asked, bored of her trinket. "Where's the rest of it?"

"I burned it." He couldn't bring himself to look at her. Instead, he drank his water and stared out the window over the sink.

"Jeremy!"

"What else would you have me do?" he asked, slapping the tumbler down on the small table. "I couldn't very well bundle it up and bring it all home, now could I? You really made yourself at home there, didn't you?"

Ruth shifted uncomfortably. "For a time," she said quietly. "But all that's in the past now." Her tone was hopeful, bordering on delusional. If she thought their plight had been magically resolved she'd find herself sorely mistaken.

"In the past? Good God, woman, what short concentration you have!"

His fury must have caught her off guard. She took a step back and brought her arms in close to her chest. She said nothing, just looked at him with doe eyes and sunken chin. It was all a ruse, he decided, a trick used many times before to dampen his displeasure. She was adept at playing to his emotions and winning him over, using his good nature to her advantage. He'd have to work to maintain his distance. He could not afford for her to get a hold over him, not again.

"Ruth, this is very much my present and quite well could be our future if you don't learn to keep your antics contained!"

She nodded her agreement but he was not interested. He

left her in the kitchen and went upstairs to fetch more pillows for another uncomfortable night on the sofa.

Chapter 8

Maggie bounced on Mercy's lap, her chubby baby legs springing back and forth as if she were propelling herself up and down. Mercy was, in fact, the one bouncing her but she did so absentmindedly, her hands positioned in Maggie's underarms, the baby gleefully enjoying the game. The child had been flourishing under Constance's loving care. In the week since her parents died, she'd gained weight, her eyes grew more attentive, and she had even learned to laugh, something she did heartily while on Mercy's knees.

Mercy noticed none of this. She had been trying to enjoy her visit with her sister, but her mind kept wandering back to the scene at the train station, Maxwell's incarceration, and then the moments leading up to Walker's sudden departure from her house the day before. Mercy tried in vain to bring her attention about.

Constance was rambling on about the child, about her and Lottie's routine for her. Like any newly made mother, Constance could think of nothing else but the child's care. She was wholly in her element. She paced the room tidying a few blankets and cloths that had been strewn about. With her hands finally free, and company to boot, she busied herself while Mercy held the baby.

"She is hardly sleeping at all, of course," Constance said. "Not at night, at any rate. Which makes things dreadfully difficult for Alexander, as you can imagine."

For just over a decade Constance and Alexander had lived above the funeral parlour his parents had started and ran the business together, having no children or concerns besides the daily turnover of clients requiring embalming and funeral processions.

"He hasn't been able to keep up with the workload, you see, what with so little sleep and all."

"He's finding it difficult because his wife is no longer

doing so much of the work," Mercy said, her tone even. Her brother-in-law's dependence on Constance had been no great secret for some time. Mercy wasn't the least bit surprised that he now struggled.

Constance paused in thought. "I do believe you may be right on that account," she said. She paused for a moment more and then offered a shrug. "He'll just have to adjust or hire someone."

It pleased Mercy to see her sister so unaffected by the change of her role. Constance had wanted to be a mother for as long as Mercy could remember. It nearly broke both their hearts as her marriage to Alexander grew longer and no children came. Maggie may not have been a child of her own body but within a single week she was Constance's child in her heart.

"For the first few days Alexander refused to even look at the child," Constance explained, retrieving a basket of clean linens from a corner of the room. She brought it to the ironing board next to the stove and worked quickly, taking advantage of her free hands. "This morning I found him leaning over her cradle peeking at her."

"Positioning to smother her, more like," Mercy said under her breath.

"What did you say?"

Mercy's eyes widened, surprised her sister had heard. "It's no great secret that he is jealous of the babe," she said, hoping she'd not be asked to repeat her mean comment. "He's had your undivided attention for quite some time."

"Yes, I suppose. Not that I had much choice in the matter. I'd have welcomed children sooner."

"I know, Connie darling." Mercy offered a soft smile. "I am so happy to see you so happy."

"Yes... yes, it is wonderful, isn't it?" Her smile faded for a second and then quickly reappeared. "It's hard work, of course... well, yes, you know. You've had Edith. But despite all that, I am really hopeful for the future. It won't be midnight feedings and nappy changes forever, will it?"

"Thank the heavens, no!" Mercy laughed. "You will get to the fun parts soon enough."

"But this is the fun part," Constance said, moving fast through the pile at her side. "I really am enjoying it... most of it, in any case. Seems cruel to be enjoying it so much when clearly Alexander is at odds with it."

"Who cares what Alexander thinks?" Mercy said, dismissing her sister's words with a wave of the hand.

"I should care. He is my husband. His needs are equally as important to mine, perhaps even more so."

Mercy lurched forward at her sister's words, before breaking out into a fit of coughs. Within seconds Constance had come to take Maggie from her. "Pardon me," Mercy said breathlessly, "I wasn't expecting you to say that."

Constance eyed her from a few steps away. "Why shouldn't I say it?" she asked, putting Maggie down on a soft blanket on the floor near her work. "It's the truth, is it not?"

Mercy shrugged. "If you say so."

"Perhaps you feel this way because you are not married," Constance offered. "I imagine you'd feel differently if things hadn't been so unconventional for you."

"You mean if I hadn't found myself pregnant and out of wedlock," Mercy said.

The direction of the conversation seemed to make Constance nervous. She was unable to look at her sister directly. "Yes, perhaps," she offered quietly, "among other things."

Mercy smiled at her sister's words. "I suppose I should expect nothing less from you."

Constance blanched. "What?" she asked abruptly, setting down a towel on the ironing board. "What does that mean?"

Mercy waved her hand and scooted to the edge of the chair she had been sitting in.

"No, really, Mercy, what did you mean by that? Just because I happen to be contented as a female and I enjoy my role as wife and now mother doesn't mean I think any less of you."

"No less than you did before," Mercy added, a smirk on her lips.

Constance furrowed her brow, disturbed by Mercy's frank words on the subject. "You can't tell me after all these years you've come to realize you would have enjoyed domesticity. You've had suitors. Scores of them."

Mercy scoffed. "Oh yes, which one would you have

preferred me to marry? The one who not so subtly demanded I send Edith away to boarding school in America during his proposal, or the one who told me I should never speak of my abilities with the dead in his presence? I may have had men willing to overlook my negative traits, but I could scarcely overlook theirs." She stood. "I realized long ago none of this was in the cards for me. I've come to terms with it, and you should too." She gave her sister a soft kiss on the cheek and then limped across the room to the exit.

"What about Detective Walker?" Constance asked before she reached the stairs. "Could you see yourself with him?"

Mercy paused, her hand on the banister, her heart in a knot at the mention of his name. "He's married, Constance." She fought back tears as she spoke. "He's married and as much as I don't think she deserves him, I'll not have him break his vows to her, not on my account."

"Oh, Mercy—"

Mercy did not let her finish. "I have to go, Connie," she said. "I have a long walk home."

As she made her way down the stairs she could hear her sister call out to her. "You should take the omnibus on account of your leg!"

In an effort to avoid running into Alexander, Mercy left by the front door. She stepped out into the busy city street just as a man was approaching the funeral parlour and they collided.

"Oh!" Mercy felt herself thrown off balance and clung to his arms to hold herself upright.

"Pardon me, miss," the man said, waiting a moment to see she was steady. "You all right then?" He crouched down slightly as if to look her in the eyes.

Mercy nodded. "Yes, sorry. I should really watch where I am going." She felt his grip loosen at her elbows and slowly they drifted apart.

"No harm done, miss."

For a brief second their hands touched as he turned, and Mercy was blinded by a flash, a vision that attacked her consciousness. The noise of the city abruptly ended and she saw the man walking the length of the train terminal. He was scanning, looking for someone, his hand in his pocket, his fingers grasping the grip of a gun. The image ended as abruptly as it began. The noise of the passing carts and shouting people, the murmur of the street, snapped her back. She used the wall of the building to keep herself upright as she adjusted to the sudden change.

Such a thing had only happened to her a few times before and always when she least expected it.

A woman stopped alongside her. "Are you all right, love?" she asked, her British accent thick.

Mercy forced a smile as she corrected her stance and pulled away from the wall of the building. "Yes," she said, as lightheartedly as she could muster. "Quite all right."

The woman continued on her way and Mercy could not help but to move in the direction of the man. Pushing past loiterers, she quickened her pace, racing against the pivotal seconds she had lost. Finally, she spotted him looking in a shop window. She started for him but stopped herself. If he was the gunman from the train station what did she expect to do? As she contemplated her choices, he turned, revealing himself fully and she realized it was a uniformed police constable. He made eye contact with her and must have recognized her from their brief encounter.

"Can I help you, ma'am?" he asked.

He couldn't have been the gunman. The gunman had a ginger-coloured mustache, whereas the officer was clean-shaven. Mercy turned on her heels and fled, embarrassed by her mistake.

The vision was brief, so brief that by the time Mercy reached the street where she lived she wasn't entirely sure it had happened at all. And yet she had smelled the coal from the train cars and the scent of coffee from behind the ticket booth. The memory of it was his, but the vision was Mercy's. She had seen it as if she had been there. She had felt the gun in her hand, the gun that, at one point, was meant to shoot her.

Mercy stopped on her porch and placed a hand on her stomach. Her mind waffled between heading back to Walker's station house or heading inside and leaving well enough alone. Suppose she was wrong. Suppose it was all just a mistake, a result of her trauma. She'd never forgive herself for that type of error. She'd risk looking wanton, desperate for any excuse to visit him.

She fished inside her reticule, looking for her key to the front door, but before she could locate it she heard the latch on the other side pop. Edith appeared, eyes red, lips pouting,

"Edith what is it?" Mercy asked, pushing her way inside and closing the door behind them. "What's wrong?"

"He didn't show up," Edith said, working hard to suppress her tears.

"Oh, honey." Mercy removed her gloves and tossed them to the hallway table before encircling her arms around her daughter.

"I don't know where he could be," Edith said between sniffles. "He's never not shown up before."

Mercy looked on sympathetically. She had known he'd never show up. Mercy knew he was not at liberty to keep appointments, not even with girls he fancied. Internally, Mercy chastised herself for not telling Edith sooner. Her daughter was distraught. Had Mercy been truthful the entire situation could have been avoided. But there had been a cost to the truth, a cost Mercy wasn't so sure she was willing to pay.

"How long did you wait?" Mercy asked, stalling while she figured out a way to break the sad news to Edith.

"An hour."

"An hour?" Mercy couldn't hide her surprise. Patience was not her daughter's strong suit and yet the child had managed to sit by herself in a park, waiting for a boy. Mercy should have known it would take such enticement.

"I tried to think what you would do if you were there and figured I'd wait a little more. I had some readings from school to finish."

"Well, that's good news at least."

"Mother, I'm so worried. This is not like Maxwell," Edith said, her eyes pleading.

Mercy found herself running her hand up and down her daughter's arm. "Darling, there is something I need to tell you," she said after a moment.

A knock sounded at the front door.

"That's a client," Mercy said. "Please wait, don't do anything rash. I am just as concerned as you are, all right?"

Edith nodded, and used her palm to brush away tears.

"Try not to get yourself worked up," Mercy said.

Edith gave a weak nod.

Chapter 9

Mercy's client was a man of few words when not in the reading parlour, but once seated opposite Mercy, with his hands on the table, eager to hear from his departed love, he could scarcely be contained. Jane Anderson's death had been unfortunate, Mr. Moore's connection with her even more so. When alive, Miss Anderson had been pursued relentlessly by Mr. Moore and others. Sensing his competition circling in to snatch her away, Mr. Moore proposed recklessly, only to find out Miss Anderson did not return his favour. She denied him his one wish and refused him a second time shortly thereafter. Not long after that she contracted the Spanish Influenza, dying a few weeks later.

"She'd have changed her mind," Mr. Moore confessed to Mercy on their first meeting. "Had she been given enough time to think it over she would have sent for me. I know it."

Mercy hadn't been entirely sure. Mr. Moore hadn't many attractive qualities. While in readings with Mercy he was pushy and relentless, often talking over her and telling her what to do. He certainly wasn't very handsome not in the slightest, with a long skinny nose that came to a point and a deep receding hairline one wouldn't expect on someone so young. He was miserly as well, counting out each payment to the penny, which was very unlike many of Mercy's other clients, who were often so pleased by her services they increased her usual fee by twice as much.

"Do you think she may have more energy today?" Mr. Moore asked, smiling. There were only two occasions with which Mercy would ever see Mr. Moore smile: when he anticipated a conversation with Miss Anderson and when Mercy told him she was giving him a discount for his reading.

Mr. Moore insisted on disrupting poor Jane Anderson's eternal rest on a weekly basis. He had been coming to Mercy's reading parlour for nearly two years now and Mercy was beginning to wonder if she shouldn't just put his pestering to an end. It did not matter that she was not actually bridging the gap between their communications. It was all just smoke and mirrors in the end. What really bothered Mercy the most was his relentless pursuit of Miss Anderson, real or imagined, without the slightest regard for her wishes on the matter.

"We shall see." Mercy contrived a smile while simultaneously trying to think of a way to broach the subject of leaving Miss Anderson to rest.

The room had dimmed considerably after Mercy pulled the drapes. To ease their eyesight, she placed a small lamp on the edge of the table, turning the flame high enough to illuminate the table and the cards, but little else.

"Did you hear a knock?" Mr. Moore asked. "I just heard a knock."

Mercy paused with the cards in her hands and listened. She could hear nothing.

"That was Miss Anderson," he said. He started to tap his finger on the table in front of him. "She's telling us to hurry. Her time is only so long."

Mercy nodded and did as she was bid. Setting the cards aside, she reached over and took Mr. Moore's hands. 'Let us open the circle," she said before closing her eyes.

A vision flashed into her consciousness. A gun pointed at her face. A smile prickling at the edges of a man's set of lips. And then a train whistle, loud and booming that shook her to her very core.

Mercy opened her eyes to rid herself of the image but the feelings it provoked persisted. She shook her head slightly, a set of awkward contortions that probably made her look apoplectic.

"Ms. Eaton, are you all right?" Mr. Moore asked.

"Yes, just..." She could feel the muscles in her neck tightening. "Give me one moment, to gather my thoughts." She reached a hand behind her neck and soothed the spasms with a gentle rub.

"Jane, are you here?" Mr. Moore asked, happy to circumvent Mercy by going directly to the source. "Come forward. Make a sign."

Flustered, Mercy reached over the tabletop and placed a

hand on top of Mr. Moore's. "She's come forth," she lied. "I can feel her presence." It was the only way to bring the reading back under her control. She couldn't have clients believing she was superfluous. That wouldn't be good for business at all. And she needed to direct the results and not let the reading get away from her.

Mr. Moore's smile was genuine. "I knew she'd come."

A dark shadow passed in the hall, its shape through the glass of the parlour doors catching the edge of Mercy's field of vision. By the time she turned her head, the shadow was gone.

Mr. Moore followed her gaze and then leaned across the table. "Is she here?" he asked, swallowing hard. "Is she standing in the doorway?"

"No," Mercy said, before she could stop herself. "She's standing right behind you."

Mr. Moore smiled and squared his shoulders. "Tell her I love her and I always will. Tell her I won't abandon our love even though she's gone. Tell her—"

"Mr. Moore, stop. She is giving me a message, but you must listen very carefully and do as she says, yes?" Mercy was careful to keep her expression serious and her tone even. "Jane says you must stop coming here."

"Certainly not! Never. I will never abandon her."

Mercy reached over and clasped his wrist. "She says you must end this. She wants to rest. She needs you to move on with your earthly life."

"I can't..."

"You must. For Jane's sake. You summoning her each week is making her weak."

"That happens?"

"Oh yes," Mercy lied. "Especially because of her weakness when she died. Her spirit must re-establish strength. Your summoning her back to earth is... well, it's just draining on the soul. There is no other way to say it."

Mr. Moore looked genuinely struck by the revelation. Mercy, of course, was merely making it all up as she went, but to Mr. Moore it had farther-reaching repercussions.

"She wants you to love others," Mercy explained.

"No. I'll never."

"You must. She demands it of you. She needs you to

move on. It's the only way her spirit may grow strong."

Tears welled up in the young man's eyes.

"It's for the best, Mr. Moore," Mercy said softly. She truly did feel he needed to move on. Had Jane survived she most likely would have married another by now, and Mr. Moore would have been forced by circumstance to move forward with his own life. Jane Anderson's death and his incessant need to contact her was impacting his life negatively. As much as Mercy needed the income his weekly visits brought, she could not under good conscience let this man flounder for years in such a state of mourning. Mercy needed to help him come to terms with Jane's death.

"Let her return to her eternal rest, so you may return to the land of the living." She squeezed his hand once more

After a moment's pause, he gave a weak nod. And then he started his final goodbyes. "I won't forget you, Jane Anderson," he said. "Not for a million years."

The air in the room grew lighter as he spoke and the flame inside the round globe of the lamp flickered ever so slightly. For being merely hocus pocus, there were times when Mercy herself believed her own fibs. As Mr. Moore gathered himself, sliding his final payment across the table, Mercy had no doubt she had done the right thing. Already his features looked lighter, his expression less burdened. He wept silently as he put on his hat and made for the door. There was still a process ahead of him, Mercy realized, but at least now he could mourn and eventually move on with his life.

"Thank you, Ms. Eaton," he said as he stood on her front porch. "You have been most helpful."

"Take care of yourself, Mr. Moore."

He flashed a weak smile and turned to his waiting carriage. Mercy pulled the door closed.

"Do your clients know the extent of your true abilities?" Detective Walker asked from behind her. The sound of his voice made her jump and forced her back into the door.

"My apologies," he said, trying to suppress an amused smile. "I thought you knew I'd arrived."

"When I am with my clients I try to make the outside world disappear," she explained, glancing out the window in the door to make sure Mr. Moore had gone.

"Is that so you can make them believe better?" Walker asked.

Mercy decided to ignore his question. He'd probably never understand the true nature of the services she provided. "What are you doing here?" Mercy asked, pulling him away from the foyer and effectively the front door. "If you keep showing up like this, my clients are going to think I'm up to something." She crossed her arms over her chest and returned his stare.

"I have no desire to tarnish your reputation—"

Mercy huffed.

"I only came to ask a single favour."

She knew it. Mercy had known it was only a matter of time before he came again seeking something from her. She had sworn him off, but her resistance to him only seemed to achieve the opposite.

"Trust me when I say I would not ask were it not absolutely necessary." His expression was sincere, his demeanour humbled, somewhat.

Before Mercy could give a reply, Edith appeared in the hall. "I don't mean to interrupt, but I wanted Detective Walker to know his tea is ready and that I put it on the table in the kitchen."

Mercy raised an eyebrow. "Tea, is it?"

Walker looked apologetic. "She offered. I wasn't sure how long you'd be with your client."

"Did I do something wrong?" Edith asked.

Mercy shook her head. "No, darling, you've done exactly as I have raised you. Why don't you go upstairs and finish your homework?"

Edith slid between them but at the last second turned to her mother. "Maybe we could ask about M—" she said in a low voice.

"Edith!" Mercy gave a nervous laugh and then tried to regain her composure. She stole a glance over her daughter's shoulder to Jeremiah. "I don't think that's a wise idea," she said, in a low voice.

"Why isn't it a wise idea?" Edith pressed, her voice growing louder with each word.

Normally, it took quite a bit to get Mercy angry with Edith but that day Mercy was ripe with frustration.

Between Mr. Moore, Detective Walker, and now Edith, it appeared no one was willing to accept Mercy's authority on any subject matter. "Because I said so, now go do your homework like I asked."

Edith paled at the sound of her mother's tone. She didn't venture to argue. Her eyes narrowed a touch, a non-vocalized challenge in her face, before she turned and went up the stairs. Mercy had no doubt they'd share words about it later.

Mercy rubbed her forehead, willing away a threatening headache. What a pickle she had found herself in. How exactly was she going to talk to Edith and now Walker about what she knew about Maxwell?

"Is there something I can help you and Edith with?" Walker asked hopefully. "Perhaps we can arrange an exchange of favours."

Oh my. Mercy hid her smile by walking ahead to the kitchen. What a turn her life had made in recent weeks. At one point she'd never have allowed herself to converse with a policeman and now she was contemplating exchanging *favours* with him.

Walker's tea was set on a saucer at their square, wooden kitchen table. Four pressback chairs sat empty. Mercy poured herself some tea from the cream-coloured teapot set on the counter next to the sink. She heard Walker come in the room behind her.

"Edith was supposed to meet a friend of ours this afternoon after school," Mercy said over her shoulder as she stirred her tea, "but he never showed."

"Oh."

Mercy turned, saucer and teacup in hand, and gestured for him to take a seat. By the time they were settled in their seats, Mercy realized she was not very good at pretending nothing was wrong.

"I'm worried because—"

"I can look into it, ask around, check the hospitals," Walker offered, somewhat eagerly.

"No." She waved off his offer. "No, that isn't necessary." Her heart was threatening to pound from her chest. She took a breath, exhaling slowly in an effort to calm herself. "I know exactly where he is." She raised her gaze and found

Walker listening attentively. He seemed as equally concerned as she was but she doubted he would be so fretful once he found out what she meant.

She pressed down on her knee to end the incessant bobbing.

"Walker, there's something you need to know about yesterday," she started, still unsure what wording to use in her explanation.

"You're hurt more than you are letting on?"

"No, please stop interrupting. This is difficult enough without you"—she looked to him again and quickly turned away—"being you."

This confused him.

"This isn't about me, well, not entirely. It's about one of the men from yesterday... at the train station."

"Yes?"

"His name is Maxwell... Maxwell London. He's known to me, very well known. He's like a son to me," she said, fighting a dryness in her throat. "He's disappointed me beyond words. I can't express to you how much seeing him there, in handcuffs, hurt me." She closed her eyes against the images. "I didn't tell you because I didn't know how to, and I definitely don't know how to tell Edith."

"You didn't tell her?"

"No, and you can't either. It will break her." Mercy put her hands up to her face, disbelieving her own words. Of course she had to tell Edith, eventually. She just needed time to think about what exactly she should say.

When she looked back to Walker she found him lost in thought. He'd pulled back from the table and sat in shock.

"I should have told you, I know. You can be angry with me all you want but just please let me tell Edith in my own way."

Edith stepped into the kitchen from the hallway. Tears were streaming down the sides of her cheeks. "You can tell me now."

"Oh, honey." Mercy stood up and limped to her, but Edith put her hands up defensively and turned from her. She circled the kitchen table so she was the farthest from her mother.

"I don't want consolation," she said. "I want to know what's happened to Maxwell." Edith's voice broke through her tears, revealing precisely how distraught she was. "What happened at the train station?"

Mercy relayed the tale with an air of submission, resigning herself to the fact that Maxwell had been involved and both Edith and Walker needed to know. "I didn't realize it was him until Walker was securing him to the train," she said. "I wanted to tell you, Edith, but I just didn't know how."

Mercy could tell Edith was struggling with this new information, slowly coming to terms with the reality of Maxwell's situation.

"Where is he now?" she asked.

Mercy shrugged. "In custody. In jail, I imagine."

"He's at Don Jail," Walker said. "MacNeal took him there yesterday." It looked as if he wanted to say more but couldn't.

"We have to get him out of there. Mother, that place is horrible. You know what these places are like—"

"I know!" Mercy rubbed at her forehead. "Walker, he's a good boy—man, I should say. He's a good, young man. Never gave a lick of trouble to anyone."

"I don't understand," Edith said. "He has no need to steal. He told me he had a new job."

Mercy scoffed. "Working for his uncle, the blackguard."

"I have to go see him," Edith said, making a beeline for the door. "I need to know."

With her sore leg, Mercy struggled to beat her to the doorway. "Edith, wait! I can't let you go there. It's not a place for young women."

"Nor is it a place for young men either," Edith snapped. By this time she was in the hallway, reaching for her hat. "I can't believe you would let him languish there!"

"I'm sorry, Edith. I didn't know what to do. I saw him with the satchel with my own eyes. Clothing, Edith! He was caught stealing clothing!"

"You and I both know Maxwell would never do such a thing."

"He did. I saw him."

"Maybe he did not do this willingly," Walker suggested from the doorway to the kitchen. "If his uncle is as bad as you say he is, perhaps he put the boy up to it."

"Yes," Edith said, as if angered with her mother for not suggesting as much herself. "Exactly, my point. He is innocent, and I'll never forgive you, Mother, for believing so ill of him."

"Edith!"

The teenager reached for the doorknob.

"Don't you dare open that door, Edith Eleanor Eaton!" Mercy hobbled down the hall in an effort to stop her daughter from leaving. "If you open that door at any time this evening I will personally see to it that you don't walk through it for the next month!"

"Mother!" Edith looked to her mother incredulously.

"Don't test my resolve."

A few seconds of silence passed as Edith weighed her options before, finally, she let out a visceral growl and turned for the stairs. "I hate you!" she said as she made her exit. She made sure to pound on each step with her foot as she climbed to the second floor. Mercy waited for the inevitable door slam and was not disappointed.

Chapter 10

Mercy's headache was raging full force at this point and her leg throbbed from all the walking she had done that day. She hobbled past Walker to the kitchen, resenting his presence even more than she had when he first arrived. She wished he hadn't witnessed that. Arguments with Edith were few and far between, but they seemed to be occurring with more and more frequency the older Edith became.

"Forgive her," Mercy said as she passed. "She's distraught... as am I."

To her surprise Walker appeared sympathetic, unlike other men in her life, such as Alexander, who would have told her she needed to deal with Edith with a firmer hand, or at least taken the opportunity to tell her these outbursts were the result of no father figure in Edith's life.

"Young people are prone to strong emotions," Walker said, following her into the kitchen. "Which is why I believe it's entirely possible Maxwell wasn't behaving as he normally would while at that train station."

"I'm grateful to hear you say that, but I don't believe our judicial system will see it the same way," Mercy said.

"Do you know how to contact his uncle?" Walker asked.

Mercy exhaled and ignored the shaking that began in her hands. "I wish I didn't." She went to the hallway table to retrieve her address book from the top drawer and returned to the kitchen. Mercy had been actively avoiding contact with Ezekiel for a number of years and wished she could have saved Hazel from having to do so. The man had made her skin crawl from the first moment she met him, a distrust that he eventually proved he was deserving of.

"Is there something I should know about this man?" Walker asked as if reading the look of apprehension on Mercy's face.

Mercy put the book down on the kitchen table and flipped through a few pages, scanning the contents for the appropriate entry.

"Ms. Eaton..." He reached over and placed a hand over Mercy's trembling fingers. She pulled her gaze from the pages before closing her eyes against the tears.

This was not a conversation she had been expecting to have when she started out the day. She wished she could keep her knowledge on the subject locked away in the cobwebbed corners of her mind. She pulled her hand from under Detective Walker's and used it to pat the undersides of her eyelids.

"His name is Ezekiel London," she said. "He's a businessman in St. James and he's a horrible man. Poor Maxwell has had to rely on him more and more since his mother's passing. When he'd told me he'd gotten work with his uncle I very nearly begged him not to continue. Nothing good can come of the connection to him."

"Why do you say that? What has Ezekiel London done?"

"It was his word, and his word alone, that sent Hazel to Mercer Reformatory for Incorrigible Women and Girls."

It was no secret women were dependent upon their fathers and husbands and brothers for their living but they were also dependent upon them for their freedom. Many men had been successful in having the women in their lives labelled mad or incorrigible with little more than their word. Once inside the asylum or reformatory, the women were subjected to unspeakable horrors: assaults, rapes, abuse, and experimentation. Many who weren't the slightest bit insane upon admittance soon found madness the only reprieve from the relentless onslaught of tortures.

"She never belonged there," Mercy said, sniffling.

"And neither did you."

Mercy's eyes shot up. She had forgotten she had told him of her own stay at the Toronto institution. "Yes, well, no one rightly belongs there, if you ask me," she said. "If it were up to me such a place would cease to exist."

More than once since her release she had fantasized about putting a torch to the place, only after ensuring all the female inmates were safe, of course, and the staff was locked up in the cells they used as their torture chambers.

She'd have seen the rats saved before ever considering pulling the doctors and head matron from the flames.

Such mental images had no place in her present life, however. Had Mercy let such thoughts persist she'd have found herself even more bitter, angry, and resentful than she already was, unable to save Edith from the tragedies of their past. As it was, they had enough to contend with making a living for themselves. Demons deserved to stay in the dark. Life was meant to be lived in the light.

"If Maxwell London is in trouble, it's due to that man," Mercy said, quickly taking the attention off her own haunted memories of the place. A few seconds later she found the address entry she had for Mr. London, a remnant from the days when Hazel returned to live there after her release and it was the only way for Mercy to contact her. "He has a building on Yonge Street," Mercy said, turning the address book toward Walker so he could see the complete entry. "As far as I know he still owns it."

What she didn't tell Walker was that Ezekiel had attacked her once. She had accepted an offer of tea from Hazel and at some point in the afternoon she found herself alone with Ezekiel. He pressed himself on her, forcibly touched her, and made lewd comments while trying to hold her to him. Young and weak, Mercy hadn't the strength to fight him off, though try as she did. She was saved by Hazel, who returned to the room. She was so shocked by her brother's actions she dropped the tea tray and sent shards of china to all four corners of the room.

Thankfully, Mercy could avoid him, never meeting Hazel at the house again, but Hazel and Maxwell had been forced by circumstance to live there. Hazel had no reprieve from the man's relentless pestering, sexual and otherwise.

These things, however, were not the sort of details Walker was looking for. There was little protection under the law for women, who weren't even recognized as persons. Walker would be more interested in facts, Mercy reasoned, not the details of yet another time someone had tried to take advantage of her.

Walker copied the information diligently. "I will look into it," he said, tucking the notebook back in his inside breast pocket.

Mercy felt a weight lifted from her, knowing Walker wouldn't condemn Maxwell as quickly as others would have.

"Now you must tell me which favour it is you ask of me," Mercy said, pulling her teacup and saucer from the table and taking them to the sink.

Walker stammered, as if forgetting entirely that the reason for his visit was to ask something of Mercy. "I need you to check in on my wife tomorrow."

Mercy's arms dropped at his words, mimicking the feeling in her heart. The china set impacted the enamel sink so fast the saucer chipped, sending a triangular piece ricocheting off all sides of the sink. "Blast!" Mercy picked up the chipped piece and held it between her fingers. The set had originally been enough for twelve place sittings. Mercy had bought it the first month after she and Edith had established their home there. With this piece now ruined, the set was down to only five complete settings.

She heard Walker walk up behind her. "Are you all right?"

Mercy was struck by the smell of him first, an intoxicating scent, and then after a time she felt his warmth at her back. It took all her strength not to turn around and wrap her arms gleefully around his neck. With his body so close, as it had been the day before, she realized how much she craved romantic human touch. As strong as she was, she wanted to be held and embraced. To have sweet nothings whispered in her ears and kisses planted down the crevices of her neck.

Walker took the small chip and broken plate from her and examined them closely while Mercy ducked out from the tight space, happy to put some distance between them once again.

"I'm not entirely sure I am the appropriate person to play jailer for your wife," Mercy said, wiping her glistening brow with the back of her hand. She circled the table and would have left the room to calm her nerves a while had Walker not been following her movements.

"I would not ask were it not absolutely necessary." He placed the saucer down on the counter and set the chipped piece on top. "I have no desire to take you from your clients."

Mercy's jaw tightened. "You believe I object for the sake of my clients," she said, her tone even despite the racing of her heart.

"I know she's difficult. I'd venture to say she's become even more so in the six months she was away. But my mother has a prior engagement."

"I see."

"I'm asking because I trust you," he said. "No one can know she's returned, at least not until I find out more about what happened in that cemetery."

"Does MacNeal know?" Mercy asked.

"No, he doesn't. And he can't find out."

"He's been assigned the case."

Walker nodded.

Mercy crossed her arms over her chest. "How long are you planning to keep this from him?"

"As long as necessary."

There was a knock at the front door. Through the lace curtains at the window Mercy could see a silhouette of someone standing on her porch. Her next client had arrived.

Walker took two steps toward her, placing his hands together in front of him—begging. "Please, I must find out what happened, but I can't do that and keep my wife safe without your help."

The door knocker sounded again.

Mercy returned his gaze and nodded before she could stop herself. "All right," she said, leaving the room abruptly and walking down the hall to the front door. "But after this I want to be left alone," she said as she went. "I want to go back to the way things were, before I had policemen showing up on my doorstep every day."

She opened the door. "Mrs. Carver?" Mercy's heart stopped at the sight of the newly made widow standing on her front porch. Mrs. Carver appeared equally surprised. Mercy quickly looked behind her and discovered Walker had disappeared from sight, probably having ducked back into the kitchen or dashing up the stairs.

"My apologies," the tearful woman said. She looked down to the small card she held in her hand and rechecked the number painted into the brick of the house. She spied the small, cardstock sign Mercy had affixed to the inside of her parlour window.

Ms. Eaton
Spiritualist & Speaker for the Dead

Mrs. Carver blanched. "I hadn't realized there were so few Eatons about," she said, her grief lacing each word. She was ill-amused, and most likely distraught from having just learned of her husband's passing the day before. "Does the Toronto Police employ a number of spiritualists?" Mrs. Carver asked, her smile almost menacing.

"Just one," Mercy answered, feeling compelled to maintain the lie Walker had insisted upon. "How can I help you, Mrs. Carver?"

"You came highly recommended by a friend," the widow said, flashing the card in Mercy's direction. "She said your readings were medicine for a weary soul."

Mercy raised her eyebrows. "Truly?"

Mrs. Carver nodded, but still appeared uncomfortable. Despite this, Mercy smiled. Medicine for a weary soul. She rather liked that description. Perhaps she'd use it as part of her advertisements.

"What is it exactly that you do?" Mrs. Carver asked, her expression flat. Her eyes were scanning Mercy's hallway, as if looking for further validation of Mercy's abilities.

"Why don't you come inside?" Mercy said, stepping out of the way to allow Mrs. Carver in. The woman hesitated. "No purchase necessary," Mercy said.

Once Mrs. Carver relented, Mercy led her to the parlour and pulled the pocket doors closed. She stood for a moment, using her body to block Walker's quick exit. Once Mercy saw that he was out on the porch, pulling her front door closed, she turned to attention to her potential client.

Mrs. Carver was occupied, surveying the room, and didn't see a thing. She lifted the tablecloth and peered under the table, checked the stability of Mercy's chairs, and even flipped through Mercy's tarot deck.

"I serve a number of clients in a number of different ways," Mercy began. "Some are like yourself, they have recently lost a loved one and are looking for the opportunity to say goodbye. Others are merely curious. I've even helped people locate missing items, such as a will or heirloom, if that is what you require." Mercy looked on hopefully, wondering which category Mrs. Carver fell into.

"Tell me, Ms. Eaton," she said after a long pause, "at the police station, you told the detective 'it's not him.' What exactly did you mean by that?"

Mercy stammered. "I'm... I'm not at liberty to discuss—"

"Did you know my husband was dead?"

"No, not at that time."

"Why did you say that then? What exactly were you referring to?"

Mercy hesitated.

"I'm not particularly keen on being the butt of someone else's joke, so if you don't mind, kindly explain to me what you meant by that comment."

Mercy released a breath and invited Mrs. Carver to sit down. For a moment it looked as if she would refuse but then she relented. Mercy sat opposite her, knitting her fingers together.

"At the time you visited the police station, Detective Walker was investigating the identity of a man found dead in Necropolis cemetery," she explained. "There was some concern that it may have been your husband—"

Mrs. Carver sucked in air and Mercy put out her hand to touch her arm.

"It wasn't the case. At that time your husband was on a train headed back to Toronto. When we met at the station house, as far as we knew your husband was still alive."

Mercy could see tears welling up in Mrs. Carver's eyes as Mercy spoke. By the time Mercy finished speaking, Mrs. Carver's chin was trembling and her emotions were ready to spill over.

"I am deeply sorry for your loss," Mercy said, still trying to comfort Mrs. Carver with a gentle touch.

"He was a good man, my husband," Mrs. Carver said, drawing her handkerchief to her eyes.

"I have no doubt," Mercy said.

"Have they told you how he died?" Mrs. Carver asked. "Do you know? I have to know. I need to understand."

Mercy shifted uncomfortably in her chair. "What exactly did the officers tell you?"

"They came to the house. Told me James had been in an unfortunate accident at the train station. They told me he died but they wouldn't tell me anymore." The woman sniffled. "The papers offer conflicting accounts. One says a man was shot, another tells us he was stabbed. Some say it was a group of bandits, another says a single gunman. None of the reporters seem to agree."

Mercy licked her lips. She was familiar with the inaccuracies found in the papers. "I'm sure that's something that's still under investigation," she said.

Mrs. Carver waved her off. "Damn the investigation! I need to know how my husband died." Mrs. Carver forcibly took Mercy's hands and placed them on her own in an awkward attempt to repeat what had happened at the station house. "Ms. Eaton, please. I'm begging you."

Mercy swallowed and resisted the urge to cry herself. The woman opposite her was distraught and suffering not only from the death of her husband but also suffering from not knowing his demise. Against her better judgment, Mercy nodded and wrapped her hands tighter around Mrs. Carver's clenched fists.

"All right," she said. "We must close our eyes and be silent. If the spirits wish to speak, they will speak. I cannot force anyone to come forward, mind you."

Mrs. Carver nodded, her gaze hopeful.

"Let's close our eyes then," Mercy said, lowering the tone of her voice and raising her face toward the heavens slightly. "Spirits, come forth," she said. "Come forth and soothe this woman's pain. You know her plight. You know the answers she seeks."

Mercy concentrated on her breathing, emphasizing her exhales just enough so Mrs. Carver would hear. "Come forth," she repeated. "Come forth."

Mercy allowed the room to fall silent. Aside from the gentle murmur of the city beyond the parlour window, the room and the darkness behind their eyes grew to become their reprieve. Mercy found the silence, the touch, the steady breathing calming. After a time, Mercy spoke.

"Mrs. Carver, I know how your husband died," she said, opening her eyes and pulling her hands away.

"Yes?"

"I'm told he was the target of some men, men who wished to possess something he had," Mercy explained.

"I don't understand. We own very little."

"It must have been something of great value," Mercy continued. "These men, three—" Mercy stopped herself, not wanting to group Maxwell in with the others. "Two men targeted him at the train station. There was a struggle and your husband..." Mercy put her hand to her chest, a dramatic but necessary addition. "A bullet. He was killed by a bullet."

Mrs. Carver gasped and pulled away from the table. Her gloved hands went immediately to cover her gaping mouth. "No," she said. "That's not true."

"Yes, Mrs. Carver, it is. Both his bags were stolen," she said.

Mrs. Carver swallowed nervously. "Have the bags been recovered? Do you know?"

"I'm sorry, I can only say what the spirits tell—one bag," she said. "One bag is in police custody."

"Which bag?" Mrs. Carver sat forward, reaching over the table. "You have to tell me, which bag?"

Mercy sat back, wanting to avoid Mrs. Carver's touch. The woman looked incensed. "I'm sorry," Mercy said. "I can't say with any certainty."

"Try again. Was it the brown leather bag or... or... or the carpetbag?"

Mercy shook her head. "I don't—"

Mrs. Carver lunged over the table, toppling the deck of tarot cards to the floor. "You have to tell me."

Mercy stood so suddenly her chair tumbled backward. She backed away to the armoire behind her. "I think you should leave now, Mrs. Carver," Mercy said assertively.

The tablecloth sat askew and the chandelier above swayed slightly. Mrs. Carver pulled herself up from the table and adjusted her blouse. The look on her face betrayed her embarrassment. "My apologies, Ms. Eaton," she said, unclipping her reticule. "How much then? How much for your insights?"

"Nothing," Mercy said quickly, still backed into the armoire. "It's on the house."

Mrs. Carver gave a weak smile, pulled out a few coins, and set them on the table. "Thank you for your assistance," she said. "You've been most ... helpful."

Mercy watched and waited as Mrs. Carver left the room. She only stepped forward when Mrs. Carver opened the front door to leave. Almost as soon as she was on the porch, Mercy pounced, shutting the door and locking the latch as quickly as she could.

Chapter 11

Jeremiah slipped out of the house after Ms. Eaton retreated to her reading parlour with Mrs. Carver, thankful he hadn't been spotted. There was a heavy feeling about him, and it was more than just the anxiety he felt for Ruth's predicament. One thing Ms. Eaton had said stayed with him the entire walk back to the station house. *"After this I want to be left alone."* To a certain extent she was right. At some point they would have to part ways, especially now that Ruth had returned. Even if he did proceed with his intended divorce he had no desire to embroil Ms. Eaton in the scandal it would cause. He saw it as a good thing he never told Ms. Eaton how he felt about her. She may now even regret having ever confessed her love for him. Perhaps she'd even take back her words were she given the chance.

His mood was made worse when he rounded the street corner and the station house came into view. From his vantage point across the carriage-strewn street he saw through the front windows that the reception area was impeded by a throng of men, reporters it looked like, with their grey suits, bowler hats, and notebooks at the ready. There were so many of them the throng spilled out the front doors and littered the street immediately in front of the building. Shouts could be heard over the general hum of the scene. After a few moments of listening Jeremiah knew they were there about the incident at Union Station.

"Why weren't any police on hand?"

"Are the citizens of Toronto not safe?"

"What of the man who was arrested?"

Jeremiah lingered on the sidewalk, contemplating whether or not to reveal his affiliation. Were he to make his way over, he'd be accosted. He doubted he'd ever make it to the front door, not on his own at least.

"Does this scare you, Inspector?"

Jeremiah turned to look at the man approaching him from the right and saw it was Alistair George, newspaperman from *The Empire*. He must have been hanging back, playing the part of a disaffected observer as Jeremiah had. George came up alongside him and, shoulder to shoulder, they took in the scene.

"I'd be lying if I didn't say yes," Jeremiah admitted.

George cracked a half smile and glanced to his own notebook that he kept at the ready. "You get used to it," he said.

The men had a contentious history. George had threatened Ms. Eaton on a previous occasion. Once word of the encounter reached Jeremiah, the officer had been less than cordial and proceeded to make threats of his own. They seemed to have reached a mutual understanding, for the time being at least.

Jeremiah stole a glance at the man's notepaper and saw some scribbling. He couldn't make anything out before George repositioned his hand and took the page from Jeremiah's view.

"How is Ms. Eaton faring after her recent scare?" George asked.

Jeremiah straightened his stance involuntarily at the mention of Ms. Eaton. "I can't rightly say," he said as evenly as he could muster. "Haven't seen her much since that day."

George chuckled. "Interesting. A few witnesses claim she was accompanying you at Union Station." He started to flip through some pages of his notebook as if to prove he'd done his due diligence.

"A coincidence," Jeremiah said quickly, feigning disinterest in anything the man had to show him. "We hardly had the opportunity to speak. That day or on any other day. Unfortunately."

"How unfortunate indeed." George seemed amused by their exchange.

Jeremiah eyed the crowd of reporters across the way and wondered how long it would take before one of them realized he was a police officer and that George might be getting the scoop they were all clamouring for this entire time. Jeremiah took a step back, deciding to keep walking down the street so he wouldn't draw attention to himself. He tipped his hat toward George before stepping on.

"Best of luck," he managed to say with as much restraint as he could muster. He wasn't two steps from George when Jeremiah heard the man call out to him.

"Your wife then, Ruth Walker, you haven't heard from her lately, have you?"

Jeremiah turned to face George, to read the expression on the reporter's face. "What sort of question is that?"

"A pertinent one. I have been made aware that your wife has been missing for some time, er, I mean, not missing exactly, just not with you."

"Ruth may do as she pleases." Jeremiah was trying hard not to show any discomfort.

"She has lovers, you know, scores of them."

Jeremiah scowled. Only a certain type of man would be so cruel as to speak publicly about such private matters.

"You knew this, yes? In fact, one of them was found dead recently. Do you have anything to say about that?"

"Not particularly."

The corner of George's mouth began to twitch and then curl. "I gather you don't care much for your wife's infidelities. It seems you may be too busy conducting one of your own."

Jeremiah rushed at him and took him up by the collar. George did not fight him. He accepted the rough treatment as if it were a daily occurrence, a means to an end. "Don't you dare besmirch Ms. Eaton. Leave her out of this. My wife and her conduct is my own affair." He drew the man closer. "Understand me?"

George licked his lips. "You've been very clear."

Aware that people were watching them, Jeremiah released him.

George smiled devilishly before Jeremiah could turn away. "You betray yourself, Detective Inspector." He straightened his overcoat and brushed off his lapels with the tips of his fingers. "It's clear for all to see where your allegiance lies."

Jeremiah left, willing himself not to say another thing on the matter. He could feel the reporter's eyes on him as he walked away. He could breathe easy once he turned the corner of the next block, but he still found his heart beating rapidly. The reporter's suspicions were either highly tuned or he'd already found out some information that put Jeremiah at risk. He needed to be more careful, for all their sakes.

∾ ∾

The Don was a four-storey Italianate structure with distinguished columns that flanked the entire front facade. Erected a few decades earlier, the building, which fronted on Gerrard Street in Riverdale, was starting to show its wear with discoloured stonework on the outside walls and chipped walkways that led Jeremiah to the portico. Once inside the double front doors, Jeremiah was confronted by iron bars from the tile floor to the top of the plaster archway. He flashed his badge to the officer on duty and was allowed through the first doorway into the rotunda. Immediately, the place felt chilled, a condition further punctuated by the dampness in the air that was only somewhat relieved by sunlight streaming down from the windows three storeys above.

Once inside Jeremiah stepped toward a desk at the side and signed his name on the ledger. Even the paper felt damp under the weight of his pen. The smell wasn't so bad in the rotunda but Jeremiah knew it would get worse, much worse, as he made his way through the maze of levels and wings of the building.

"I'm here to interview Maxwell London," he told the warden.

With his thumbs through his belt loops, the duty warden cocked his head to the side and beckoned Jeremiah to follow him. They left the sunshine and entered a dark hallway, walking up a set of stairs to the immediate left. Without an escort Jeremiah was sure he'd get lost in the maze of iron bars, staircases, and hallways. After two flights of stairs, a sharp turn, and a long walk down a darkened hallway, the warden stopped at a nondescript cell and leaned in, peering into the darkness. In a nearby cell Jeremiah could hear constricted weeping and farther away still he could hear low-volume muttering. The place itself echoed without apology, a fault of design but one purposely made. Everything was heard, no matter how far removed from the rotunda.

"London! Step forward." The duty warden placed a utilitarian chair just before the cell door and patted the back as if expecting Jeremiah to take a seat in it. "Ten minutes," he said before shuffling away.

Jeremiah watched as the duty warden pulled the iron bars at the end of the hall shut, effectively locking him in with an entire corridor of dangerous criminals. It did not ease Jeremiah's mind to know that each cell had its own locked bars. In that moment he felt just as much a prisoner as anyone else in that place.

He inched toward the bars, metal but painted white, and peered into the dark cell. The room itself was no more than four feet wide and perhaps six feet deep. Through the darkness Jeremiah could see three men occupied the space, crammed together like steerage passengers in a ship's hold preparing to traverse the Atlantic. The men looked weary with a greasy sheen to their skin, smudges of dirt, and dried blood adhering to their faces. One man was backed into a corner while the other two glared menacingly toward Jeremiah, as if one wrong move could have them pulling Jeremiah between the bars to become a prisoner alongside them.

"Who are you?" one of the men hissed.

"My name is Detective Inspector Jeremiah Walker."

"I remember you," the other one said. "You'd never have got me were it not for this bumbling idiot." He cocked his head to the side, indicating the young man behind them. It was too dark to be certain, but Walker assumed it was Maxwell in the corner.

Walker flipped some pages in his notes to find the man's name: Wendall Simpson.

Simpson pressed his face against the bars and locked down the hall from where Jeremiah and the duty warden had come. "Is that pretty little thing with you?" he asked, a wide smile revealing blackened and chipped teeth. "She's a real stunner, ain't she? All plump and round in the right places—"

"I've come to ask a few questions," Jeremiah said, ignoring the man's comments, which he could only imagine were referencing Ms. Eaton.

Simpson shrugged. "I know nothing," he said. "I saw an opportunity and I took it."

"You expect me to believe neither of you had anything to do with the murder of that man?"

Simpson blanched. "Murder? I only took a bag. I ain't got nothing to do with no murder. Theft. You can only get me for theft."

"I can get you for a lot of things, Mr. Simpson," Jeremiah said evenly. "Including murder."

Jeremiah already knew the man had been incarcerated before, petty theft mostly, a few assaults. Murder was an entirely new category. The penalty was death by hanging and it was clear Simpson knew this.

"Nah." Simpson shook his head in protest, his interest in Jeremiah more pronounced. "I heard the commotion and saw an opportunity. That's all."

Walker looked past him. "What about him?"

The two men at the bars slowly turned. Both bore bemused looks, like playground bullies who were both assured that their victim would back up the story they had fed him.

"Hey, Max," Simpson said, "you kill anyone at the train station?"

Maxwell looked up, revealing the terror in his eyes. He swallowed nervously and adjusted his position so he could look at Jeremiah. The boy had been roughed up recently, a fresh bruise on his jaw and a small cut crusted over with blood above his eye.

"Nnn..no, sir," he said, his voice quivering.

Simpson smiled and turned his attention back to Jeremiah. "See? We didn't do in nobody."

"Either of you hear the gunshots? I was outside and I heard them."

"Yeah, I heard the gunshots. Saw the men fighting over the piece too. I kept my distance. I didn't want any piece of that."

"The two men were struggling? For the gun?"

"Yeah. Each had one hand on the case, one hand on the piece. I ain't seen a better standoff since you all shut down McGregor's basement." Simpson laughed heartily, amused somehow by memories of past arrests.

"What were you doing at the train station?"

Simpson smiled, and his gaze left Jeremiah.

"Pickpocketing?"

Simpson shrugged. "There be worst crimes." He looked over his shoulder at Maxwell, a look of warning. Walker knew these well.

"Walk me through it then," Jeremiah said, pretending he was none the wiser. "Where were you when the commotion started?"

"I was opposite the ticket booth, closer to the doors to the platform. People come, and are often new to the city. They're distracted. I relieve them of their burdens."

"How magnanimous."

Simpson squared his shoulders slightly, slow to pick up on Jeremiah's sarcasm. "I saw everything. I always do. Man with the bags were in a real rush. Must have been desperate to get home to his lady or something. Banged into the other guy at full speed while looking over his shoulder." Simpson licked his lips. "Everything happened so fast too, you see? At first, I just thought it were the funniest thing, two blokes nearly take each other out after one walks into the other. Then I saw bagman with the gun and I knew, I knew things were serious."

"The man with the bag had the gun?" Walker asked.

"Yeah, that's right. He were so mad at being held up he tried to shoot the guy he walked into. If you ask me, the man, the one that got away, he's a hero for saving his own life. No knowing how many other lives he saved that day neither."

Jeremiah pondered this version of events. "All right, let's say I believe you—"

"You don't believe me? Buddy boy over 'ere will back me up. Won't you, London?" Simpson laughed and turned back to Walker. "We call 'im London."

"That's quite original," Jeremiah said, before changing the subject. "So, why'd the guy run if he were only defending himself?"

Simpson shrugged. "I don't know no one who wants to be around when the bobbies show up."

"And the bag?"

"That were his own bag. He didn't steal anything."

"I have witnesses who say he took it."

Simpson huffed, feigning shock. "Who would lie about a thing like that? What is this world coming to?"

"I don't know, Wendall," Jeremiah said. "You're in here and they're out there."

"That don't mean nothing," Simpson said. "I'm better than any of those cu—"

"All right, calm down. Just collecting the facts, Wendall, that's all." Jeremiah looked to Maxwell, who sat silent and still the entire time. Jeremiah carefully considered all that Simpson had told him. "How do you two know each other?" he asked, pointing to Maxwell with his pencil.

"Come on now, London and I go way back, don't we, London?" Simpson looked over his shoulder with a great, big grin on his face.

It may have been dark in the cell but Jeremiah could still see the tremor in Maxwell's body when he nodded. "Yes, sir," he said.

Simpson smiled. "These boys, so polite nowadays."

"See, what I don't understand is why you refused a necklace and ring from one of the female travellers."

Simpson's face hardened. His effectiveness as a thief was put into question. "Yeah, well... wasn't expecting no bluestocking to foil our escape neither," Simpson said. "Women like that should have a leash put on 'em or something."

Jeremiah narrowed his gaze at the thought and worked hard to keep himself from threatening the man for such insolence. In the back corner, Maxwell finally lifted his head to look at Simpson, most likely just as disturbed by his comment. Walker could see Maxwell clench his hands into fists at the mention of Ms. Eaton.

"You all right there, Mr. London?" Jeremiah asked. "You seem awfully quiet. Is everything Mr. Simpson telling me accurate?"

Maxwell hesitated, his gaze going to Simpson as if asking permission to speak. "Yes, sir, as accurate as can be told."

Jeremiah looked to the two others the boy shared his cell with. Two hardened criminals, both with long rap sheets, Simpson did at least and the other looked none better. A boy like Maxwell did not belong in such a place.

"Is there anyone you'd like me to get a message to?" Jeremiah asked. "A lady friend, perhaps?"

For a moment it looked as if Maxwell would not catch his meaning and then all at once the boy's face brightened. "Yes, my mother, if you don't mind... and my sister too, I suppose... tell them I am all right and I'd appreciate their prayers. And I hope they think none the worse of me."

Jeremiah nodded, his mind already reeling from the work he must do, in addition to all the other tasks that lay before him, to help Maxwell escape such a place. "Anything else?"

Maxwell thought for a moment. "No, sir."

"All right then. Consider it done." Jeremiah gave a glance to Simpson, who seemed well enough amused by their side exchange.

"Tell my mother—"

Jeremiah scoffed. "Tell her yourself." And walked away.

It was the man's smugness that Jeremiah hated the most, his unapologetic way regarding his choice of lifestyle. Jeremiah wasn't sure if he believed any words the man said. Simpson was not to be trusted. It was such a shame Maxwell was housed with him. The seasoned criminal had clearly gotten to Maxwell, roughing him up enough to ensure the tale Simpson wanted to tell was the one which came out of both their lips.

Maxwell would have to stay there, to sit in the near dark for hours on end with two men who'd been arrested for far worse than anything Maxwell London could have done. Jeremiah could hardly bring himself to walk away. The boy did not belong there.

The warden tapped his pocket watch as Jeremiah approached. "Forgive me, Warden," Jeremiah said, without feeling even a hint of remorse for going over his allotted time. "There's a man in that cell, Maxwell London, he needs to be moved to a different cell."

"Not possible... unless you want me to move him to women's wing."

"Then switch him out. Trade his place with another man's. The man he is housed with is his accomplice. We can't have them communicating, especially before trial."

With a notable lack of enthusiasm, the duty warden flipped open the ledger on the desk in front of him and scanned the entries "Fine," he said, keeping his finger on the entry. "I'll see what I can do."

"He's been housed with his accomplice. His testimony is now compromised. Shouldn't that invalidate his trial?"

"What do I look like, a judge? They bring them in. I just put them in the cells."

Jeremiah glanced up the stairs behind him, unsure if he should leave or press the issue to have Maxwell moved. The courthouse would be closed for the day. The warden was hardly in any position of authority to make a decision on the matter.

"Has anyone else been in to see him?" Jeremiah bent over the ledger again and ran his finger along the entry.

"Just you," the warden said.

"What about the man he was arrested with, Wendall Simpson? Has he had any visitors?"

"How should I recall?" The duty warden flipped the book so that it faced Walker. "Look yourself."

Walker used his finger to trace the list and found a new entry for Simpson. The entry was input just that morning at eight o'clock. Walker followed the entry to the signature box and found it empty.

Chapter 12

Mercy looked down to the key in her gloved hand as she made her way along the street where Walker lived. Mentally she prepared herself for an assignment she never really wanted to accept. Since finding out Walker had a wife, the nameless, faceless woman had become Mercy's nemesis. Her resentment deepened the more she learned about the woman. How she had left Walker six months earlier without any indication where she had gone. How she had made him worry for the entire time she was away. And now, the cryptic manner in which she conducted herself, speaking in overdramatic tones, never giving complete information and acting as if Walker were her sole hope for salvation. Even during their brief meeting Mercy could see the hold she had on him, the manipulation she used. The woman was a minx.

Standing at the door, Mercy felt suddenly aware that she was participating in something clandestine. She looked both ways down the street before turning the key in the lock and heading inside. Immediately, her throat went dry. She muttered a small curse to Walker for sending her there.

The house was dark. All the drapes had been drawn over the windows, allowing only the slimmest beams of sunlight into the room. The rest of the dark corners were illuminated by ambient light and the odd lamp lit with a flickering flame. Mercy inched into the parlour, peering around the corner as if she expected the wild animal that was Walker's wife to jump out at her unannounced. Seeing no one, she headed for the kitchen.

"Mrs. Walker?"

She smelt something cooking in the wood oven. When she opened the trapdoor, she found sausages, onions, and something else entirely indecipherable in a cast iron pan. It appeared the rumours were true. Ruth had been a decent sort of wife at some point.

"Come to claim my efforts as your own, have you?"

Mercy whirled around, inadvertently slamming shut the trapdoor to the oven. Ruth was standing at the back door in her nightdress, a long, slim cigarette between her fingers and propped up close to her mouth. She looked as if she had just pulled herself from bed, though the hour was just after four in the afternoon.

Mercy looked back to the oven, ashamed that she had been caught being so nosy. "Certainly not," she said. "Merely checking to make sure something wasn't burning."

Ruth eyed her as she drew the cigarette to her mouth for a long draw. When she exhaled, the smoke swirled around her head before dissipating into the broader air.

"Are you my new overseer?" Ruth asked.

"No... I merely came to see if you were in need of anything. I can run to the shops if—"

"Don't lie to me. Jeremiah sent you. I'm not an imbecile."

Mercy swallowed nervously, unsure how to answer.

"And look at you, came running to do his bidding." Ruth left the safety of the doorframe and came into the room. She pulled two teacups from the cupboard and snatched the teapot that sat on the warmest part of the stove top. "I expected as much from his mother," Ruth said, as she poured out tea for both of them. "But you?" She eyed Mercy sideways, a hint of a smirk on her lips. "I imagine he must have some sort of hold on you to make you come all this way to check on his wedded and bedded wife of two years."

Mercy released a chuckle if only to mask the discomfort she felt at the word "bedded."

"What has he told you about me?" Ruth asked, holding a cup of tea in her upturned palm and handing it to Mercy. No milk or sugar or honey or even a saucer. Judging by the lack of warmth radiating from the china, Mercy wasn't even sure the tea was made recently.

"Nothing really," Mercy said. "Only that you've been married a few years and that you've been missing for a few months."

Ruth was amused for a second but her smile vanished as quickly as it came.

"He asked that if I ever received a message—"

"A message?"

"From the other side, I was to tell him. He truly just wanted to know you were all right and if you weren't all right, he wanted to know that too."

"So you are one of them spirit people."

"Spiritualist."

"You converse with dead people."

"Upon occasion."

"And you are willing to tell people this?"

"Not always willingly, but it is how I make my living."

Ruth's interest perked up even more at the mention of money. "People pay you for this?"

Mercy nodded and sipped her tea.

"Bloody hell. If I told anyone I spoke with dead people they'd have me at the asylum within the hour. Why do the likes of you get away with it?"

Mercy hesitated. She could see Ruth's nipples beneath the thin fabric of her nightdress, exposure Ruth made no effort to conceal. Mercy averted her eyes and tried to concentrate on the conversation. "I suppose it's a matter of delivery," she said. "How you address people. The language you chose. It all creates an impression so they can decide if they trust you."

Ruth smiled out one half of her mouth and placed a hand on her hip. "So that's how you've done it then?"

"Done what?"

"How you won over the ice king's heart. You told him what he wanted to hear."

"No, not exactly. I—"

Ruth's expression turned sour and Mercy became aware their innocent conversation was about to turn. "Women like you make me laugh," Ruth said, her voice no longer light and amused. "You turn yer noses up at me for snagging a husband with lies but you all do it, just in different ways."

Mercy couldn't hide her confusion and Ruth turned and headed for the parlour, the wisps of her nightdress trailing behind her.

"He knew what I was before he got involved with me," Ruth said, peering over her shoulder to ensure Mercy was following her.

"And what was that?" she asked, coming to the parlour door, teacup held carefully in both hands.

Ruth let out a smile. "Lady of the night," she said, unashamedly. "Just like his mother."

Mercy jolted to attention, her stomach producing a huge, instant knot. She'd have placed a hand over it were it not for the teacup in her hands. "I'm sorry. What did you just say?" she asked, to hide her gaff.

"Lady of the night," Ruth repeated, enunciating each syllable to reveal its full impact.

"I heard that. What did you say about his mother?" A flash of heat began in Mercy's cheeks, crawling down her neck. She felt hot and sweaty and her heart rate was quickening by the second.

"You didn't know Jeremiah Walker was raised in a brothel?" Ruth appeared genuinely amused by Mercy's sudden distress. "That his mother is the infamous Mrs. Audulay of Yonge Street? Funny. I wonder why your spirits wouldn't have told you such a thing before you set your cap for him."

"I haven't set my cap for him," Mercy said without thinking. She raised her gaze and met Ruth's squarely, still somewhat shocked to find out the stoic, pious Detective Jeremiah Walker was hiding such a secret as this. A wayward wife was one thing, rare but not unheard of, but a brothel madam for a mother was something entirely different.

"Could've fooled me," Ruth answered, her tone filled with malice, her meaning quite clear. She was warning Mercy off her husband. Which was her right to do so, Mercy told herself. She had no right to involve herself with a married man, no matter how unfaithful his wife was. "He has a soft spot, you know, for damaged woman. He feels this need to fix them. Make them respectable. Makes me wonder what sort of damage he sees in you. What's in your past, Ms. Eaton?" Ruth asked, practically enjoying herself. She was playing with Mercy, like a cat would play with a wounded mouse.

"Nothing," Mercy lied.

"There must be something," Ruth teased. "Something dark and shameful, I bet, something that draws Jeremy to you."

"You can see into my past, can you?" Mercy was trying to

feign detachment but knew she was failing.

Ruth shrugged. "Some people can see into the future. Others can disassemble the past. You must have done something awfully shocking to get Jeremy's attention."

Mercy had listened, a false look of disinterest pasted on her face, as Ruth spoke. Inside, her stomach turned in knots and her hands shook. Is that why Walker continued to come to her? It wasn't affection but a need to save her

Mercy returned to the kitchen and placed the teacup in the washbasin. "Thank you for the tea," she said, loud enough for Ruth in the other room to hear. She stood at the sink a few moments looking out the window to the back garden. She felt her eyes tearing up and quickly brushed them away. She gave herself another second to compose herself before heading back to the parlour.

"Apologies for making our visit so short," she said, crossing the room for the foyer. "I really must be going—" She turned her attention to the door and saw Walker standing there. She stopped suddenly. "Oh." Mercy looked to Ruth on the other side of the room.

"Hello, darling," she said. "We were just having a cup of tea."

"Ms. Eaton, are you all right?" Walker asked, bending low to look Mercy in the eyes. Not wanting him to see her distress or inquire further, she avoided his gaze.

"Yes, of course. It's just... I must go." She placed her hands in front of her as if to keep distance between them while she skirted him in the hallway. Walker prevented her from pulling open the door.

"What did she say?" he asked in a low voice.

They were protected from Ruth's view by the wall that separated the foyer from the parlour. Walker was close enough for Mercy to smell the laundry soap used to wash his clothes. She needed to leave and she needed to do it before her emotions spilled over.

"Nothing," she said, giving him a quick glance and trying to offer a reassuring smile. "Please let me go." She raised her gaze. "I have to go."

There was no mistaking it now. He had seen her eyes, the look on her face. His expression fell as the seconds passed and then suddenly he turned the knob of the door and held it while she slid by.

"Thank you," she whispered as she passed the threshold.

She did not look back and she did not hear the door close behind her as she left. He must have been standing there, watching her, as she scurried down the street. She was careful not to move her hands to wipe away the tears. Instead, they cascaded down her cheeks, growing in intensity as she walked the sidewalk putting as much distance between her and Walker as she could. She was choking back tears until she reached the corner and by then she could hardly contain herself.

Chapter 13

Jeremiah stood on his stoop for several minutes watching Ms. Eaton hurry down the street. She didn't look back, not once, and she scarcely slowed her pace. He lingered outside his front door long after she had left his line of sight. The look on Ms. Eaton's face, the anguish he saw there, stayed with him, quickening his heart rate and setting a rock in his stomach. He knew Ruth would be wondering what was taking him so long but he stayed outside anyway, letting the distance between him and Ruth soothe him to the point where he wouldn't lose his temper with her.

So easily he could lose his temper with her. During their marriage, when her antics got his goat he'd stand outside in the back garden, go for a walk, or perform some other avoidance technique just to calm himself. Not being around her soothed him, whereas the very mention of her raised his heart rate. This was not a healthy marriage. And it never had been. He was starting to realize that.

He re-entered the house and closed the door. Ruth was waiting for him at the door to the kitchen. "I made dinner," she said, holding out a plate like a proud child who had just received a culinary lesson. She cocked her head toward the table. She was setting down the plate at his usual spot and pulled out the chair for him when he entered the kitchen. "Come," she said. "Sit."

"What was that about?" he asked.

"I can't rightly say," Ruth said, disaffected.

"You must have said something."

She pulled a frown. "Nothing out of the ordinary," she said, shaking her head.

It was difficult to tell what was actually on the plate. The house was so dark with all the curtains drawn.

"I used what I'd found in the ice box. We don't have much, do we?" Ruth asked as Jeremiah rounded the table to take his seat.

Ruth approached him and placed a fork on one side, a knife on the other. Her movements looked deliberate, as if she wanted to make sure he'd seen. All this attention, this sudden domesticity, made him wary. She'd never acted like this, not since the first week they were married. Her doting attention had quickly faded, however. Not long after their vows, she'd given up making hot meals and eventually gave up preparing food altogether. She'd not even stoop so low as to fetch sundries from the shops, leaving that chore, and many others, to fall onto Jeremiah.

"I didn't ask you to do this," he said. He couldn't see the expression on her face clearly. He had no idea if she intended to poison him or, more likely, if this was an attempt to win him over.

Ruth took a seat opposite him. "Tuck in," she said. "I've been waiting for you."

"Waiting for me for what?" he asked, slicing into one of the sausages.

"Jesus, Jeremiah, you'd think no one has ever tried to be nice to you before." She sat back in her chair, sulking. "I make a meal and this is the thanks I get." She leaned forward again, her agitation clear, her jitters having returned. "You know, this suspicion is exactly why I stopped playing housewife after we got married."

Jeremiah's fork and knife clattered to his plate. "Oh no," he said, nearly laughing. "My suspicions came about after years of your neglect."

"Neglect? Oh, don't be so dramatic! I was as good a wife to you as anyone could be."

"Was? Your memory must be failing you. You are still my wife, by law, in any case. You can't just leave and call it done."

"I left because I had no choice!" Ruth stood and turned from the table, slowly pacing away.

"And you came back because you had no choice!"

The room fell silent and suddenly Jeremiah wasn't at all hungry. He pushed his plate away, which only seemed to make Ruth angrier. "I can't believe you, Jeremy, after all I have done, this is how I am treated. Like a caged animal... a slave!"

Jeremiah stood, pushing his chair back into the wall. "Absolutely not," he said, exiting the kitchen and traipsing through the parlour for the front door. Ruth followed him more out of curiosity than anything else. "If you want to leave, then leave!" he said, pulling the front door wide open, so the noise and the soot found its way inside. "I'll not hold you prisoner," he said. "By all means, if you feel you can do better on your own, then do so and I can be done with it "

Ruth pulled the opening of her dressing gown tight around her body and hugged herself as she stared beyond the doorframe to the street.

Jeremiah recognized the look of terror, a glint in her eye that told him he had been right, that her fear of containment wasn't greater than her fear of the gallows.

He closed the door. "I am not keeping you here against your will," he said evenly. "You came to me, remember that."

Ruth kept her gaze on him as he crossed the room to the small cupboard where he kept the blanket and pillow he used to sleep on the couch.

"I think it was a mistake to come here," Ruth said, her voice as quiet as a mouse.

"That's certainly something we can agree on."

ə   ɕ

Early the next morning Jeremiah left his home and headed for College Street. He took the omnibus down Yonge and walked the rest of the way. Ezekiel London, Maxwell's uncle, owned a three-storey, well-appointed red brick building with a business space on the lower level and living quarters above. Once a public house, the business was boarded up with butcher's paper plastered over the windows, preventing pedestrians from seeing inside.

After knocking at the front door without response, Jeremiah found an opening in the paper on the window that allowed him a limited view inside. It was a construction site mostly, with boards and cans of paint, odds and sods, as well as large framed pieces of artwork yet to be hung. Down the hallway, thanks to a bit of light, Jeremiah saw a moving shadow cast on the wall, signalling that indeed someone was in there.

Jeremiah rounded the corner into the alley and saw two men loitering near the side of the building, a cart pulled up along a single door in an otherwise solid brick wall.

As Jeremiah approached, the two men threw down the remainders of their cigarettes and stomped out the embers.

"I'm looking for Mr. Ezekiel London," Jeremiah explained. "Is he here?" He gestured inside the opening of the building, a double door, each side propped open opposite each other with heavy crates. One of the men pointed feebly and then both men stood at near attention as an older man emerged from the dark of the building.

"I'm Ezekiel," the older man said. "Can I help you?"

He was stout and slightly shorter than Jeremiah but he did not lack in confidence or authority. He sported a well-developed beard of black with some grey and a receding hairline that hadn't any grey at all. He wore a suit, a shirt, tie, vest, and matching dark grey trousers but no jacket. His shirtsleeves were rolled up to his elbows and his hands were slightly dusty. He wiped them off on a cloth as he spoke.

"I'm Detective Inspector Jeremiah Walker with the Toronto Police."

The man's face remained stoic, neither surprised nor worried. Usually, when a police officer arrived at a person's front door, guilt or worry would be written on their features. This man betrayed nothing.

"I met a young man yesterday at the Don. He says his name is Maxwell London, your nephew."

"What's he done now?" Ezekiel asked. He gestured for the two men to get inside the building. They obeyed without a word.

"He was arrested, possession of stolen property," Jeremiah said, watching as the men went.

Ezekiel let out a short laugh. "Of course," he said, tossing the cloth he was using to clean his hands to the side.

"You are not surprised?"

"No, I'm not. He's always getting himself into trouble. I always imagined the boy would get himself arrested one of these days. He's a ner'do well, just like his mother was."

Jeremiah felt his jaw clench at the mention of Ms. Eaton's late friend. That scared young man in the jail cell seemed hardly the type to get himself into trouble without some sort of help along the way. Jeremiah stole a glance over Ezekiel's shoulder, trying to see into the darkness what the man housed in his building.

"If he expects me to get him out of the mess he created, he's in for a big surprise," Ezekiel said, shifting his body to prevent Jeremiah from seeing past. "Do you think I am being unreasonable, Detective?"

Jeremiah shrugged. "I can't rightly say. I don't know the boy. I only promised I would come by and let you know where he was."

"That's very kind of you," Ezekiel said. "How's he holding up? I've never been to one of these places but I hear tell they are mighty uncomfortable."

"Oh yes, they are. Miserable places these jailhouses."

"Good. Can't have criminals thinking they can do anything they want without consequences, now can we? If they wanted the lap of luxury, they should work for it, like the rest of us, hey boys?" Ezekiel twisted his round body to look into the building.

The two men and a few others were crisscrossing the room, carrying implements this way and that without a defined purpose to their movements. Jeremiah's access to the room was cut off when Ezekiel squared his shoulders again. "My boys here, they're the good ones. Too bad none of their virtues rubbed off on Max."

"Mr. London, your nephew has an opportunity to post bail—"

Ezekiel scoffed before Jeremiah had finished his sentence. "You think I wish to waste my time and money on that riffraff. Nah." He twisted his face into a grimace. "He can rot in there. Pay for what he's done. I ain't getting him out."

Jeremiah's neck grew warm as he faced off against the man. London was just a boy, most likely only doing what his uncle had told him. He was polite and both Ms. Eaton and Edith seemed to care about him a great deal. Were London his own nephew he'd not have him in Don a minute longer than necessary. Jeremiah hadn't the freedom to say all this, though. As far as Ezekiel knew Jeremiah was merely an officer of the law and knew nothing of Maxwell beyond an encounter at the jailhouse.

"Fair enough," Jeremiah said. "I did my duty then. I told him I would find you."

"And so you have." A slight smile came to Ezekiel's face. "Is that all, Officer?"

Jeremiah hesitated and allowed his eyes to drift beyond the man in front of him. The other boys had gathered around, further barring his view. Jeremiah turned his attention back to Ezekiel. "What sort of business are you in, Mr. London?"

Ezekiel pulled a grimace and shrugged. "The construction business, it would seem. Can never seem to get closer to having the damned thing open. Too many snags."

"What's your vision for this place then?"

"A gentleman's club, a social place to eat food, have a drink, play billiards."

"Do women," one of the young men coughed from behind Ezekiel.

Ezekiel cleared his throat and shot a glance to the gathering of young men that had formed behind him. "Don't you boys have something you should be doing?"

Chastised, the workers dispersed. Walker heard muttering but no one openly protested their dismissal from the conversation.

"I gather you've secured your liquor license?" Walker asked, shifting his stance in the hope it would allow him a better view of what was inside the building.

"Yeah... I thought this house call was about my nephew?"

"For the most part," Walker answered.

"Let 'im rot." Ezekiel raised a hand to the sliding door, as if preparing to close it. "Good day, sir."

Jeremiah stepped back just as a woman rushed past him from the sidewalk. He turned in place just in time to see Ms. Eaton enter London's outbuilding.

"Mr. London, you are a scoundrel of the highest degree!" Jeremiah could hear her yell as she entered the darkness of the building. Instinct brought him back to the doorway. Ms. Eaton stood inches from Ezekiel nearest the centre of the large, dimly lit room.

"I have no need of a dressing down, least of all by you, Ms. Eaton." Ezekiel's laughter laced his words. He pushed forward, as if he intended to knock Mercy to the ground, but his gaze caught Jeremiah at the door and he stopped short.

Closer now, Ms. Eaton continued to yell. "I know what kind of man you are and you don't scare me. Not in the least."

Ezekiel backed away, his hands up as if providing proof he would not instigate a tussle. "I haven't the slightest clue to what you are referring. I am a businessman, nothing more."

"You are the devil incarnate! Always have been. You let your sister rot in Mercer and you are letting Maxwell rot in the Don!"

"My sister was a trollop!"

"Because that's how you liked her!"

Jeremiah knew the look of a violent man. They rise against any challenge, any slight with a gleam in their eye, a fist ready at their side. He saw such a look in London's face, a look that told him he did not care that an officer stood right there. He'd have hit Ms. Eaton and not felt the least bit guilty about it had Jeremiah not pulled her back from him.

"Is this woman bothering you, sir?" Jeremiah asked.

Ms. Eaton turned her gaze to him, most likely recognizing the sound of his voice. Before she could say anything to reveal their connection, Jeremiah spoke again. "Come with me, *miss*."

She pulled her arm back from his grasp, looking at him with a sudden disgust. "Unhand me," she said. "Arrest this man for enticing a minor to commit a crime."

"I did no such thing." Ezekiel laughed. "Take her out of here, Officer. I have no interest in arguing against female hysterics."

"Hysterics?" Ms. Eaton's face flushed beet red and the muscles in her neck tightened. "How dare you behave so flippantly while Maxwell suffers for the sake of your *pocketbook.*"

"Officer?"

Jeremiah tried to guide her away again but she pushed away all his attempts. "You are pure evil, Ezekiel London, and I will see you destroyed even if it's the last thing I do. I will burn this building to the ground!"

Jeremiah pulled out the handcuffs he kept in his inside jacket pocket and slid one around her wrist. She looked to the piece of metal and then raised her gaze to meet his eyes.

"You are under arrest," he said, grabbing her other wrist, "for disturbing the peace and uttering threats."

Chapter 14

The sound of the fastening metal and the feel of the cold steel on her skin raised a panic inside her that she hadn't felt in over a decade. As Detective Walker pulled her arms behind her back, Mercy's legs began to shake and her knees threatened to give out from under her. She could see an undeniable smirk on Ezekiel London's face. A second ago she had been propelled by fury. But now, restrained so forcibly and surrounded by authoritative men, she felt powerless, as if she could be consumed and wiped from the earth without anyone taking notice.

Mercy felt herself being yanked toward the door.

"This way, miss," Jeremiah said from behind her. His voice was devoid of the friendliness she had grown accustomed to. How had he known she'd come here? Had he been following her? Was he somehow involved, perhaps on Ezekiel's payroll?

"Thank you, Officer," Ezekiel called out, following them to the door. "You may want to check with Mercer. Perhaps they will take her back and actually teach her how to behave like a lady this time." His voice was laced with laughter. He was thoroughly entertained.

As Mercy was led down the alleyway, she fought back tears. Her footsteps grew heavy as they turned onto the busier street. Jeremiah led her past open shops, a butcher's and grocer's, a small tea room where couples sat at intimate tables next to the front windows. Everyone stopped what they were doing to watch as Mercy and Jeremiah passed. Mercy saw the looks of consternation, the disapproving shakes of the head, the *tsk-tsk-tsk* that sat on the tips of their tongues.

If Detective Walker expected her to walk the entire twenty-odd blocks back to the station house he was sorely mistaken. She doubted her wobbly legs would transport her another block before finally giving out altogether. She'd rather be dead than be back in a place such as Mercer. One block away from Ezekiel London's building Mercy began hatching her plan of escape. She'd not suffer again at the hands of such a place. She'd not endure the filth, the abuse, the starvation ever again.

Suddenly, she was directed to the left, Walker pulling on her arm and guiding her to a parkland with a black iron gate and ornate gardens hidden by large hedges. Within seconds he was pulling at her handcuffs, freeing one wrist then the other.

"Ms. Eaton—"

Before he could say another word, she rounded on him, raising a determined hand to the side of his face and hitting him as hard as she could muster.

"Don't you dare speak to me, Detective Jeremiah Walker!" she commanded, watching him recoil from the pain she inflicted. "Don't you come near my daughter or set foot on my porch ever again!" She pushed him back from her. "Do you hear me, Detective?" She turned before he could give a reply. She knew nothing he could say would ever make up for the humiliation she had just endured. What an idiot she had been. To think she had once thought so highly of him.

She made determined strides across the grass, charging deeper into the park, praying Walker would not follow. With her gloved hands she patted the undersides of her eyes, wiping away tears until there were too many to effectively stem the flow. Eventually, she gave in, slipping onto an empty park bench and throwing her head into her hands. For a long time her body shook as she gasped for air.

The memory of Mercer washed over her as she cried. The stench. The sickness. The hopelessness. Edith had been the driving force in her life ever since her release, a vow on her lips made to her infant daughter to never be so vulnerable ever again. While in Walker's handcuffs, standing before Ezekiel London, all her worst fears were realized. She'd never be free of the whims of men. She'd never truly have autonomy over her own life.

After a time, her tears dried up. Though still overwrought, physically she couldn't cry anymore.

Eventually, she raised her head and blinked against the sunlight to find Walker seated next to her, a look of deep concern on his face.

Mercy could not bring herself to look at him, nor could she summon the strength to walk away. They sat quietly for some time. A couple on an afternoon stroll passed them, not knowing the tension that rose up between the pair.

"Please accept my sincerest apologies," Walker said, his voice low. Mercy felt him shift his weight on the bench and then heard him release a controlled exhale. "I hadn't thought my actions would affect you so deeply."

"Of course you wouldn't," Mercy answered indignantly. "Your life has always been your own. Mine has only ever been at the pleasure of men."

She had been locked away without a proper hearing because of the word of her stepfather. Her sentence had been open-ended, her reputation declared "wanton" because of the baby that grew inside her. She'd been a ward of the province until they finally saw fit to release her, though this was done more due to a technicality than any actual reformation on her part. She may have played the part of a docile, obedient inmate, but inside she seethed. Nightly she dreamt of a great fire that would one day consume them all, even her, if it came to that.

She had endured the hardship for her growing baby-to-be and then for its care after Edith was born. She'd fought with the nurse who'd helped deliver her. She'd not let the baby out of her hands for fear they would take her. She kept vigil for weeks, denying herself sleep, keeping the child on her at all times even during chores that had her scrubbing the stone floors on her hands and knees. They could take her freedom, they could wrestle for her hope, but they would not take her child.

The memory of Mercer Reformatory had never left her. Despite her ability to move on in body, the place stayed with her in spirit. It had etched itself into her soul so deeply she was surprised no one saw it when they looked into her eyes.

Eventually, the dank halls of Mercy's memories faded and the lush green of the Toronto park in summertime returned. Mercy could still feel her heart beating rapidly and took in a few steady breaths to calm herself.

"I'm so sorry," Walker repeated. "I should have thought this through better. Ms. Eaton, please believe me, I had no intention of arresting you. I thought you knew that. I only needed Ezekiel London to think I was arresting you."

"Why on God's earth would you need Ezekiel to think that?" she asked, turning her head to look at him squarely.

"He would not allow me past the door," Walker said. "When I saw you walk right in I knew that was my chance."

Mercy pulled a handkerchief from her reticule and patted her face. "Your chance for what?"

"My chance to see what he was hiding."

"And what did you see exactly?"

"Oil paintings... lots of them."

Mercy did not bother hiding her confusion. "Why on earth...?"

"That's the same thought I had," Walker admitted.

"Could this be related to Mr. Carver, the artist?"

"I'm not sure. I've been wanting to enquire about Mr. Carver with the Ontario Art Institute... would you care to join me?"

She looked at him, doubtful. Walker raised an eyebrow.

"What makes you think I would willingly go anywhere with you?" she asked, still angry.

"Well, you can accompany me to the institute or I will accompany you home." Walker gathered himself from the park bench and offered a hand of assistance to Mercy. "In any event, you won't be getting rid of me anytime soon."

Mercy stared at his offered hand, and repeated his words in her head. With one quick exhale she reached up and allowed him to help her. Goodness gracious! How weak-willed she was when it came to him.

Chapter 15

"Never heard of him," Mr. Tomlinson said when Walker asked him if he was familiar with a local painter by the name of James Carver. Mr. Tomlinson was vice president of the art institute, and was a pious, snooty-looking man who was clearly unsettled by the idea of breaking with his normal duties to talk with a man behind a badge.

"Neither Mr. Carver nor Mr. London have an association with the Institute," Mr. Tomlinson reiterated. "I would know, as I am personally responsible for memberships and acquisitions."

Almost as soon as Mercy had entered the nondescript two-storey building she was taken in by the artwork on the walls. She only had a passing interest in the conversation that was taking place a few feet from her. Instead, she was standing before a large canvas with the image of a woman, almost entirely naked, entering a washbasin of water that was set in a nearly empty room. Beyond her, a window streamed in a ray of sunshine, while a door was left open. Farther down a hall stood another woman, a maid, preparing a pitcher of water, presumably to bring down to the room for her mistress.

It looked like France, she decided, though Mercy had never been.

"I've seen this painting before," she said, breaking into the conversation between Walker and Mr. Tomlinson. "Where have I seen it before?"

"The papers, most likely," Mr. Tomlinson said, as if he'd answered this very question hundreds of times before "It was stolen from us four years ago from a travelling exhibit at—"

"The Queen's Hotel. I remember," Walker said.

"We thought we'd never see it again," Mr. Tomlinson said, closing his eyes and shaking his head as if to banish the memories.

"How did you find it again?" Mercy asked.

"A change of heart, I suppose," he answered. "It was left at the side door not eight months ago, wrapped in paper with string. Now, I won't let it out of my sight. This piece is too precious. It's to stay here, in the lobby of our building until we can secure funding for a true gallery for the city."

"It was missing for three years, then," Mercy said.

"If only the canvas could tell us where it went," Mr. Tomlinson said, half joking.

"Does art theft happen often?" Walker asked.

"This piece of art is worth thousands, Mr. Walker," Mr. Tomlinson said. "More than you would make in your entire lifetime."

"It's 'Detective Inspector' Walker."

Mr. Tomlinson didn't seem to care for the correction. "Art thieves know the value. They profit from stealing and selling to people who either don't know it's been stolen or to people who do know and don't mind."

"Perhaps they could not find a buyer for this one," Mercy offered, "so they returned it."

"I highly doubt it. This is one of Booth's most famous pieces. Anyone would want it in their collection."

During their entire exchange Mercy did not take her eyes from the artwork, not once. She let her gaze trace the brushstrokes. She followed the light and sought out further meaning in the shadows. Mr. Tomlinson was right. It was an incredible piece.

From the corner of her eye, Mercy could see Walker taken in by something else that was framed and on the wall. When Mercy drifted toward him, she saw it was a class photograph, people in slate-coloured gowns and light-coloured sashes arranged in rows and layered so that everyone's face could been seen.

"What's this?" Walker asked.

"That is a portrait of our membership," Mr. Tomlinson said. "It's out of date and we are due for another one. Several of these people have moved on to other parts of the continent."

Mercy noticed Walker studying each face carefully, with far greater desire for detail than she could have mustered.

"Not many women in your institute, Mr. Tomlinson,"

Mercy observed.

"Women haven't much desire to pursue the arts," he said. "Not with cooking and cleaning as their primary objective."

"You mean men's primary objective they've placed on them," Mercy answered.

He gave her a pinched-mouth smile.

"Thank you for your time, Mr. Tomlinson," Walker said, nudging at Mercy to move on. He guided her down the hall toward the door from which they had entered.

"There is one piece that hasn't made it home," Mr. Tomlinson said, seeing the advantage of befriending a police officer.

Walker and Mercy turned at the door and found him coming toward them.

"A still life, a mixed bouquet of flowers in a vase," he said.

"Just a vase of flowers?" Walker asked.

"It's a stunning piece," Mr. Tomlinson said, turning his attention to Mercy, who clearly had a greater interest than the detective. "It evokes a feeling of something sinister It's the shadows behind the vase. It's about where the light doesn't reach. Some people said they could see faces in the brushstrokes of the flowers, gnarled and deformed faces. On the surface the piece looks whimsical but... the more you take it in... the darker it becomes." Mr. Tomlinson spoke as if in a trance before finally snapping back to attention. "I tell you this in case you happen to stumble upon it, in your travels. It was on loan to us from the Creighton family, who'd very much like to see it returned."

"When did this one go missing?" Walker asked.

"A year ago."

Walker scoffed. "You aught to beef up security around here if this is going to be a regular occurrence," he said.

Mr. Tomlinson bristled at the unsaid accusation. He opened his mouth, most likely to offer a sharped-tongue rebuke, but Mercy cut him off.

"We will certainly keep an eye out for it," she said with a smile.

***

"Why did you say we'd keep an eye out for it?" Walker

asked as they left the quiet of the building and walked down the street. "I haven't got time to look for rich people's collections."

"Is that all you think about artwork?"

"I'm saying, if they cared for it so much, and it's worth so much, why don't they keep it hidden away so no one can steal it."

Mercy very nearly laughed. "Because artwork is supposed to be viewed. The more people who view it, the more people will appreciate it."

"People, the average person, don't concern themselves with art because they are too busy trying to put meals on their tables. Men like that, those like Mr. Tomlinson, don't have any idea what life is like beyond their art-filled mansions."

"That may be true," Mercy agreed, "but that doesn't mean the rest of us can't appreciate art or see its value to society."

She could feel him eyeing her sideways. "How did you become such an art expert?" he asked.

"Hazel," she said. "She was the art expert, not me. Those exhibitions Mr. Tomlinson was talking about, Hazel took me to all of them and eventually we started bringing the children along. It felt like she knew everything. She could tell me what made a painting remarkable. Sometimes she could tell me an artist's life story, which only added to the allure. I guess I couldn't help but pick up some of her enthusiasm." Mercy laughed. "She had this sketchbook she took with her everywhere. She was always jotting down notes in it." When Mercy looked to Walker he seemed distracted. Her speech must have jarred something in his memory.

"That bag Maxwell stole—"

"Walker."

"No... it had a notebook in it, but there were drawings too. I didn't know what it was at first but now I think it might have been a sketchbook. Did Maxwell ever keep a sketchbook?"

Mercy shook her head. "Not that I recall. He never picked up his mother's interest. Why do you ask?"

"Simpson, the man arrested alongside Maxwell, said the

bag was not Mr. Carver's but Maxwell's. I had my doubts from the start."

"It must be Mr. Carver's sketchbook."

"Let's go find out."

Walker took Mercy to the police storage house, a discreet facility tucked in the back of a building that fronted on Queen Street. Walker bypassed the double doors on casters and led her to the main door farther down. The alleyway floor was fortified with brick, remnants no doubt from the construction of the building, but time and traffic had made its mark, creating an uneven surface riddled with indentations in the once-smooth ground, creating pools of standing water and places for dirt and debris to accumulate. Mercy found herself staring at the awkward pattern of the bricks, some crammed together on the crests of uprisings, but most pulled apart with large gaps between. There was mud and gunk filling up any available space. The smell of rotting leaves and garbage overwhelmed her and she was beginning to second-guess her decision to accompany Walker to inspect the confiscated evidence.

The padlock on the door was easily enough opened and Walker led her inside. It took a moment or two for her eyes to adjust to the dim light offered from the line of windows along the one wall. The room itself was small, large enough for a few bulky items and some shelving units but nothing more. Their entrance had brought the dust to life, sending it into the air, floating, twisting, and turning in the beams of sunlight. Mercy began to cough and covered her mouth against the onslaught of dust. Walker looked to her with concern but she waved him off. She'd not have him fussing over her.

"It's over here," he said, leading her toward a sturdy shelf on the other side of the room.

Together they scanned the items on the shelves before Walker finally spotted something on one of the higher shelves. He scanned the room for a ladder.

"The carriage," Mercy said, pointing to an unhitched carriage with a flatbed.

It was a low carriage. The wheels were no larger than half the size of the hansom cabs that roamed the city. There was a single wood bench, rough and splintered, at the front and an open platform at the back. Together Mercy and Walker lifted the dust cloth that covered the back. Walker used one of the spokes of the back wheels to hoist himself over the outer planks and then offered a hand to Mercy to bring her up alongside him.

"Are you able to get it?" Mercy asked, trying to stabilize herself from the rocking of the carriage as they moved around. "This seems to be an easy place for things to go missing, don't you think?"

Walker looked to her.

"No officer on guard, just a simple padlock on the door." Mercy very nearly laughed at the absurdity. "All this evidence with cases pending in court. This place is a gold mine for anyone looking for it."

Walker looked nervous. "I should have come sooner," he said, conceding Mercy's point. He reached up as far as he could and slid the leather satchel from the dusty shelf.

The dust sent Mercy into a fit of coughing, forcing her to sit with her skirt and legs over the back edge of the flatbed. She felt Walker jump down and come to her side.

"I'm all right," she said through a tightened throat. She covered her mouth with her handkerchief to prevent another outburst.

Walker put the satchel beside her and opened the clasp.

Empty.

Mercy looked to Walker, unsure what was happening. He looked equally as confused.

"I don't understand." He reached in the darkness of the bag and found nothing. "Son of a—" Walker backed away from the satchel and turned from Mercy, hiding his true frustrations.

Mercy took the opportunity to search the satchel herself and again found nothing, "You looked at this before?"

"Yes, in my office. There was clothing, a shaving kit, and a book, a book with blank pages, a few scribbles, and some drawings. It was there, I swear to you."

"I believe you," Mercy said with a smile. It was rather shocking how much she trusted him, truthfully. She turned the satchel upside down and examined every stitch and crevice before setting it back down. Mercy stood up on the flatbed of the carriage and tried to see if the contents had fallen out on the shelf where they found it. The carriage rocked slightly from her shifting weigh.

"See anything?" Walker asked.

Mercy turned to the driver's bench and decided to climb on for the extra foot in height it would give her. She held the shelf for balance. "Nothing," she said. "Not even dust, which is saying a lot for—" The shelf shifted and Mercy's hand slipped. She let out a yelp and felt herself falling but caught herself at the same moment Walker appeared under her. He had grabbed for her legs and arm.

He looked up at her with a peculiar smile.

"Does my plight amuse you?" she asked.

"Not at all."

She looked about. There was no way for her to right herself or climb down to the flatbed again.

"You have to jump," he said. "I'll catch you."

Mercy nearly groaned at her predicament. He was right. The only way to get down safely was to let him catch her. She used his shoulder to hold her steady as she gathered her skirt and prepared for her jump. His one hand was holding her steady under her arm, while his other arm encircled the back of her knees, ready to catch her.

The distance was short, her journey smooth, and her dress was completely covered in filth, but she noticed none of this because all she could see was Walker's eyes staring at her. By the time her feet were firmly on the ground their bodies were pressed together, her hands still on his shoulders.

"I can't apologize enough for my behaviour this afternoon," he said after a moment of silence. "I have no wish to do anything that causes you pain, physical or otherwise." His words come slow, his intention emphasized.

Mercy struggled to find appropriate words for a response. She was not overly vexed with him. Her emotions spoke more of the trauma left over from that god-awful place and the mark left on her because of her experiences there.

"Walker, I—"

A high-pitched screech rang out, the distinct sound of metal-on-metal as the wheels of the large barn-sized doors were forced to move along their guide rail. Sunshine streamed in. Mercy was so blinded by the stream of light that she did not back away from Walker as she should have, as society expected. Instead, she stood dumbfounded, and may even have stepped a hair closer to Walker as if seeking protection. Her fear was quickly replaced by embarrassment when she saw MacNeal walk in with another uniformed officer following closely behind. She felt Walker step back from her; instinctually, she did the same. A cold air quickly rushed into the gap between them, while her hips and arms burned with the memory of his warmth.

"What's this?" MacNeal asked, his Scottish accent even more pronounced than usual. A small smile teased his lips.

Walker looked to Mercy, at a loss for words, probably as equally embarrassed as she.

"What are you doing here, Walker?" MacNeal asked more directly.

"Reviewing evidence for a case," Walker answered.

MacNeal nodded but his expression betrayed a hesitation. "Is that so? Did you find what you were looking for?"

"As a matter of fact, we did not," he said. "It's missing."

The officer beside MacNeal shrugged. "It's probably here somewhere," he said.

"We need a better tagging system," MacNeal said.

"Yes, we do." Walker gestured toward the door. "If you don't mind following me, Ms. Eaton."

Mercy felt the eyes of MacNeal and the other officer burn into her as she stepped forward, her stride matching that of Walker. Once outside the doors she was finally able to breathe normally.

"Who was that with MacNeal?" Mercy asked as they walked the alley toward the road.

"Constable Green, a transfer from another station house." Walker was slightly ahead and turned to look at her, another apologetic expression on his face. "I did not know they were coming," he said.

"Of course not," Mercy answered.

If she were honest, she'd admit how upsetting the encounter had been. Neither of them were doing anything wrong by being there or being there together, and yet something in the way MacNeal and the other man looked at them told her they believed something more was taking place, something intimate between them. Their opinion of her shouldn't matter in the least. She was a grown woman, a woman of means. She could do anything she damn well pleased. But Walker, he was a married man and should not be found alone in the company of a woman who was not his wife.

When she looked to Walker again, she found him staring at her.

"What did Ruth say to you at the house yesterday?' he asked.

Mercy could not bring herself to answer. She wanted to, and had even opened her mouth to speak but everything she formulated in her head would only further emphasize her affection for him. She needed to continue to distance herself for both her and Edith's sakes.

"Whatever she said about me she's probably lying. She's a vindictive woman, Ms. Eaton, and she'd say anything to destroy any happiness I find, especially if she feels threatened by it." He studied her face, forcing Mercy to close her eyes against it.

"She said something about your mother."

"My mother?"

"She told me she was a... a... prominent businesswoman."

He looked shocked by Mercy's euphemism. "She's done quite well for herself, yes... Did Ruth say what type of business my mother is involved in?"

"I am rather fond of women of independent means. It bodes well for Edith and I." She couldn't look at him.

"You didn't answer my question—"

"I doesn't matter to me what your mother choses to do to make her living," Mercy said quickly. "There are a number of people in this world who disagree with my choice of employment and there was a time, when I first met you, when I disagreed with yours." She met his gaze squarely. "I decided last night that I don't care if your mother is a lady of the night or if you are a product of her choices. What matters is that she was able to put food on the table and shoes on her little boy's feet... just as I have done with my little girl. We do what we have to do. What society sometimes forces us to do."

Walker did not respond. Instead, he stood dumbfounded and most likely somewhat relieved to hear what Mercy had to say on the matter.

"I promised I would visit my sister," she said, thinking up a reasonable excuse to leave him. "She lives just around the corner. Now is as good a time as any. Thank you, Walker, for the... *illuminating* afternoon." She sped up her pace and made for Queen Street.

"Let me walk with you."

She could hear him coming up behind her and she turned around. "That isn't necessary."

His expression fell. "Are you angry with me?"

"No, not at all." She bit her lower lip. The opposite was true. She'd never felt more in love with him. "It's just my brother-in-law doesn't like you very much and I'm afraid if he saw us together I'd never hear the end of it." She pulled out her gloves from her purse and started to pull them on. "Oh, don't look so hard done by. Alexander doesn't like me very much either and I never did anything to the man besides advise my sister not to marry him."

Chapter 16

The front pavement of the funeral home was crowded with people dressed in mourning clothes. Women in wide hats and wispy black veils cried into lacy handkerchiefs while the menfolk mingled, patting each other on the upper arms and shoulders. It was a melancholy scene Mercy wished to avoid, but just before she darted for the back door she saw a large framed portrait being brought in the front doors of the funeral home. She only caught a glimpse of the man before the piece of art was whisked away and knew instantly who it was: Mr. Carver. His likeness was etched into her memory, the man himself splayed out on the marble floor lying in a pool of his own blood.

Mercy took a steadying breath before making her way into the funeral parlour through the back door. Two other bodies lay in wait in the preparation room, one to be embalmed, the other already dressed. Their funerals must be scheduled for the next day. Mercy passed them without even a second glance and went for the door that would lead to the hallway. Opening the door a crack, Mercy peered out and easily spied her sister standing at the entrance to the parlour, shaking hands and offering a warm welcome to everyone who walked by.

"Connie." Mercy's voice came out like a whispered hiss. "Connie!"

Her sister stirred, confused.

"Psst!" Mercy was half out the door now, waving her arm to catch Constance's attention. Dutifully, Constance came, smiling at first. But her pleasant demeanour changed the closer she came to Mercy and the farther she was from her clients.

Once in striking distance, Mercy grabbed her arm and pulled Constance into the room with her, closing the door more harshly than she intended.

"Whatever it is, Mercy, I really don't have time,"

Constance said. She looked even more poised than usual, her back erect, her clothing some of the best Mercy had ever seen her wear. You'd never have guessed both Constance and Mercy had grown up on the verge of poverty. Mercy, on the other hand, looked much less put together and Constance was quick to notice. She gave her sister an apprehensive once-over before taking a sly step back as if the dishevelled look was catching. "What on earth have you gotten yourself into?"

Mercy brushed the dust on her skirt with her gloved hand and unintentionally marred the white fabric of her glove. Now she looked even worse. "I was with Detective Walker," she said. "We were investigating."

"Investigating what? Every attic in St. Andrews?"

Mercy shrugged. "Something like that."

Constance looked to the door, anxious to return to her work. "I'm happy you found a new outlet for your time but I don't have the same luxury. I have to get back. The funeral is about to start and I need to be there to welcome the reverend."

"Why can't Alex do it?"

At the mention of her husband, Constance stiffened.

"Where's Alex, Constance?" Mercy pressed.

"I wish I had time to explain but"—she looked to the door again—"I really must get back."

"Wait." Mercy grabbed her sister's arm, forcing her to look at her. "I need to read the body."

Constance started. "Whatever for?"

"It involves the case Walker and I are working on."

Her sister looked doubtful. "If Walker wanted you to read this man, he'd have brought you here himself. The fact that he didn't only proves this is your desire, not the desire of the police."

"Constance, please. It will just take a minute."

Her shoulders slouched as she exhaled, her patience for Mercy at a low point. "That man is going six feet under in less than an hour. When exactly do you expect me to give you access to him?"

Mercy shook her head. "I don't know. Roll him back here briefly."

Constance pressed her lips, looking down on Mercy with

a look of disdain. Mercy knew her request was unreasonable. Her suggestion had been more of a whim than of any real use.

The alley door creaked open and Alexander sidled in, his steps unbalanced and his demeanour off-kilter. He didn't notice the two women watching him until he was halfway through the room. "Hello, wife," he said, his speech audibly distorted. His gaze turned to a glare and slight snarl as he took in the image of Mercy. "Trollop." He was drunk. He only ever called Mercy that when he was too inebriated to stop himself.

Mercy bit her tongue, preventing a harsh retort, and stepped back to allow Constance to direct him from the room. Alexander could always be counted on to shirk his duties, leaving Constance to run what was legally his business. This was nothing new. He was a horrible husband, and Mercy had told her sister so many times, but nothing changed.

Mercy watched from the door as Constance directed her tipsy husband across the hall, steering him away from the ballooning crowd gathering in the funeral parlour. "There's some paperwork for you to sign, husband," Constance said, practically pushing him through the door. "I've set it all out for you to have a look at."

Alexander was easily appeased. He was in no condition to see to anything pertaining to the business but Constance often used this tactic to get him out of the way. A visibly drunk undertaker would not present the best image for the parlour. It was best if he remained unseen.

Seconds later Constance returned, intent on closing the door and shutting Mercy away from the guests. The strain of her duties, the absence of her husband, and now Mercy's absurd request was apparent in her eyes.

"Stay here," Constance said. "I'll see what I can do."

Mercy heard the hum from the packed room soften and then the voice of the minister called them together in a prayer. As Mercy waited, she leaned against the counter that overlooked the two bodies laying on the enamel tables in front of her. The room was dark, the late-afternoon sun having drifted to the far side of the building, leaving nothing but muted light to enter the slim windows that skirted the top of the one wall. In the morning the light streamed in at just the right angle to illuminate everything. More often than not, Constance would do her work on the bodies then, when the light was best. She washed them, embalmed them, and dressed them, often combing their hair and applying a bit of makeup so they looked more lively. For all intents and purposes, Constance ran this establishment. Alexander just said he did.

Time ticked by. Mercy could hear the minister droning on. She contemplated taking a peek to see if in fact the man had put all the mourners to sleep. She hovered by the door, ignoring the souls of the departed who shared the room with her. She felt their call. Their desire to have the stories known. Their insistence grew with each second that passed. After a time, Mercy found herself begging for deliverance. This type of self-control was akin to torture for someone like her.

Finally, the door opened and Constance rushed in, pulling Mercy toward the alley. "Hurry," Constance said, pulling against Mercy's natural resistance. "We don't have much time." She guided Mercy down the alley to the street and then pressed her against the brick wall of the building at the corner, keeping her hidden from view of anyone on the sidewalk. "Wait here," Constance said.

Mercy nodded and Constance rushed back inside.

Mercy could hear the front doors of the parlour open, followed by a steady stream of people filing out into the street. Curiosity got the better of her, and eventually Mercy stole a peek around the corner just in time to see the six pallbearers escorting the casket out to the horse-drawn hearse waiting at the curb. The hearse was a boxy carriage, similar to a stagecoach, with glass walls and black curtains inside. The driver, in posh livery complete with top hat and pure white gloves, sat up front on a high bench ready for the signal. Constance appeared, opened the back door to the hearse, and stepped aside to let the pallbearers set the casket inside. Mercy watched from her hiding spot, her one eye visible around the corner if anyone was paying attention. Luckily, everyone was so engrossed with their tears and consolations no one saw Mercy lurking in the shadows.

Soon the mourners at the back of the hearse thinned, and Constance waved for Mercy to come forward. Constance drew the curtains to cover the glass windows and ushered Mercy inside.

"Stay low," Constance whispered. "If you move too much the driver will notice."

Mercy nodded and slid in beside the casket. The roof was so low she could not have stood up even if she wanted to. She heard the door latch and suddenly Mercy was in the dark.

"All set, driver," Constance called out from somewhere on the sidewalk.

And then the carriage was moving, tossing Mercy's body back and forth with each rut on the road. Small slivers of light came in through gaps in the swaying curtains, enough to help Mercy find the lid to the casket. It sat heavy on her arm as she lay down, reaching into the unknown. At first she felt the man's sleeve, and she began feeling around in the dark for his bare hand. Before she realized it, her skin touched his and her mind was captured, held hostage by unrelenting images that flashed as quickly as she could comprehend them.

A boy staring back at her from a distorted mirror. A prayer at a church altar. A church wafer in a hand. Then a girl, a young woman, smiling, laughing, a dainty paintbrush in her hand. A room of half-finished canvases, cans, and jars of paint covering every available surface. Mercy winced as the paintbrush touched her nose, a blot of paint left behind.

A train, barrelling down tracks. Nervousness. Anxiety. A checked satchel. Unclasp. Clasp. Unclasp. Clasp. A pocket watch on a bouncing knee. A whistle followed by compressed air streaming out onto a wooden platform. Mercy's hand grasped a suitcase so tight, so desperately, her hand hurt. And then, in the lobby, a gun pressed to her stomach. A struggle for the case. Bent fingers that struggled to keep hold. Shattering glass. A shot. A final image of the gunman running from the scene, the case now in his possession.

Darkness.

A few seconds passed before Mercy was aware enough to

pull her hand away, allowing the casket lid to collapse back into place. Slowly, the warmth in her hand receded but she knew the pain in her stomach would remain for a day or two.

The man was a painter. Mercy had known this. Mrs. Carver was a pivotal part of that. Something in his satchel must have been very valuable for him to display such anxiety over it. Perhaps the sketchbook Walker spoke of, perhaps something else. The image of what lay in the case was gone, flashed for Mercy's benefit but removed too fast for Mercy to realize what she was seeing. She knew it was valuable but that was all.

Something else nagged at her. A feeling there was more that needed to be told. She placed her palm on the side of the casket and closed her eyes. She wondered if she needed to do it again.

The hearse lurched, which nearly drove Mercy into the side of the casket. She hit her head off the wood and recoiled in pain. She put her palm to her forehead and immediately her skin felt wet. Still wincing against the pain, she stole a peek out of the edge of the curtain and saw that they had made it to the cemetery. She'd have to make her exit soon or risk being discovered.

Half crawling on the casket, Mercy pivoted her body around and used her hand to feel around the back door for a lever or latch to let her out. There was none. Of course not. The dead had no need of such things. The dead merely went where the living put them. Mercy groped blindly for something to get her out but felt nothing. She pushed on the door at each corner. She felt it give slightly but, in the end, nothing budged. Her desire to leave morphed into insistence and then gave way to an all-out panic. Suddenly, the air felt stale, the box even more suffocating. She needed out, and she needed out immediately.

She did not notice when the carriage finally stopped. The back door opened, nearly sending her head first to the ground had the hearse driver not caught her and held her up.

"Oh my goodness, thank you," she managed to say breathlessly.

"What on earth were you doing in there?" the man asked,

helping Mercy climb out.

Mercy exhaled a breath of relief once both her feet were firmly on the ground. The warmth of the sunshine had never felt so good. "I'm sorry," she said, out of breath and stumbling away. "It won't happen again." Her apology was feeble, her excuse non-existent. She needed to get out of there before any of the mourners spotted her. A hearse driver could be appeased by his employer, but mourning family members would only ask more questions.

Mercy staggered to a wide tree farthest from the paved road through the burial grounds and perched herself on a root jutting up from the ground. Careful to ensure she could not be seen, Mercy leaned her back against the trunk of the tree and closed her eyes. She held her stomach where the bullet had pierced her skin and willed away the pain that radiated there.

What an absolutely horrifying way to go. He had watched the gunman leave and was conscious when Walker entered the same way but not for long.

What on earth had been in that case?

By the time Mercy's heart rate returned to normal, mourners had begun to arrive. From her hiding spot, Mercy could see the pallbearers gathering near the back of the hearse, awaiting their cue.

Such scenes were a familiar sight to Mercy and her siblings. Their childhood home was across the street from one of the city's busiest graveyards. Periodically, her normally quiet neighbourhood would be transformed and play host to large gatherings of mourners. Carriages would line the streets and a murmur from those gathered would rise up, indecipherable sounds mostly interlaced with weeping from the most distraught.

More than once Constance and Mercy had been caught unaware while playing in the front yard. At the first sight of a horse-drawn hearse, Constance would gather her paper dolls and rush inside, but not Mercy. Mercy would rise to stand, her feet firmly planted on the ground in their front garden. She'd hug the bottom of the iron railing and watch intently as if mesmerized. For as long as she could remember she had done this. Sometimes her mother would try to coax her inside. She'd grab Mercy's hand and attempt to pull her up the steps to their front door.

"Have some respect for the dead, will you?" she'd scold.

But Mercy wouldn't budge. Being intrigued by the recently departed was not the same as disrespecting them. Mercy had known this from a young age, though it wasn't until her own family had made a mourners' walk across the street to bury her father that she knew she could communicate with them.

As if a child again, Mercy watched from her hiding spot. The casket was guided out from the confines of the hearse. The pallbearers lined up neatly, taking their positions on either side. They began their careful shuffle toward the freshly dug grave. From a distance the casket looked odd, unlike others Mercy had routinely observed as a child and as an adult. It appeared almost too big for a single man. In that instant Mercy caught sight of Mrs. Carver, the dead man's widow, and sank back into hiding. She closed her eyes and hoped she had not been spotted.

She waited a long while before looking again. They were no longer standing near the carriages but had made their way along the grass to the gravesite. Mercy knew she had to leave then or she'd be stuck hiding behind the tree for the better part of the afternoon.

With care, Mercy clamoured over the enlarged roots jutting from the ground. As she did, her eye caught a glimpse of something in the grass. A cameo pendant. She brushed soil from the carved ivory with her thumb and saw lettering engraved into the gold, filigree frame.

Ruth

Mercy's heart quickened at the realization and she glanced about her, only to realize she had been hiding in the shadows of the same tree where she and Walker had discovered Ruth's murdered lover.

A sound from one of the waiting horses, a whiny followed by the clomp of hoof on the gravel walkway, snapped her attention back to the present. Mercy gathered the broken chain that dangled from the pendant and stowed it safely in the pocket of her skirt. She left the cemetery by the closest gate and was soon swallowed up by the midday traffic.

Chapter 17

"Tell me what you know about Ezekiel London." Jeremiah was seated on an emerald-green velvet sofa in his mother's office, a tumbler of whiskey in his hands.

Vivian Audulay was pouring herself a concoction of her own at the sidebar, the crystal decanter still in her grasp when her son suddenly spoke. "Is that the true reason for your visit? And here I'd thought you'd finally taken pity on your lonely mama."

"You can hardly call yourself lonely," Jeremiah said.

His mother lived in three-storey building, a building she herself owned free and clear. Her office was across the hall from her suite of rooms, with only the best appointments paid for with money procured via ill-gotten gains. Beneath them was the common room, a bar of sorts where clients could imbibe and mingle with women who also had rooms on the upper floors. Mrs. Audulay made money from the liquor and the women, and on rare occasions from men who chose to spend the night in one of guest apartments.

Mrs. Audulay's wealth had also procured three other buildings on the block, none of them cathouses. The various tenants paid her money each month, which further expanded her security. Many times Jeremiah had entreated her to move into one of those buildings if only to improve appearances. "But then who'd watch over things here, deary?" she'd asked. "You forget, Jeremy, this place is my bread and butter."

Once finished pouring her drink, Vivian grabbed her crystal glass, and made her way over to sit with her son.

"You didn't answer my question," Jeremiah said, as he watched her sit down.

"Do I have to?" she asked with a sigh.

"Yes." He had decided to give her no way out. She'd answer his questions and help his investigations or his next absence would be longer than the last.

"He's not a client, if that's what you are expecting," she said, raising her glass to her lips.

Jeremiah raised an eyebrow.

"Not anymore at least. He's rough, let's just put it that way. He scared the girls and I don't like it when my girls are scared. This is an upscale place," she explained. "I know what those other places are like. That's where I got my start and when I finally struck out on my own I knew I wanted this place to be different."

"You've succeeded, Mother."

"Yes, I have." Her voice raised a notch, eager to accept that she had accomplished what she'd set out to do. "And I don't think Ezekiel London or his lot accept my authority in this city."

"Did he cause trouble?"

"Trouble? He damn near had this place shut down all because I wouldn't hire his thugs to man my doors. He offered them to me at a premium too, said he'd be getting a ten percent finder's fee in perpetuity. Ten percent! Jesus, that man has some balls." The contrast between the upscale room they were seated in, the Paris-made gown she wore, and the profanity-laden speech she gave was not lost on Jeremiah. He was used to such scenes. He had grown up in those very rooms and her vocabulary hadn't improved much over time.

"I take it you said no," Jeremiah offered.

"Damn right I said no. I can get men, good men, for pennies on the dollar, men with loyalty to me and my girls, not some middle-aged ruffian with a small winky."

Jeremiah chuckled at the insult. "What'd he do?"

"Ah, he made such a fuss," she said. "Hit one of my girls, threw another down the stairs. Took four of my guys to remove him from the building. His goons wouldn't leave until Harold pulled out his knife."

"Good ol' Harold."

"Yes, thank goodness he's got some sense. Now, all my guys are packing guns *and* a knife. I can't... I just can't leave ourselves vulnerable like that." His mother clenched her jaw at the memory.

"What happened to the girl he threw down the stairs?"

"Broke her hip. Walks funny now. Makes very little

money for me since, but what I can I do? I can't just toss her, not when it was my lack of sense got her into that mess."

"That was a good decision," Jeremiah said.

"Yeah, well, look at me and my bleeding heart." Her drink was finished. She stood up and went to refill her glass. "Jesus, men like that think they run this town, think they don't have to answer to anyone but themselves. I heard tell he got another girl pregnant, some girl at another house in the north end. He refused to pay to end it. Fought tooth and nail so the girl was forced to go through with it. He shows up, after nine months and all..." Her voice trailed off and she looked upset. "He takes one look at the baby and..."

"No." Jeremiah's stomach churned at the thought. "He didn't."

His mother nodded.

"Ah, Jesus." He lowered his head into his hand. Jeremiah felt queasy, his insides tumbling at the very thought. It was just a rumour, he told himself, but he also knew rumours were often rooted in truths or at least partial truths. "Why didn't anyone contact us? I could have arrested him."

"It's a cathouse, Jeremy, and not a nice one like this. You think your boys would have believed a woman like that? Not arrest her for solicitation? There's a whole world out there that you don't even know about. There's people living just outside the law and those people who are completely untouchable."

"You believe Ezekiel's untouchable."

"I know it... He's opening his own cathouse now, so I'm told," Vivian said. "I guess he can do whatever he'd like to those girls and no one's going to stop him."

"I met him for the first time today," Jeremiah said. "Saw the building he's renovating."

"Oh really?" She smiled. "Bet he was all graces and manners for a boy with brass buttons."

Jeremiah couldn't argue with that. Ezekiel seemed well versed in playing the part of an upscale businessman. "I don't know what to make of him—"

"Stay clear of him," his mother warned.

"What if he's breaking the law?"

"The street will take care of him," she said, taking a sip of her drink.

"How long will that take?" he asked. "I don't have the conscience to sit on my hands while he gets another kid like Maxwell London sent to the gallows."

She shrugged. She'd never been one for doing what she was told or overly concerning herself with the plight of others. When Jeremiah first told her his intentions of joining the force she was distraught, believing he'd be giving his talents to an ungrateful public. If she had her way he'd join the family business, manage her properties, and help her expand. Turns out, he wasn't one for doing what he was told either.

"You can't save them all, Jeremy," she said. "I believe I said as much about Ruth as well."

"I didn't come to argue." Jeremiah pushed himself from the comfort of the sofa and returned his empty glass to the sidebar.

"Rumour was she was with him," his mother said, her voice low.

"Come again?"

"Ruth. She's attached herself to Ezekiel in some way."

Jeremiah shook his head. "Impossible."

"Is it?" She took another sip of her drink. "If she were interested in returning to work, you know she wouldn't come back here."

Just the thought of Ruth aligning herself with such a man made Jeremiah's blood rush to his feet. His mother was right. Ruth had been all but banished from the property shortly before their nuptials, partly because of his mother's vexation with her for marrying her only son, but also because of another drunken episode that ended with Ruth's hand in the cash box in Vivian's office.

"I told you, she's a hard case," she said.

"Yes, Mother, I am aware." Jeremiah leaned in and planted a gentle kiss on the crest of her cheek.

"Then do something, Jeremy," she said as he walked to the door.

"I'm doing my best," he said. When he looked back she had one hand on her hip, the other was positioning the tumbler at her mouth so she could finish the rest in one gulp. "You might want to take it easy with those," he said, watching her pound the tumbler into the top of the sidebar.

"I'm doing my best," she said, with the wispy exhale of a thirst thoroughly quenched.

An hour later, Jeremiah was seated at his desk, the papers in front of him spread out like autumn leaves. As hard as he tried to concentrate on the case at hand, he couldn't keep his mind from returning back to thoughts of Ms. Eaton. When asked for her assistance she obliged right away, despite his heinous mistake. He should have never put those manacles on her, no matter his intentions. He was aware of her history with the law, and he had always sympathized with the injustice of it. He hated to think of Ms. Eaton in such a place as Mercer Reformatory and it chilled him to the bones to think the lovely Edith had been born there. What an outright ass he had been.

And yet, she had willingly accepted his apologies, though she never exactly said so. She accompanied him to the police storage house, and took great risk to her reputation for doing so. She was, undoubtedly, the most amazing woman—

KNOCK KNOCK

Jeremiah's attention snapped to the door where MacNeal stood. "Am I interrupting anything?"

Jeremiah sat up taller in his seat. "No, no," he said as lightheartedly as he could muster.

MacNeal stepped inside. Walker gathered some papers that he had scattered over his desk. MacNeal leaned over for a quick glance. "Train station murder?"

Walker let out an exhale. "Yeah, one of the boys we arrested, I'm trying to figure a way to get him out."

"Get him out?"

"Maxwell London." Jeremiah handed MacNeal the single-page file they had on him. "He doesn't belong in there, not with these types. No prior charges, not even a warning. I bet the chap still has all his teeth, he's so clean."

MacNeal chuckled as he looked over the file. "Did you

speak to him?"

"As well as I could. Simpson, his fellow thief, wouldn't let him say more than two words to me when I asked my questions."

"They're connected?"

"They probably both work for Maxwell's uncle, Ezekiel London. He's putting together a gentleman's club on College. A real hard case."

"Money?"

"Lots of it. Found out he'd been elected alderman two elections before last. Served one term and then stepped down before some accounting scandal hit the newspapers. He's been a private citizen ever since." Jeremiah left out the bit his mother told him. No sense in stirring the pot with rumours. The official information they had on him was already enough to paint him in a very bad light.

"This kid, Maxwell, how old is he?" MacNeal asked.

"Sixteen."

"You'd think with an uncle like that he'd have a number of priors."

Jeremiah tapped his fingers on the papers in front of him. "Apparently, his mother's been keeping him clear. Ms. Eaton tells me she passed away last year and he'd only just started working for Ezekiel."

"Ms. Eaton, is it?"

"Her daughter is a close friend of Maxwell's. As I understand it, he's like a son to Ms. Eaton. The children grew up together."

MacNeal smiled. "I see. You feel obligated to get him out of there."

"He doesn't belong there, MacNeal," Jeremiah said.

"So cut him a deal in exchange for telling us all he knows about his uncle's operations."

"He doesn't know anything. He only just started working for the man. And anything he did know I'm positive Simpson has beat out of him while in the confines of that cell." Jeremiah rubbed his face. "I demanded he be moved but you know these types. They're forced to put three or four men to a cell meant for two, they don't care who is housed with whom."

"He at least knows what happened that day. He may

know why he and Simpson were there. He may even know who the shooter is. That would be enough to set him free, if he agrees to testify."

"And if Ezekiel gets to him?"

MacNeal looked ready to wave off Jeremiah's concern for the boy's safety.

"This is a man who sent two young men, boys really, to a train station to kill someone in broad daylight. He had his own sister declared incorrigible and I don't know what he did to Ms. Eaton but she is terrified of him."

MacNeal handed the file back to Jeremiah. "Have him testify on the record in front of the judge before he even sets foot outside that jailhouse," he said. "Hopefully, nothing will happen, but if it does, you and the court will have a record of his testimony."

Jeremiah leaned back in his chair, his mind turning over MacNeal's solution. "That could work."

"Really?" MacNeal perked up.

Jeremiah shifted some papers to find a blank page. He wanted to write it down.

"I suppose I am good for something after all," MacNeal said with a nervous laugh.

"Who's been giving you a hard time? Not Chief Johnson."

"Nah. Green. I keep making mistakes on this investigation and Green is riding me about it."

Jeremiah raised an eyebrow. Green was a lower rank than MacNeal. He shouldn't be saying anything about MacNeal's manner of investigation. "What sort of mistakes?"

"We were at the storage facility today to re-evaluate some evidence found at the scene. The box is gone. It's like it never made it there. I know I tagged it. I itemized everything."

"How strange."

"And that's not even the half of it. My notes keep getting misplaced. Entire pages in my files gone. Pages I personally wrote out myself. It's like they never existed, but I know I created them." MacNeal shook his head, disbelieving his own carelessness. "I can't tell you how many meetings where I have shown up late."

"Late?" This was unlike MacNeal. As his partner for years, Jeremiah knew MacNeal with quite punctual.

"I'll make an appointment to interview a witness. I show up and Green's already there, nearly finished the interview. I swear, Walker, I'm starting to lose my faculties." MacNeal gave a weak laugh, part amusement, part worry. "It's the funniest thing."

"It's the job," Jeremiah said, slapping his pen down on the table. "It can get to you."

"Ain't that the truth... There is one thing that came up... something that I noticed before I started having so much trouble..." MacNeal's voice trailed off, as if building the courage to say what he was really thinking.

He closed the door, effectively cutting them off from the bustle happening farther down the hall.

"Forgive me for asking," MacNeal said, making up his mind to talk, "but I wanted to check with you to see if you had heard from Ruth recently."

Jeremiah struggled to keep his expression even. "No," he said easily, "I've heard nothing." He waited a moment, studying MacNeal's face for signs of mistrust.

"Nothing's come of your searches? Nothing at all?"

Jeremiah shook his head. "No... well, I thought I might have found someone who knew something but... that turned out to be nothing."

MacNeal nodded, his gaze drifting along the wall, his eyes not entirely focused.

"Should I have heard from her? Is something wrong?" Jeremiah shifted to the edge of his chair. He hated lying to his partner in such a way. The man would never forgive him if he found out Walker had been harbouring a suspected murderess at the centre of his investigation. He needed to keep playing the part of an estranged husband who hadn't seen his wife in months.

MacNeal put his hands out in front of him, entreating Jeremiah to remain calm. "No, nothing is wrong. Not that I can tell. It's just..." He paused. "I have reason to believe she may be involved in some way."

"You think Ruth killed your victim?" Jeremiah stood, sending his chair scraping along the floor behind him.

"No, no, nothing like that. Sit, Walker, please." MacNeal had a pained look on his face. "This is exactly why I have been avoiding talking to you about it." He ran his hand through his hair and stood with both hands at his hips.

Walker settled back into his seat, trying to pretend that the information MacNeal wished to tell him was new to him, that his wife hadn't been hiding from the law at his house this entire time.

"The man's name is Edward J. Dubois."

Jeremiah raised an eyebrow at this. "Dubois?" he repeated.

MacNeal waited for the possibility Walker might recognize it. "Several witnesses have told us Dubois is known to Ruth... intimately known." MacNeal's words were slow, and deliberate, delivered in a way that wouldn't set off Walker in a rage. He didn't know Walker's rage had all been spent in the months before when Ruth's whereabouts were truly unknown.

Jeremiah turned his gaze away. He had known, but now others knew. Ruth's behaviour was shameful and Walker would pay the price for her lack of care. He'd lose the respect of the men he worked with. Once word got out, he'd never be able to hold his head high in the station house again.

"I've kept this a secret from everyone," MacNeal said. "In my notes I've only written her down as R.W. If nothing comes of it, no one ever has to know."

Jeremiah looked up, appreciation in his eyes. "Thank you," he said.

"But, Walker, if something comes of it, I'm going to have to tell the Chief. I can't hide it from everyone forever."

"Do you know what she did? Or where she might be?"

"She's in hiding, we know that. We have reports of a man and a woman spotted in the cemetery the same night Dubois's body was found."

Jeremiah started. "A man and a woman?"

MacNeal nodded.

It could have been Ruth and Dubois, but more likely the witnesses had seen Walker and Ms. Eaton.

"Who told you this?"

"Residents in the area. They may have just been looking for a secluded place... you know how it is."

Jeremiah nodded coolly but his mind was awash with thoughts regarding his and Ms. Eaton's discovery. He had no alibi and no excuse to have been in the cemetery so late at night. If questioned it would eventually all point back to Ruth.

"You think my Ruth was the reason this man died?" Jeremiah managed to ask.

"I don't know for certain," MacNeal said. "I'm not even supposed to be talking to you about it given the conflict it presents me."

"Yes, of course. I understand."

"I thought I would let you know. Thought maybe Ruth had made contact or returned home. Maybe that would explain why you suddenly decided not to move in with me and Kirkpatrick."

"Huh? No, no, nothing like that. Just cold feet, I guess."

MacNeal nodded. "Thought as much." He turned to the door and pulled on the knob. "Oh, I should say, he was shot."

"Come again?"

"You never asked but Dubois was shot. Twice. Right here." MacNeal pointed to his chest. "Close range too, we reckon."

"Whoever it was he knew them well enough to get that close," Jeremiah said.

MacNeal nodded. "That's how I see it too."

"Good." Jeremiah smiled. "You're learning."

"From the best."

Jeremiah's throat went dry at his words. MacNeal closed the door after sliding into the hallway and thank God for that because then no one would see Jeremiah drop his head into his hands from exhaustion and worry. He should never have agreed to let Ruth hide out at his home, their home. He should have sent her on her way and let her troubles be her own.

Chapter 18

Mercy caught a glimpse of herself in her bedroom mirror and nearly gasped. Inching closer, she saw that her hair had released some pins, making the knot on her head appear lopsided and extremely loose. Her bodice was tinged with streaks of soot and dust and one glance to her skirt showed it was soiled even more so. The previously starched fabric was crimped and no longer sat on her shoulders and curves at it should. She looked like the worst version of herself, unkempt and deranged. She touched a hand to the side of her face and marvelled at the dark shadows under her eyes. She wondered if she had looked as bad when Walker had been with her. Had he seen her in such a state, so intimately close too?

"Goodness, Mercy," she said quietly to herself. "Why can't you be more like your sister, Constance?"

She was forced to look away from her reflection and began pulling at the buttons down the front of her bodice. She could have cried then, thinking about the state of her appearance, remembering all whom she'd interacted with, all whom had seen her in rush hour no less. Worst of all was the thought of the impression she had made on Walker. He must have thought so ill of her. Never before had she allowed him to see her so dishevelled. Well, once perhaps, but that was a special circumstance.

As she dressed in a freshly laundered skirt and blouse, she told herself to not worry about what Walker might or might not think of her. It wasn't as if Ruth was so well put together, now was she? And with Ruth back in his life, it wasn't exactly like he was looking at Mercy in any other way than friendship. He'd asked for her help because he trusted her. There couldn't be any other reason but that.

Mercy washed her face in the basin and then pulled at the remaining pins in her hair.

She'd miss him when it was all over. Once he no longer

needed her help protecting Ruth he'd have no further reason to stop by, not unless he chose to become a client of hers. Mercy very nearly giggled at the thought. A man such as that would never require her services. He was too assured, and far too skeptical. He'd never take her advice, not that she trusted herself to give the proper advice he needed. She was too close to him to be a fair judge. If she didn't watch herself she could easily tell him to divorce his wife and marry her instead.

Mercy raised her hands to her mouth, startled at her own thoughts. Where on earth had that come from? He was a married man, and therefore off limits. It did not matter if she didn't care for his wife. Ruth was the choice he had made and he was making good on his vows to take care of her. Mercy should not be getting between them in any way.

She quickly pulled her hair back, twisting it skillfully to create a knot and setting it in place with copious amounts of pins.

"Mama!" Edith voice came from the foyer, followed by the sound of the front door closing hard. "Are you home?"

"I'm up here, Edith," Mercy called out, patting the sides of her hair to make sure her knot would stay in place. She heard Edith pounding up the stairs before her head peered around the corner of the doorframe. "Any word about Maxwell?"

Mercy's shoulders sank. "I'm sorry, darling. It was just as I thought. Did you really expect a man like Ezekiel to stand by his nephew?"

All hope drained from Edith's features as she stood there.

"Detective Walker and I are working on it."

"You asked for Walker's help then?"

Mercy couldn't help but sigh. She met her daughter at the door. "He's a very busy man, Edith," she said. "Besides, I'm not sure there is much he can do."

"Mama!"

"Maxwell is to appear in court tomorrow," Mercy said, forcibly directing her daughter from the room. "Maybe we can make an appeal to the judge."

"And failing that?"

"We are going to have to start raising money for his

defence fund then." Mercy looked her daughter in the eye and saw the beginnings of tears welling up in her lower lids. "I'm not going to let him rot in there. Not while there are still things we can do out here, understand?" Mercy pulled her daughter in for a hug. "Are you hungry?" Mercy asked, still holding her daughter close.

"Famished."

"Let's get something on the stove. We can conjure up a game plan while we eat."

Mercy felt Edith nod but she did not move from her mother's embrace.

"I love you, Mama." Edith's words came out muffled against Mercy's shoulder.

"What was that?" Mercy asked, pulling her daughter away slightly.

"I love you," Edith repeated, wiping tears from her cheeks. "I'm sorry for what I said last night. I didn't mean it... any of it."

"I thought as much," Mercy confessed. "But it is very nice to hear you say it."

"I also wanted to say that I don't think anyone else has a mother quite like you."

Mercy chuckled. "Now, isn't that the truth?" She turned her daughter toward the stairs. "Come now, we can't save Maxwell on empty stomachs."

Edith went ahead, bounding down the stairs before turning to the kitchen. In the hallway Mercy paused at the narrow table and fished inside her pocket for the cameo pendant she'd found in the graveyard. The entire walk home she'd hoped she had been mistaken about the name but looking at it once more she clearly saw "Ruth" etched in gold.

Mercy held it in her hand. She'd heard her grandmother tell a story once of a woman who was able to hold an object in her hand, even briefly, and immediately know who had owned it. It was said she could give intimate details of the owner's life beyond the object in question. Mercy held it in her palm for some time, willing images to come forth, wanting to confirm the necklace was indeed Ruth Walker's, but she came up blank. Reading objects was not her gift.

Mercy opened the single drawer of the table in front of

her, careful to not make a sound, and deposited the necklace inside. As she closed the drawer she ran all manner of excuses through her head, but in the end she could only conclude that Ruth must have been there, in the graveyard. She'd have seen everything. She'd either pulled the trigger, or knew the person that did.

A knock sounded at her front door, startling Mercy enough to send her back from the hallway table. She composed herself quickly and was surprised to find Walker standing on her front porch. He was holding a small posy of flowers he must have purchased from the florist a block away.

"I've come to apologize," he said, "for my behaviour earlier." He handed her the posy. "And for other things."

"Other things?"

Walker stepped out of the way, revealing Maxwell standing directly behind him. Before Mercy's mind was able to register what she was seeing, Edith pushed past her. "Max!"

Although dirty and scruffy from his stay in jail, Mercy had not seen a better sight than Maxwell standing free on her front porch. He smiled broadly as Edith came to him and then flushed red when she hugged him tightly.

"I don't understand," Mercy said, looking to Walker. "How did you manage to get him released?"

"I met with the judge he was slated to see in the morning, I spoke on his behalf and, in exchange for his testimony against his uncle, we managed to get his charges downgraded on account of his age." Walker looked to Maxwell. "He has some restitution to give but he won't have to see the inside of that cell anymore, and that's what matters."

"Restitution?" Edith asked from Maxwell side. She looked between her mother and Walker in confusion.

"I still need to pay back my debt to society through community work, that sort of thing," Maxwell explained.

"That's not fair."

"It don't bother me none," Maxwell said. "As long as I never have to see that place again."

"But... they expect him to testify against his uncle?" Mercy hugged herself at the thought. "Walker, I don't—"

"It's a risk, I am aware," Walker said.

"It's a risk I'm willing to take," Maxwell said, puffing out his chest with a slight bravado.

"Max, this is Ezekiel we are talking about," Mercy said.

"I don't care. I've seen enough and heard enough over the years to know he has to pay for what he's done. It ain't right. He's not the upstanding citizen he wants everyone to think he is."

Mercy watched as Maxwell's features hardened. Gone was the innocence of youth Mercy had seen in him not two days before. Jail had hardened him somewhat. Secretly Mercy hoped he'd soften up before long and become the youthful optimist he once was.

"First things first," he said, brightening the mood, "I need to find a place to stay."

"You are staying here with us," Mercy said decisively.

"Ms. Eaton, I can't—"

"Oh, hush," Mercy chided. "You are staying here with me so I can look out for you, like I promised your mother." She reached over and touched the side of his face, marvelling at how much he looked like Hazel.

Edith beamed. "You can have the room beside mine."

Walker blanched.

"No," Mercy corrected, playfully pulling Edith away from Maxwell. "He can have the room off the kitchen. It's cozy but it'll be more than warm enough from the heat of the kitchen."

Maxwell nodded. "I'm much obliged, ma'am."

"Ah, don't you dare call me ma'am," Mercy said with a laugh, directing Edith into the house. "It will be Ms. Mercy, like your mother asked you."

"Yes ma'am, er, I mean, Ms. Mercy."

Mercy stepped aside to allow him to follow Edith inside. Once alone, she turned her attention to Walker. "Edith and I were just going to put down some supper, you are free to join us."

Walker hesitated to accept. He glanced over her shoulder to the cheery conversation happening behind them. "I wouldn't want to intrude."

Mercy waved away his refusal. "Not an intrusion at all." She reached for the posy and purposely graced his hand with her own. The brief touch sent a warm sensation through her hand and up the length of her arm. She raised her gaze and for a moment they locked eyes. Internally, Mercy begged him to stay. Each time they left each other she felt a gaping hole in her chest, one that remained empty for as long as they were apart. When they were together, even just standing opposite each other, she was content, almost giddy, something she hadn't felt in a very long time.

"All right then," he said, a sheepish smile on his lips. "I'd like that very much."

Over the two hours, the group of four remained in the warm glow of the kitchen lights, sharing food and laughter, each one of them ignoring the hardships they'd endured earlier in the day. At the table Mercy and Walker sat opposite each other. Every so often Mercy would find Walker stealing glances at her, looking intently while all other attention was on Max or Edith, whomever was telling a story at the time. Once caught, Walker would smile and drop his gaze. Sometimes, to cover up his intensity for Mercy, he'd ask the speaker a question, or offer a joke and send the table into laughter.

The mood was exuberant. Maxwell was finally out of that wretched place and life seemed less chaotic in the warmth of Mercy's kitchen. Around the table, the minutes slowed and the outside world felt like a distant memory, so much so that when a knock sounded from the front door everyone paused but no one seemed willing to break their reverie. The disruption both surprised them and yet came as no surprise. Mercy and Walker matched eyes, their mood crestfallen, their willingness to answer to the door non-existent.

Finally, Edith said what they were all thinking. "We don't have to answer it, Mama," she said.

Mercy surveyed the reluctant looks around the table but ultimately knew she'd have to go answer the door. She laid her hand gently over Edith's and gave a slight squeeze as she stood. Walker met her at the threshold of the kitchen.

"Your daughter has a valid point," he said, a pained look on his face. "Perhaps we should take her advice." He appeared the most reluctant of all of them.

In that moment she realized how much he had needed

such an evening, a time of friendship and laughter, to break bread and bask in the welcoming warmth of a chosen family.

A second knock came, this one louder and more persistent than the first.

"And what if it's MacNeal, or Ruth, would you have me not answer for them?" Mercy asked.

"Damn them," Walker said sternly. "I don't care about them. I only care about..." His eyes searched her face, taking her in, looking for something. "I only care about..."

Mercy waited, knowing he longed to profess what she had told him a week ago.

A third knock, harsh and demanding down the hall, drew his attention and broke their spell. With a heavy heart, Mercy turned from him and made her way to the door. The night air rushed in, the reality of the outside world sending barriers up around them.

Standing on Mercy's front porch was Mrs. Audulay, ill at ease and agitated. "My son," she said quickly, "I must speak with my son."

Walker came to the door at the sound of his mother's voice. "How did you know I was here?" he asked.

"Your partner, Mac-something, he told me where I'd most likely find you." Her tone matched her scowl. Her patience was at an end. "It's your wife," she said. "She's gone."

"What do you mean 'gone'?"

Mercy stepped back, giving the pair some distance, but remained close enough in the hall to hear what was said.

"Gone, as in no longer there where you left her." Mrs. Audulay raised an eyebrow, unimpressed. "I went to check up on her, well, on you actually, and I found the door open and your parlour ransacked. Ruth is very much gone."

Mercy watched as Walker's shoulders sank as if resigned to this inevitable outcome. She turned to the hallway stand and pulled at her gloves and shawl. "We will go see what can be done," she said, pulling on her gloves.

Walker placed a hand on her arm. "I can't permit you to come," he said.

"Then it's a good thing I didn't ask for your permission." She returned his gaze squarely, unflinchingly resolved to assist in whichever way she could. She shook off his hand when she raised her shawl over her head and draped it over her shoulders. When she looked to Mrs. Audulay on the porch she saw the older woman give a slight smile.

"Mama?" Edith came into the hallway, with Maxwell close at her heels, and a look of trepidation on her face. She surveyed Mrs. Audulay at the front door. She came alongside her mother and leaned in close. "Is that Mrs. Audulay?" she asked in a low voice.

Mercy looked to her daughter, surprised she would recognize her.

"Sister Mary warned us to steer clear," Edith explained, again careful to keep her voice low.

Mercy looked to Mrs. Audulay and saw her pull back her shoulders in defiance. A practiced maneuver, Mercy realized. "Your notoriety precedes you," Mercy said, her tone apologetic.

"It usually does," Mrs. Audulay replied with a closed-mouth smile.

"Should we come?" Maxwell asked, breaking the awkward silence that had fallen over them.

"No, absolutely not."

"I'd like to help." Maxwell stepped forward as if to pass her in favour of the door, but Mercy stopped him.

"I need you here to watch out for Edith, yes? Can you do that for me?"

Maxwell nodded.

Mercy stepped out onto the porch. "Let's go, Walker," she called out over her shoulder. "She couldn't have gotten far."

Chapter 19

"She's gone." Jeremiah ran his hand through his hair and rubbed his face in anguish.

"Isn't this exactly what I already told you?" his mother asked.

They stood in the parlour, the heavy drapes still drawn over the windows, a few of Ruth's things dotting the sofa and side tables. Her shawl, a broach, and a single, stained glove. The lamp was overturned, the frosted globe broken into a hundred pieces, and the oil spilled out over the floor. It was a miracle nothing had been set ablaze.

At the centre of the room was a small pool of blood, about the size of a cast iron frying pan, unmistakable and difficult to miss.

"Someone found out where she was," Ms. Eaton said, from the archway to the room.

Jeremiah noticed a teacup spilled over next to the sofa, a crumbled biscuit with jam ground into the carpet as if stepped on. He placed a few fingers on the side of the cup to feel what remained of the tea. "It's not entirely cold," he said. "Not yet."

His mother seemed surprised by his finding. "This couldn't have happened but a few minutes before I came," she said.

Jeremiah stood back to take in the scene in its entirety. In his mind he tried to lay out the attack. Was she approached from behind or the front? Where was she standing? Probably nearest the lamp, he imagined. It would have needed the most amount of energy to overturn, whereas the spindly side table legs could have easily been bumped as a later part of the struggle. But the bloodstain didn't fit. Whoever it was who attacked Ruth must have thrown her that way and she must have fallen. And then...?

"When I came to visit she had been startled, by what I don't know. It wasn't unlike how she had been the night she came back."

Mrs. Audulay scoffed. "Ruth is never startled by anything. So self-assured, that one. Too self-assured, if you ask me." She looked to her son. "When I came she had all the piss and vinegar I remember and then some."

"But that's exactly my point," Ms. Eaton explained, taking a step forward. "She was terrified when I first met her. Then once she feels safe she reverts back to old habits. She gets complacent. Until something happened to remind her why she was hiding."

"But the door is intact," his mother said. "No one forced their way in."

Jeremiah went to the front door and examined the framing. There were no new marks on the wood or the brass of the knob and latch. The small window was untouched as well. He went to the rear door and discovered it was still locked from the inside.

"How did you find the door when you first arrived?" he asked.

"Wasn't latched all the way," his mother said. "Not locked. Just hovering there between open and closed."

Jeremiah stood frozen in his living room, his mind conjuring up the image of Ruth answering the door to someone she knew, someone she might have trusted enough to get her out of trouble. But then why hadn't she gone to that person instead of coming back to him? Why had she come back to him after all that time, when their marriage was merely a statement in the church ledger?

"Or maybe this was part of her plan all along," he suggested. His mother was preoccupied with adjusting the cushion on the sofa, so he turned to Ms. Eaton, knowing she would understand. "She came back just long enough to put my position on the force in jeopardy."

"Just long enough to leave this."

Jeremiah looked to his mother and saw a small pistol held up in her outstretched hand.

"Where did you find that?"

"Here, under the sofa," she said. "Just now."

Jeremiah took it from her and brought it closer to the window so he could examine it under the light of the streetlamp. It wasn't his. His was locked in his desk drawer in his office at the station. He sniffed it. It smelled of gunpowder.

"It was used recently," he said. "I think they shot her."

"Who shot her?" his mother pressed.

"And why?" Ms. Eaton added.

"We know why. She's a fucking embarrassment, that's why."

Out of the corner of his eye, Jeremiah saw Ms. Eaton sink back.

"I knew it," his mother said. "I knew that little vixen would be the undoing of all my hard work."

"What are you saying, Mother?"

"I'm saying she's deliberately left this shit, all of this," she said gesturing to the blood on the carpet and the state of the room.

"We don't know that," Jeremiah was quick to say.

"Fucking open your eyes, Jeremy!" His mother stood. "She's conned you once again just like when she had you believing she actually loved you."

"Mother, please."

"I can't do it anymore, Jeremy. I can't watch as you ruin your life, your career, everything because of some unearned belief you have in this woman, a woman who has done nothing but use you for years." She reached for her shawl. "You aught to throw that thing in the Don River and be done with it. Be done with her for good." She marched to the hallway as if to leave and suddenly turned to face Ms. Eaton. "It's been charming to meet you, Ms. Eaton, but if you are half as smart as you have demonstrated you are, you'll clear yourself of this man and never think twice about it." She gave a sideways glance to Jeremiah. "He'll never leave his wife, no matter how much she abuses him."

"Mother... please."

Mrs. Audulay said nothing more. Seconds later the door slammed, signifying her departure.

Jeremiah collapsed into the sofa behind him, lowering his head into his hand, while the other held the gun out in front of him.

"Do you really believe Ruth is in trouble?" Mercy asked, still hovering near the door.

"She is very troubled," he said, almost refusing to look

up. "But this?" He alternated his gaze between the gun in his hand and the bloodstain on the floor. "I can't tell what's real anymore and if you listen to my mother I never could, not when Ruth is involved." He wondered if Ms. Eaton would heed his mother's advice and leave him to his misery. He tossed the gun to the carpet and saw it land a few inches from the blood. "She wasn't always like this—Ruth, I mean. When we first met, she was kind and attentive. Which, to be honest, was the opposite of how I was raised. My mother kept me at a distance. She was a businesswoman and I was a hinderance."

Ms. Eaton inched into the room as he spoke and took a seat on the sofa nearest him.

"Ruth gave me the attention I wish I had received from my mother. I was smitten from the first hello." He released a nervous laugh. "She was happy enough at first but things changed quickly. My mother warned me then that Ruth had grown tired of me. It was her way. Ruth grew bored easily, she said. I didn't listen. I proposed in an effort to keep her interest. I don't know why she said yes. I convinced myself that after the wedding things would go back to the way they were but they never did. My attempts to retain her attention changed into cleaning up her antics. I made excuses, offered apologies... many, many apologies." He laughed again. "Once she was caught stealing a crate of liquor from behind a bar. She had sewn pockets in her bustle, folds in the fabric where she could place each bottle. Well, one fell out and tumbled to the floor. I paid the barkeep fifty dollars, my entire savings at the time, to not contact the police."

"You must have been angry," Ms. Eaton said.

"Very angry. Angrier than I ever thought possible. I never struck her. I could never do such a thing, but I thought about it for a brief moment. I was that angry. Then I felt shame for being so angry at the woman I loved. Every evening I begged her to stay home. I begged her not to go and she left anyway. She'd look me right in the eyes, see my pain, and leave anyway."

"And one day she never came back," Ms. Eaton offered.

"I didn't know where she was or what had happened to her. I'd hear rumours but nothing came of any of it. I chased her around the city, took out newspaper ads asking for information. It was like even after she left I was begging her... begging her to come home, begging providence to return things to the way they were and ignoring the way it actually was. I was a fool, an absolute fool."

"We all do stupid things for the ones we love."

When Jeremiah looked up he realized Ms. Eaton had put her hand on top of his own, which was resting on his knee.

"No," he said suddenly. "She was like a dream I cooked up for myself, made up of bits and pieces of a woman I wanted her to be but never was. I don't love her," Jeremiah said. "I thought I did once, but"—he took in Ms. Eaton's face, tracing the curve of her cheek and returning her hopeful gaze—"I know better now."

He turned his palm up and wrapped his fingers around hers, solidifying her hand in his. With a gentle pull he drew her toward him. They came together slowly, pressing their lips together first, and then he placed a hand on her waist and drew her body even closer. She submitted to him easily, draping her free arm over his and reaching for his neck, holding him to her.

It was the most natural thing he could imagine—having her in his arms. Now that he had her he was afraid to let her go. When they finally pulled apart her gaze dropped.

"I'm sorry," he said, wondering if he had read her signals wrong. "I didn't mean—"

She pulled her hand away. "You're still married," she said, her voice barely a whisper.

A knock rang out from the front door, harsh and persistent. "Walker!"

Jeremiah's eyes widened at the sound of MacNeal.

"Walker, open up!"

Ms. Eaton jumped to her feet in panic.

"It's all right," Walker said, going to her to calm her down. "You didn't do anything wrong," he said softly, wrapping his arm around her waist in an effort to comfort her. He saw the tears, the panic. "They aren't here for you," he said. "They are looking for Ruth."

She gave a feeble nod and used both hands to rub the tears from her face.

"Walker!" MacNeal hit the door again, rattling the small

window encased in the frame. Suddenly, he burst in without apology. His gun was drawn. Two uniformed officers filed in around him, each with their own gun in their hands, ready to take aim.

It took a moment for MacNeal to take in the scene: the overturned lamp, the gun, and blood.

"Jeremiah Walker, you are under arrest," he said, his features hardening at the sight of his partner among the wreckage. "Turn around."

Jeremiah stood stunned as MacNeal pushed on his shoulder, trying to force him to turn. "Arrested for what? Ms. Eaton and I just got here. We had nothing to do with it."

"MacNeal, stop," Ms. Eaton said. "There's been a misunderstanding."

"There's no misunderstanding," MacNeal said, fastening the handcuffs around Jeremiah's wrists. "Ruth told us what happened—"

"Ruth? Where is she?" Jeremiah asked, trying to look over his shoulder at his partner.

"She's at the hospital with a bullet wound in her arm, a bullet wound you gave her. Now, let's move."

Chapter 20

Mercy left Walker's house at the behest of the two uniformed officers intent on securing the scene. She was escorted to the porch in time to see MacNeal retreating from the police carriage. Through the window she could see Walker seated on the bench.

"MacNeal, there's been a mistake. I didn't—"

MacNeal snapped the door shut. "Take him to the station. I'll question him there," he said to Officer Green, who quickly climbed up to the driver's perch. "I won't be long," MacNeal said, as the carriage rolled into motion.

Mercy made her way to MacNeal. "You can't just arrest him with no evidence."

"Ms. Eaton, I have signs of a struggle, a pool of blood, a gun, and a woman in an extreme amount of pain who says her husband shot her. What more do I need?" MacNeal brushed by her and headed for the front door to Walker's house.

"Walker is your partner!" she called out after him. "Doesn't he deserve the benefit of the doubt?"

If Mercy's words gave MacNeal pause, it was short-lived. "No, ma'am," he said. "Not in this case." He turned his back to her and headed inside.

"Rough evening, Ms. Eaton?"

Mercy turned toward the voice and found Alistair George standing beside her, his notebook out, his pencil scribbling away furiously already.

"Care to make a comment regarding the events of this evening and the recent arrest of one of Toronto's finest police detectives?" he asked.

Without any thought to what she was doing, Mercy grabbed the pencil from his hand and pressed the graphite into the stone step in front of them. She made sure the tip was broken clean before handing it back to the newspaperman.

She walked away before he could ask anything else and headed in the direction of the station house.

***

Steps from the station house Mercy heard a single-horse cart pull up alongside her.

"Mercy Marigold Eaton! What on earth are you doing out here at this time of night?"

When Mercy looked she saw it was Constance and Alexander peering down at her from the bench seat at the front. It was Constance who had spoken, exasperated and panicking.

"Constance, I haven't the time," Mercy said as Connie and her husband clamoured down from the cart.

"Haven't the time? I haven't the time to drop everything and go running around looking for you."

"Mighty fine of you to have your sister and I scouring the streets for you at this late an hour," Alexander said, huffing slightly from his descent.

"I certainly never asked you to," Mercy said, stepping back slightly from Alexander's overbearing stance. He smelled of gin, and more than a single bottle.

"You forced us to when we came by your house this evening and my niece tells me you aren't in. She was babbling something about a woman who's gone missing, and you running off with Walker and some lady of the night."

"Calm yourself, Constance, I am all right," Mercy said, stealing a glance toward the glow of the station house. "It's nothing as dramatic as that," she lied. It was much, much worse.

"Mercy, it's after midnight," Constance said. "What woman of reputation is caught out after midnight?"

"You should be at home," Alexander interjected, "with your daughter."

"And you both should be at home with yours!"

"Mercy," Constance nearly growled. "Stop making such a fuss and get in the cart." She came alongside Mercy and grabbed her arm in an attempt to lead her. Mercy shrugged herself free and retreated a safe distance.

"My escort is waiting for me inside," she said sternly. "I have no need for another."

"You are a wanton, wanton woman," Alexander snapped.

"And you are a drunkard and... and a leech!"

"Mercy!"

Mercy refused to listen to another word. She marched into the station house, bypassed the desk sergeant, and went straight down the hall. Both Walker and MacNeal's offices were empty, so she headed for the large common room at the back of the building.

"I'm telling you, I didn't shoot her!" she could hear Walker shouting. When she rounded the corner she saw him seated, his hands still cuffed behind him, forcing him to sit on the edge of the seat they gave him.

Both MacNeal and Green stood over him while other officers observed from a distance. It seemed all other police work had stopped and everyone was invested in this interrogation. When Mercy walked in, Walker's face alighted at the sight of her; it was slight, but it was enough.

"The bullet in Mrs. Walker's arm proves otherwise," Green said. His tone was assured, displaying a bravado as if he alone had solved the case.

"I'm not arguing she was shot," Walker said. "But you cannot say it was I who did it."

"How long has she been at your house, Walker?" Green asked.

"I don't know. Probably just today. I wasn't home," Walker answered without missing a beat.

"The blood on the carpet proves something happened to Mrs. Walker in that house," MacNeal said.

"But that isn't my gun. Please, MacNeal, go check. Bottom drawer in my office. My key is on the hook behind the door. My gun is there where I left it."

MacNeal eyed him, as if pondering whether such a search would prove him weak in front of the others.

"I can check, MacNeal," one of the other uniformed officers said.

MacNeal pondered this. "No," he said. "I'll go."

Mercy sank into the wall to allow him to pass. She turned slightly and saw that her sister and brother-in-law had followed her in. Mercy moved away but couldn't move so far as to draw attention to herself.

Seconds later MacNeal returned, a black pistol in his

hands.

"See? I couldn't have done it. I only own a single gun and I never take it home with me," Walker said.

"What sort of officer of the law doesn't have his gun on him at all times?" Green asked.

"A responsible one." The look Walker gave Green sent a chill up Mercy's spine. It was clear these two men would always be at odds.

Mercy felt Constance's hand on her arm. "Mercy, you have to come with us," she said.

Mercy pulled her arm away and sidestepped farther along the wall and away from Constance and her brother.

"Mrs. Walker tells us you are responsible for killing her lover, Edward Dubois."

"Absolutely not!" Walker stood, as if unable to contain his anger while seated. "Why would I do such a thing?"

Green shrugged. "Jealousy? Revenge? Perhaps both."

"Can you account for your whereabouts on the night of June seventh?" MacNeal asked, looking to his notes.

Mercy clasped a hand over her mouth. June seventh was the night she and Walker had found the body in the graveyard, the night Ruth had returned home and gone into hiding.

"I wasn't killing Edward Dubois, if that's what you mean."

"Can anyone verify that?" Green asked.

"No—"

"I can." Mercy stepped forward. Her sudden courage froze slightly at the sight of all the men in the room turning to look at her. Even Walker's gaze was not encouraging. She could feel him begging her to stop with wide eyes and a pleading look. "He was with me," she said, in defiance.

"She's lying," Green said. He tapped MacNeal's arm. "She'd say anything—"

"This is the truth!" Mercy snapped. "He was with me."

MacNeal gave a quick chuckle and rubbed the back of his neck. "May I ask what you were doing?"

Mercy kept her gaze on him, positive that if she showed any hesitation they'd accuse her of lying. "Having relations," she said, as straight as she could muster.

She saw Walker close his eyes and bow his head.

"I knew it!" Alexander yelled from behind her. "I knew you were a trollop from the moment I first met you. A trollop and a whore!"

"Call me all the names you want, Alex," Mercy said, solidifying her defiance. "I can't be sent back there, not by you or anyone else. I'll never set foot in that place again, no matter how much you wish you could sign me over."

"What place?" MacNeal asked.

"Mercer Reformatory for Incorrigible Women and Girls," Mercy said.

"You were an inmate there?" MacNeal asked.

"Edith was born there."

MacNeal blanched, familiar with the rumours if not the reality of such a place.

"The truth is, Walker wouldn't say anything because he is trying to protect me," she said. "He was with me, MacNeal."

"It's their word against all this evidence," Green said.

"What evidence?" Mercy asked. "You have proven it's not Walker's gun, and any woman with foresight can fake a bloodstain."

She saw Walker smile.

"The gunshot to her arm?" Green asked incredulously.

"It's her left arm," Mercy pointed out. She approached the desk, picked up Walker's gun, and aimed it at her left arm. "My guess is the wound is self-inflicted."

"Self-inflicted." MacNeal repeated Mercy's words slowly, as if allowing the possibility to sink in.

"How did Ruth say it happened?" Walker asked.

MacNeal looked to one of the uniformed officers. "I only spoke with her briefly," the officer said. "She seemed to be in a lot of pain."

"What did she say, Benson?"

"She said Walker had been keeping her locked up and she wanted to leave. He shot her."

"Was she standing or sitting?" Mercy asked.

"Huh?"

"Standing or sitting? Was she standing or sitting when he shot her?" Mercy demanded.

"I dunno... standing, I guess."

Mercy smiled. "MacNeal, when you were at Walker's

house did you happen to see where the bullet ended up?"

"In the doorframe leading to the foyer."

"How high was it off the ground?" she asked.

"A couple feet," he said.

"She was sitting, probably in the middle of the rug. But she was sitting because she knew the gunshot would hurt and she didn't want to fall."

"Well, I'll be..." MacNeal exhaled as he took it all in.

"Is that what had your attention at the house?" Walker asked, a slight smile on his lips.

Mercy shrugged. "Didn't seem like I was needed for that part of the conversation," she said quietly.

"You aren't actually believing this claptrap?" Green asked.

"It's plausible," MacNeal answered.

"When was Mrs. Walker admitted to hospital?" Mercy asked.

Benson looked to his notebook. "Seven-ten."

"That settles it," Mercy said with a smile. "Walker couldn't have shot her because he was with me"— Constance gasped—"and my daughter and a family friend, at my house *having dinner*."

Mercy looked to her sister, who still wasn't appeased by the revelation that it was only dinner.

"Since when do we allow women to do the work of police officers?" Green asked, clearly more upset than anyone else.

"Since us police officers couldn't be trusted to be objective enough," MacNeal said.

Green left the room, muttering something under his breath.

MacNeal turned to Walker. "I'm sorry, Walker," he said. "It's this case. It's just getting to me." He motioned for Walker to stand and turn so he could remove the cuffs.

"Is Ruth going to be in trouble now?" Mercy asked.

"I'll have to speak with Johnson," MacNeal said. "But filing a false report, dangerous discharge of a firearm within city limits. It doesn't look good."

"What's the trouble with the case?" Walker asked, rubbing his wrists now that the cuffs were off.

"I don't—"

"The body's missing, for one thing," Benson said, moving toward them.

"What? The body's missing?" Walker looked to MacNeal.

"Mercy, it's time to go," Constance hissed from behind her.

"Go yourself. I'm not leaving," Mercy snapped back, trying to listen to the conversation between Walker and MacNeal.

"Dr. Bishop sent a messenger this morning," MacNeal said. "He showed up at the morgue to do the necropsy and Edward Dubois was gone."

"How could such a thing happen without someone noticing?" Walker asked.

Mercy felt a heavy hand on her arm, pinching her skin and pulling her backward. "Let's go, you trollop."

Mercy struggled against the strong hands of her brother-in-law. "Don't touch me," she said, squirming as he tried to get a hold of her other arm to lead her away. "I can take care of myself." She imagined if he could wrestle her into one of his coffins he would, and he'd ensure the lid was nailed shut.

Her mind went to the graveyard that afternoon. She remembered sitting by the tree, the odd-looking coffin being led toward the grave site. The feeling she had while in the hearse, the feeling that there was more to be told, another soul to be read.

"Walker, I know where the body is!" she yelled out, yanking her arm out of her brother-in-law's grasp.

MacNeal and Walker looked to her.

"I didn't visit my sister this afternoon like I'd said. Well, I didn't just go to visit her. Mr. Carver's funeral was today," she said. "Constance was the one who dressed him and prepped him for burial."

His expression soured. "You read him, didn't you? Your sister granted you access and you read him without my consent."

"I didn't see the harm in it," she said with a desperate air. "I only wished to help."

"What does 'you read him' mean?" Benson asked.

MacNeal opened his mouth as if to explain before finally waving him off. "It's complicated," he said.

Walker looked stern. "If Mrs. Carver found out—"

"She won't. Connie and I were discreet. No one saw."

"Ms. Eaton, you know I don't want you getting involved."

"But why not? I have this gift. Let's use it. I can help."

MacNeal snorted. "She seems pretty involved already, don't you think, Walker?"

"She's going to get hurt!"

Mercy recoiled slightly at his emphatic response. Walker's expression softened immediately.

"I didn't mean to frighten you." He took a breath as if to steady himself. "I remember what happened last time. It's all well and good when you are reading people who died from consumption or old age, but the corpses that I come in contact with have much more traumatic stories. You can't handle it."

"You don't know what I can handle."

"Ms. Eaton, please."

Mercy had been ordered about all her life by men who thought they knew better, who somehow saw her as incapable of making her own decisions. They expected her to obey and, if she didn't, they made her obey. Walker was different, though. He spoke from genuine concern for her safety, concern for her as a person. It was something Mercy was not used to.

"Do you want to know where your missing body is or not?" she asked, crossing her hands over her chest in defiance.

Chapter 21

In the end Mercy allowed her sister and brother-in-law to see her home but only after Walker's insistence. He had promised not to act on the information she shared until he came to see her the next day. "You *will* come see me?" she asked, keeping her voice low, wanting to ensure he wasn't making a false promise. A smile tickled his lips as he locked down at her. "Yes," he said, tucking a loose curl behind her ear, "Nothing could keep me away." She saw him give a quick glance about the room before leaning in to kiss her gently on the cheek. His lips were warm and soft on her skin. It took a great deal of restraint not to lean into him and demand more. She knew the others in the room watched them, Alexander and Constance especially.

The cart ride home was awkward, to say the least. Sandwiched between her equally vexed sister and brother-in-law, Mercy endured nearly twenty minutes of admonishments from them, both warning her regarding her behaviour, the reputation she was creating for herself, and the consequences were she to continue in such a manner. By the final blocks of their journey their words had morphed to mumbles and then background noise. In the morning she couldn't even remember uttering goodbyes to them or bidding them farewell in any manner.

"I still can't believe Constance and Alexander followed me into the station house," Mercy said, sliding some fried eggs onto two breakfast plates she was making for Edith and Maxwell. "Did they really expect me just to drop what I was doing and let them take me home?"

Edith slid Maxwell's plate across the surface of the table to where he sat. "Did I do something wrong?" Edith asked.

"No, honey, you were only being truthful," Mercy said quickly. "You could have left out the bit about the lady of the night, though."

Edith pressed her lips together. "That's what Maxwell

said."

Mercy offered Maxwell a smile. "And this is why he and I get along so well." She set a fork down beside Maxwell's place setting. "Come now, both of you, dig in."

Raven was curled up in the fourth seat at the table. Mercy gave him a long stroke from his head to his tail as she passed him and went to the hall. Inside the hallway table she found the cameo pendant and slipped it into her pocket. After the events of last night, she knew Walker would want to have it, and know where it was found.

A soft rap sounded from the door. When Mercy answered it she found Walker on the other side. She couldn't help but blush, thinking upon their kiss the evening before, followed by her confession in front of the entire police force that happened to be on duty. She had no doubt that anyone who was not there was by then privy to her confession.

"Good morning, Detective Walker," Mercy said with an air of formality. She stepped aside, inviting him into her parlour. "Edith and Maxwell are having breakfast."

Walker was slow to say anything as he followed her into the room.

"I hope you slept well," she said as a means of keeping the silence from becoming too awkward.

"Not a wink," he answered. "MacNeal's sofa is not very comfortable."

She found him staring at her curiously, as if something lay on the tip of his tongue.

"About last night—"

"I didn't have to lie like that?" she said, quickly cutting him off.

"Well, no, but... yes. You didn't have to do that."

"Yes, I did. In my experience, men are quicker to believe a woman capable of improprieties than they are to believe in her virtue. I could have said things were innocent between you and I—"

"Which they are."

"Or I could have told them what they wanted to hear anyway. I personally feel the story I told them was more effective. What sort of woman would risk her reputation by confessing so willingly to such deeds with a married man? A truthful one."

"You could have told them the actual truth."

"But then we'd both be in shackles, now wouldn't we? Everyone believes it of us anyway. Why fight the current?"

Walker smiled. "Why indeed?"

Mercy slipped her hand in her pocket and pulled out the cameo. "I found this at the graveyard yesterday," she said, handing it over to Walker. "It was near the tree where... well, Mr. Dubois was found. Last night I was so excited about Maxwell getting out of jail I forgot all about it."

Walker took it and looked closely at it.

"Was it a gift from you?" Mercy asked. It seemed like a gift a young, newlywed husband would give.

"One of many," he said.

"She must have been wearing it that night," Mercy said.

"She told me she wasn't there," Walker said. "She swore to it."

"She also swore to a police officer that you shot her," Mercy said.

Walker gathered up the chain and put it in an inside pocket. "Thank you," he said.

The mood between them was laced with words left unsaid. Gone was the easy manner with which they conversed not the day before. In its place there was embarrassment and perhaps a bit of shame. For the first time Mercy second-guessed her false confession and wondered if perhaps it had caused Walker to think less of her. Perhaps he feared she was just another wanton harlot like his wife.

"She's gone, by the way," he said.

"Ruth?"

"She left the hospital without permission. Bypassed the officer watching over her and slipped out a back stairwell." Walker appeared resigned, as if it were just another impediment he'd have to overcome.

"Someone must have told her that her story was proven false," Mercy said. "That we'd figured her out."

"Who would do that?"

"Any number of people. A police officer, no doubt."

His face froze with an expression somewhere between disbelief and irritation.

"Walker, you give others too much leeway. Not all officers

are like you."

"Not all officers are like your stepfather."

Mercy closed her eyes, willing herself not to get angry. "You have to entertain the possibility," she said, after a moment. "Maybe I'm wrong," she said, when Walker didn't reply immediately. "Maybe she just overheard someone talking with the officer assigned to watch over her."

Walker's mood alighted at this suggestion. Somehow it was far easier to believe the breach was innocently done than the result of something sinister. "Are you ready then?" he said. "We have to stop at the station house early. The Chief is expected in meetings all day."

Mercy hesitated. "The Chief? I thought we were just meeting MacNeal?"

"You'll be fine," he said, moving toward the door. "You'll be with me." When he saw she wasn't following him he stopped. "I realize you must be busy." He made a gesture with his hand indicating the room.

Mercy's business had suffered slightly in the previous weeks. She hadn't been as readily available for appointments or drop-ins as she would have liked. Thankfully, she had a sizable savings account that could tide her over a while longer.

"I'd appreciate any time you could give," he said.

Mercy suppressed a smile. "Sure, yes, of course," she said. "Anything." As soon as she said "anything" she regretted it. It made her look eager. And yet, when he went for the door, she followed, grabbing her hat and gloves before she slipped out the door.

❧ ❦

"I thought we already had MacNeal's blessing," Mercy said once they arrived at the station house.

Walker shook his head. "No, it's more complicated than that." He had led her up to the second floor and stopped at a closed door at the end of a long hall. He placed his hands on the brass knob. He gave a quick rap with his knuckle before pushing the door in. Inside, MacNeal stood behind Chief Johnson's desk, while the chief sat as if expecting them both.

"Come in, Ms. Eaton," Johnson said, adjusting the papers on his desk slightly. "I hear you have some information for us."

Mercy sidestepped inside, and stood awkwardly at the door.

Johnson gestured to the chairs opposite where he sat at the desk. "Please have a seat."

Walker handed MacNeal the papers he was holding as Mercy took a seat. Walker, however, did not sit. He stood alongside MacNeal, who was skimming the pages just handed to him. When Mercy looked to Johnson, he raised his eyebrows expectantly. "Yes?"

"Well... I just happened to notice... er, I was at the funeral for Mr. Carver yesterday. Well, not as a guest, more as a silent observer, really." Her mouth went dry as she spoke, unsure how precisely she should set the scene for her presence at the Necropolis cemetery. Walker had not coached her in any way. "I saw the pallbearers struggling with the coffin first," she said. "Seemed like a very heavy coffin."

"Heavy compared to what exactly?" Johnson asked.

"Well..." Mercy glanced to Walker, who gave her a simple nod, a slight encouragement. "I've been around many coffins in my lifetime," she said. "I know what is normal, and Mr. Carver's coffin was not normal. It was large, larger than most others and deeper by half a foot at least."

He raised his eyebrows at this. "Your sister is married to the undertaker, is she not?"

"Yes." Mercy bounced to the edge of her seat. "But I don't think they have anything to do with this," she said. "They make the arrangements for the families, they lay out the deceased, that's all."

She watched as the chief scribbled something on the paper before him.

"You realize, Walker, we are going to have to exhume the body," he said as he wrote.

"Yes, sir, and I would like to be at the gravesite while it's done, if it's all the same, sir."

Johnson's eyes shot up at Walker's words.

"MacNeal and I agree there has been enough

contamination in this case to warrant closer scrutiny," he explained.

"And you are all right with this, MacNeal?"

"Yes, sir. There's no one on the force I trust more, sir," MacNeal answered. He handed the papers to Johnson.

"I would like to be there as well," Mercy said quickly.

The room fell silent at her request. Out of the corner of her eye Mercy saw MacNeal offer a smile to Walker.

"Chief Johnson, Ms. Eaton brings an expertise unprecedented to the force," Walker said. "Her presence will be valuable."

"And MacNeal?"

"Yes, I agree," MacNeal said, stammering slightly.

"All right then, you have my permission to be present, Ms. Eaton, as long as you obey the direction of these two gentlemen, understood?"

Mercy nodded. "Yes, sir."

"Detectives, you know what to do, I'm sure you can handle the rest." He scribbled his signature on the papers presented to him and quickly handed them back to MacNeal.

Walker released a breath of relief. "Yes, sir." He moved to the door and held it open for both Mercy and MacNeal to follow him.

In the hallway Mercy couldn't help but smile. Both Walker's and MacNeal's relief was palpable.

"So, that's it, we're headed to the gravesite now?" she asked.

"No, not exactly," MacNeal said.

"We need Mrs. Carver's permission first," Walker said.

"What if she says no?" Mercy asked.

"Oh, she will say no," MacNeal said. "They all do. It's yours and Walker's job to convince her." MacNeal slipped past them and continued down the hall at a quicker pace.

"Aren't you going to join us?" Walker called after him.

"It's your case, Walker," he said, turning slightly to look at them. "Besides, I'm sure Ms. Eaton is more than persuasive enough."

Mercy took in air quickly and stopped in the middle of the hall, realizing the onus that was just placed on her. She felt Walker's hand on the small of her back.

"It's all right," he said. "We can do this."
Mercy returned his smile and gave a nod.

Chapter 22

The Carver residence was quiet when Mercy and Walker knocked on the front door, so quiet Mercy wondered if anyone was at home.

"She's probably staying with family for a few days," Mercy offered, remembering how extended family rallied around her mother when her father passed. In fact, Mercy would have preferred for Mrs. Carver to not be there. She hadn't told Walker of Mrs. Carver's request for a reading, nor had she told him how disastrously it had ended.

Walker leaned one ear closer to the wood of the door. He used the iron knocker and knocked again. This time Mercy heard a shuffling noise inside. She expected someone to come within seconds, but the seconds passed and they were left to stand on the stoop listening to the hurried movements inside.

"You never did tell me what information you gathered from your graveside reading," Walker said as they waited.

"It wasn't entirely graveside," Mercy said, suppressing a smile. They could see the doorknob on their side moving and hear the many latches and bolts on the opposite side. Finally, the door opened and Mrs. Carver appeared, out of breath and slightly dishevelled.

"Detective, Ms. Eaton... may I help you?" Mrs. Carver asked, brushing a few wisps of hair that had fallen over her forehead. She had only opened the door wide enough to wedge herself within the open space.

"Sorry to disturb you, Mrs. Carver," Walker said. "We have something of a very serious nature to ask you. May we come in? It will only take a minute."

Mrs. Craver looked over her shoulder. "It's really not a good time," she said. "I'm afraid I haven't seen to much of the housework since James died."

"We won't judge you, Mrs. Carver," Mercy said. "I'm not known for the best housekeeping even in the best of times."

Mercy saw a hesitant smile on Mrs. Carver's lips before she took a step backward and invited them in. The room was just as Mercy saw in Mr. Carver's memories. Canvases and paint cans littered on every available surface. Glass jars of mud-coloured water stood as receptacles for used paintbrushes. A palette sat atop a stool splattered with layers upon layers of paint, dried and encrusted, flaky and cracked. Turpentine permeated the air of the room, as if every rag, floorboard, and soft cushion had been doused in it at one time or another.

For a moment Mercy stood marvelling at the collection of artwork that hung on the wall right up to the ceiling. On the floor sat numerous canvases, all in various states of completion, set up like dominos against the walls, as many as six or seven canvases layered upon each other. Two easels took up the majority of the room, one enormously large, big enough to display a canvas larger than a carriage, the other much smaller, meant for daintier pieces. On this smaller easel sat a canvas no more than two feet by two feet, a pretty pastoral scene already nearing completion. Mercy found herself drawn to this particular painting more than the others. Without an invitation to look, Mercy leaned in close to take in the strokes of the brush and scalpel, which had created a three-dimensional effect on the otherwise flat canvas.

When Mercy realized both Mrs. Carver and Walker were watching her, she blushed and backed away. "My apologies," she said. "I was just so taken in by this piece."

"It was nearly done before my husband died," she said. "Now he shall never finish it."

"It's quite a collection, Mrs. Carver," Walker said. "What are your plans for it all?"

"I have a mind to sell it," she said. "It may buy me some time until the creditors come calling."

"What will you do when you have no more of your husband's paintings to sell?" Mercy asked, always keen to learn how independent women earned a living without the assistance of a man.

"I shall manage," Mrs. Carver said, her jaw tightening slightly as she spoke.

"Of course," Walker said. "Is there a dining room table or

some other area in the kitchen perhaps where we may sit and speak with you?"

Mrs. Carver led them to the back of the house and invited them to sit at a small table for two crammed into a kitchen about half the size of Mercy's. Their host procured another chair from an adjoining room and offered them tea, which both Walker and Mercy accepted.

"Mrs. Carver, we've come to ask a question of a sensitive nature," Walker said once they were all seated with teacups in front of them.

Mercy watched as Mrs. Carver steeled herself against the inquiry. Her shoulders stiffened and her grip around the teacup tightened. "I am an open book, Detective," she said, lifting the china to her lips.

"Mrs. Carver, first, I'd like to know how you went about choosing your husband's coffin," Walker said. When Mrs. Carver knit her eyebrows, he went to explain his meaning. "Did someone at the funeral home help you? Perhaps they made a suggestion..."

Mrs. Carver shook her head. "I didn't want anything to do with it. I simply told them to chose something nice but that I was a woman of limited means."

"You didn't see his coffin until the day of his internment?" Walker asked.

"That's right."

"Did anything seem odd or out of place?" he asked.

Mrs. Carver divided her gaze between them, a look of doubt on her face. "I'm not entirely sure what you are referring too."

Mercy noticed the woman grew more and more agitated the more Walker spoke. Her hand that lay next to her teacup had scrunched up in a tight fist, pulling the lace tablecloth into her grip. It was unnerving, especially when Mercy knew how Mrs. Carver behaved in Mercy's reading parlour. Walker saw her hand, but changed nothing of his demeanour.

"My colleague and I believe your husband's remains may not be alone in his grave," Walker said.

"We believe someone may have been buried with your husband," Mercy explained further.

A stunted breath escaped Mrs. Carver and immediately

her shoulders slumped and her grip loosened. "Are you sure?"

"Yes," Mercy said. "I am quite sure."

The change was almost immediate. The woman's entire body relaxed and her hand uncurled to lay flat on the tablecloth. "How on earth could such a thing happen?"

Walker took in a breath before trying to explain. "There have been two investigations of a serious nature taking place of late, one involving the death of your husband—"

"Whom you've yet to pinpoint a culprit," Mrs. Carver interjected.

"Yes, well, trust me when I say we are giving your case our full attention. The other case involves a man whose body had disappeared from our city morgue."

"How does one lose a body, Detective?"

"That remains under investigation but at this point we now believe this body may have been interred alongside your husband, as a means to cover up a crime of a serious nature."

Mrs. Carver nodded and began tapping her finger on the edge of her saucer. Mercy found herself following her movements and then snapped her gaze away, turning her attention back to the conversation.

"Well then..." Mrs. Carver seemed more than a little elated at the revelation. "I suppose there's only one thing to do... dig him up, of course. I'd hate for him to be forced to spend eternity next to a man involved in a serious crime "

Mercy saw Walker smile and pull back from the table, pleased to have reached an understanding so easily. "We have some paperwork for you to sign," Walker said, reaching into his inside breast pocket.

Mrs. Carver received the papers across the table and accepted the pen Walker provided for her.

"As always, family members are permitted to be there—"

"That won't be necessary, Detective," Mrs. Carver said quickly. "I have the utmost trust in our men in blue. I am sure you will treat my husband's remains respectfully."

"Of course. I will see to it myself."

Mrs. Carver seemed pleased enough by this, handed Walker back his papers, and stood up from the table. "If that is all then," she said, "I thank you for stopping by."

"Mrs. Carver, is everything all right?" Mercy asked, getting up slowly from her seat.

"Yes, of course."

Walker and Mercy filed out into the hall, Mrs. Carver close at their heels. At the door, Mercy turned for one last view of the room with the canvases and artwork. "Let me know when your husband's paintings go up for sale, once you've organized everything and decide how much you want for them."

Mrs. Carver nodded and pulled open the door, standing to the side to see them step out onto the street. Walker went out but Mercy hovered inside the door, maintaining eye contact with Mrs. Carver. "Your husband was quite the artist, Mrs. Carver. Must have been a challenge to be married to someone who outshines everyone around them."

Mrs. Carver winced slightly at Mercy's words. "A challenge, indeed."

"Well, then, good day, Mrs. Carver." Mercy presented her hand to Mrs. Carver, who shook it reluctantly.

"Good day, Mrs. Eaton, Detective." Mrs. Carver closed the door slowly. Mercy could hear the latches and bolts clasping as soon as the door was closed.

"That was far easier than I expected. What did you mean when you said Mr. Carver outshone others?" Walker asked as Mercy looked down to her hands. "I don't think she liked it when you said that."

"She didn't like it because Mr. Carver isn't the creator behind all those paintings," Mercy replied.

"How do you know that?"

Mercy raised her hand for Walker to see. "Because Mrs. Carver just got wet paint all over my hand."

୶   ୶

By mid-morning Walker, Mercy, and MacNeal were gathered at the gravesite. Four men, professional gravediggers judging by the scruff of their clothing, waited with shovels. Mercy watched Walker give the nod and they set to work. Thankfully, the soil was still loose from the interment the day before. The burly men made quick work of it, but even still Mercy was anxious to get to the bottom of the hole, so anxious she felt she could have snatched a shovel from one of them and started working herself. She knew, however, her assistance would not speed anything along. It would have only satiated the jittery feeling in her stomach.

Halfway through the dig, doubt crept into her consciousness. What if she had sent everyone down a fruitless path? What if Mr. Carver's coffin was just extravagant? Mercy closed her eyes against her doubts. She knew what she had seen and felt. Another soul wanted to tell their story, they were begging her, and she hadn't realized what it meant at time. He was there. She could feel him even then, clamouring to get out of that hole in the ground.

After an hour of digging one of the men's shovels made a THUNK on something hard. Walker inhaled a breath of triumph when the four men stopped to look up. "Come on, now, let's get that thing out of there," MacNeal yelled, waving his arm for the men to hurry.

Minutes later the dirt had been removed enough in order to feed the straps underneath. The men climbed out, divided the straps between them, and gingerly pulled the coffin from underground. In the final steps MacNeal and Walker assisted, guiding the coffin to the grass at the side. Seeing it again in the sunlight Mercy was sure this was no ordinary coffin. The pull she felt was even stronger the closer she stepped toward it, like a snare had caught her midsection and refused to release her.

MacNeal and Walker positioned themselves along the same side, kneeling in the grass. One of the gravediggers presented them with a tool to pry open the lid. With hurried anticipation Walker and MacNeal worked on each nail before finally they had loosened enough that the lid lifted. Inside lay the body of Mr. Carver, just as Mercy had left it, save for a blueish tinge to his skin that the makeup Constance applied no longer covered.

Mercy watched as Walker examined the depth of the coffin on the inside, sliding his hand down the velvet that cushioned the coffin's wood shell. With his hand in place he looked to the outside of the box.

"It's almost a foot deeper than needed," Walker said.

"But how do we get to it?" MacNeal asked, searching within the box as well for an access point.

"There's a hole here, in the floor," Walker said from Mr. Carver's feet. "I can get my hand in it."

"I have one too," MacNeal said from the head.

Walker nodded. "We lift," he said. "Ready?"

MacNeal repositioned himself, bracing his other arm on the edge of the coffin, and then nodded. "Ready."

With gritted teeth, both men lifted their handhold upward, pulling Mr. Carver's corpse from the coffin. After a few moments of stunned silence, the gravediggers stepped forward to assist. Once Mr. Carver's body was safely on the grass Walker turned back to the coffin but Mercy was already standing over it.

"What is it?" Walker asked.

Mercy's throat went dry at the sight, unable to comprehend what it was she was seeing. Walker came to her side and stood equally stunned.

"What do you see, Walker?" MacNeal asked, struggling to get his hand loose from the board that held Mr. Carver. "What is it?"

Walker shook his head and finally pulled his gaze away. "It's nothing," he said. "There's nothing here."

By the time MacNeal rushed over, Mercy was on her knees beside the coffin, slipping her hand inside the pine box. With her palm facing down she touched the wood.

"I don't understand," MacNeal said behind her, "why construct a coffin with so much space. Why bother wasting the materials if it's unnecessary?"

Walker didn't answer.

Mercy could feel something in the wood, not as strong as she had in the hearse the day before. It was the same energy, she realized. It was as if something had been there but no longer was. She closed her eyes against the noise and the light and immersed herself in the feel of the wood, the memory imprinted there. "He was here," she said, opening her eyes. "They took him."

"What are you on about?" MacNeal asked. "Who took 'im?"

Mercy looked to Mr. Carver's body, which lay a foot away.

"There, on his shirt collar," she said, pointing with her gloved hand. "A smudge of dirt." She knew with all her being Constance would never have allowed such a stain to mar the pristine white of any man's burial garb.

Walker went to the opposite side of Mr. Carver and touched the fabric of the collar himself. Grains of soil brushed off onto his hand.

From her crouched position Mercy watched Walker's face sour, as if he had been hit by a rogue wave but refused to buckle under its strength. Without a word, Walker turned. He went straight for the path that would lead him to Amelia Street and charged forward, propelled equally by rage and desperation.

"Walker, where are you going?" MacNeal called out. "What should we do with this?"

"Document it!" Walker called back. "All of it. Measure the box, the cavity. All of it. Then put him back."

"But where are you going?"

"I'm going to find our body."

Chapter 23

At the road Jeremiah hailed a hansom cab to the curb, but before he could utter the address of the funeral parlour Ms. Eaton was at his side.

"What are you doing?" she asked, breathless and more than a little panicked.

"I can't let him get away with it," Jeremiah said, climbing aboard. Ms. Eaton scrambled in and sat on the opposite bench.

"Alexander had nothing to do with this," she said, watching him tap the ceiling to let the driver know they were settled.

"Didn't he?"

Ms. Eaton's face went sour at the suggestion but she said nothing.

"Your silence is very telling, Ms. Eaton."

"If he did have something to do with this, you can be certain I haven't," Ms. Eaton said in protest.

Jeremiah took in a steadying breath. "My apologies if that's what you thought I implied." He leaned forward and braced his elbows on his knees. "Think of it, who was there when you told me about the depth of the casket? Who else could have known we were planning an exhumation? It's him, Ms. Eaton. I'll bet my shirt, it's him."

They were at the funeral parlour within minutes. Jeremiah wasted no time jumping from the carriage and dashing in through the front door. "Wait here," he yelled to the hansom driver as he went. Charging in, Jeremiah went methodically, room to room, knowing Ms. Eaton was close at his heels. Finally, in a back office, he found him, seated before a weeping couple, a widow and an adult son come to make arrangements. Jeremiah cared little for any disturbance he might cause.

Alexander stood when he saw Jeremiah was coming at him. The man even tried to back away farther into the room, but the abundance of office furniture allowed him to go only so far.

"What the devil?" Alexander raised a defensive hand but did little to stop Jeremiah, who grabbed him by his collar and pulled him from the room. In the hallway Jeremiah pushed Alexander's body into the wall, sending the framed portraits rocking back and forth on their nails. Alexander groaned and tried to push Jeremiah's hands from him.

"Where is it?" Jeremiah asked.

Ms. Eaton was trying her best to get between them to pull Jeremiah's hands away as well, but Jeremiah was not about to release him. Not yet.

"Walker, please, you're hurting him," Ms. Eaton said.

"Oh my God!" Mrs. Doyle came running down the stairs. "Mercy, what's happening?"

Ms. Eaton retreated to her sister's side, which was so much the better for Jeremiah, who would have feared hurting her had she not moved away.

"Mr. Carver's body... there was an extra body... hidden in his coffin. It's gone," Ms. Eaton explained, while puffing for air.

"That's preposterous. There was only one body. I saw to his needs myself," Constance said.

Jeremiah, however, was not about to let go. "You heard what Ms. Eaton said to me last night. You knew she had figured you out," he said, before pulling him away from the wall and then pounding him into it again. "Who'd you run and tell, Mr. Doyle?"

"I don't... know what... you're talking about," Alexander gurgled.

"Detective, please. My husband had nothing to do with it, whatever *it* is. Let him go."

"He's not going anywhere other than the station house," Jeremiah said, loosening his grip slightly. "He and I are going to have a little chat."

Ignoring the look of consternation directed at him from Ms. Eaton, Jeremiah guided Alexander down the hall, past the women and toward the awaiting carriage.

"Mercy, do something," he heard Mrs. Doyle say as he left the building.

"I'm trying, Connie. I really am trying."

☞ ☜

Jeremiah couldn't bring himself to look at Ms. Eaton the entire carriage ride back to the station house. He was not angry with her. She couldn't have known her brother-in-law would betray them and jeopardize their investigation. It was not her fault, but even still he could not manage her emotions in this situation and fulfill his duties as an officer of the law. Not that Ms. Eaton would be very receptive to anything he might say; any words of consolation would prove a fruitless exercise at this point. Instead, he focused his hardened stare on Alexander Doyle, already whittling down his resolve so when it came time to interrogate him he'd fold like a letter home to his mama.

At the station house, Jeremiah paid the hansom driver and promptly escorted Alexander into the building. Thankfully, MacNeal was already there from the graveyard.

"I'm not understanding, Walker," he said, sidestepping out of the way so Walker could guide Alexander to his office.

"He was there, MacNeal," Walker said gruffly. "He was there when Ms. Eaton told me about the size of the coffin."

Ms. Eaton appeared at the door then, out of breath and on the verge of crying.

"Not now, Ms. Eaton," Walker said, waving his hand so MacNeal would close the door, shutting Ms. Eaton out. Thankfully, she did not protest, but Walker could tell her heart was broken. Mrs. Doyle rushed into the hall, stopping short of Ms. Eaton. Walker saw Mrs. Doyle collapse into Ms. Eaton's arms in tears.

"Mr. Doyle, how long have you been an undertaker?" Jeremiah asked, circling the desk and taking a seat in his chair.

Mr. Doyle cleared his throat and patted a bead of sweat from his brow with his handkerchief. "Since before or after I took over for my father?" His voice cracked partway through his sentence. Walker could tell he was nervous. Perhaps his interrogation would be much easier than he previously thought.

"For the sake of argument, let's say since you took over the family business."

"That will be twelve years then, sir."

"How many bodies have you disposed of during that time?" Jeremiah asked.

He saw a smile pricking at the corners of Mr. Doyle's mouth. "Thousands, I suspect."

"All single burials then?"

The man gave a glimpse to MacNeal and pulled at his collar. "I don't know what you mean."

"How many coffins have been buried with *extra baggage*?"

Ms. Doyle swallowed. "I... I don't know."

"You don't know or you didn't keep count?"

"I don't know what you are talking about."

"Yes, you do," MacNeal said. "That coffin we pulled out of the ground was custom-made to fit another body. Two men buried in one grave, with only one grave marker. Sounds like an ideal way to get rid of something you never want found."

"How many undocumented bodies have you buried?" Jeremiah asked.

"I... can't... I don't know what you are talking about."

"How many bodies are there?" Jeremiah slammed a fist down into the surface of his desk, sending a wave of items jumping into the air.

Mr. Doyle shook his head uncontrollably, his jaw slack, his eyes wide.

"I bet there's murder weapons as well down in those graves. Guns, knives," MacNeal said, sneering. "We have no idea who this man is working for."

"That's right," Jeremiah said, leaning forward and knitting his fingers together to lean them against the edge of his desk. "We know you aren't the man behind all of this. You'd never kill anyone, would you? You're just a go-between, a pawn. Who are you working for, Mr. Doyle? Who has you on their payroll?"

His eyes went to the floor as he gave a shake of his head. "I... I don't know what... you are talking about."

"The coffin you made to hide an extra body. You heard what Ms. Eaton said to me last night. You heard her say the coffin was too big. You knew we were set to exhume the body this morning," Jeremiah said.

"Where were you last night?" MacNeal asked.

"At home with my wife."

"We know that's a lie. You were out looking for Ms. Eaton in your business cart until at least one in the morning. What'd you do after that?" Jeremiah asked.

"I slept."

Jeremiah offered a doubtful look. "I don't know. You look pretty tired today, sir. I see dark circles under your eyes. Do you see dark circles under his eyes, MacNeal?"

"I certainly do."

"So where'd you go? Who'd you speak to?" Jeremiah waited but didn't get an answer. "Did you have help or did you dig up that grave all on your own?"

MacNeal snorted. "Do you see that stomach, Walker? A man like him ain't going to be moving that much dirt without help."

Mr. Doyle looked offended. Jeremiah saw one of his hands clench into a fist.

"You can tell us," Jeremiah said. "We understand. You're just doing right by your family. You have a business, a wife, a new baby. What's a man supposed to do? Turn down offers of payment?"

The entire time Jeremiah spoke he studied him. He watched which words evoked feelings, which words made him angry, which made him sad. Most people wore their emotions in their eyes, their mouths, and their eyebrows. A slight twitch here, a sudden clench there. Minute facial movements were often all Jeremiah needed to determine if his questions were headed in the right direction. He didn't need vocal answers a lot of the time because visual answers were often enough to get him the information he needed.

Jeremiah turned his attention to MacNeal. "Send a team to his home. I want his clothes from yesterday found. If they've been laundered, I want to see the tub of water. I want his maid interviewed." He looked to Mr. Doyle. "Lottie, isn't it?"

Mr. Doyle's jaw tightened as he turned away.

"I want her brought here," Jeremiah said. "I want her to see we aren't messing around before she even considers covering for her employer."

MacNeal glanced out the window in Jeremiah's closed office door. "And Mrs. Doyle?"

"Find another interview room for her. I'll speak with her next." Jeremiah watched Mr. Doyle out of the corner of his eye, anticipating a reaction once his wife was mentioned.

Mr. Doyle did nothing.

Chapter 24

Mercy's heart nearly stopped when the door to Walker's office finally opened. Both she and Constance could see inside through the long line of windows, but only certain words could be heard through the glass, mostly what MacNeal and Walker said. They heard none of Alexander's responses. While they waited, Mercy could feel Constance tensing up. Her hand clutching Mercy's would tighten, her palms grew sweaty, and a slight tremor developed in all of Constance's body.

"It's taking so long. Why is it taking so long?" Constance asked more than once.

"Be patient," was all Mercy could manage in reply.

When the door finally did open, Constance clenched Mercy's hand even tighter. Before Mercy could stop her, her sister crossed the hall and went straight for Walker. "How dare you!" she yelled, striking him on the chest with a closed fist. "My husband was in a meeting with clients. How dare you barge in in such a fashion."

Mercy could hear the tears but only saw the anger and frustration.

MacNeal slipped past them, heading for the front of the station house, an agreement between him and Walker evident by the purposeful way he left.

"Mrs. Doyle, calm yourself—"

"Calm myself? Calm myself? My husband has done nothing wrong. Mercy, tell him how good a man my husband is."

Mercy's defense of the man was slow to come forward. Obviously, Mercy knew more of the evidence than Constance. All of it pointed to Alexander as a guilty party, unless Constance herself was behind the duplicate burials and that was something Mercy was loathe to contemplate.

"Alexander didn't do anything, Detective Walker," Constance said, letting the tears fall at last, "He didn't do anything."

She collapsed in Walker's arms, crying into his lapel.

"Come with me, Mrs. Doyle," he said, gesturing to his right. "Let's have a seat. Maybe we can clear this whole thing up." Walker looked to Mercy as he guided her sister down the hall. Mercy offered a nod, reassurance that he was indeed approaching things properly. She'd open up and tell everything she knew if she thought it would help her husband.

"Ms. Eaton, would you care to follow us?" he asked.

"Yes, of course."

Constance was handed off to her while Walker used a key to open an oft-unoccupied room. There was a circular wood table at the centre, with six or so basic wooden chairs pulled up around it. Mercy guided her sister to one of them. By the time they were both seated, Walker had returned with a teacup and saucer, which he placed in front of Constance. Then he pulled a handkerchief from his inside pocket and offered it as well.

Chagrined, Constance accepted his offering and used it to pat her tear-smeared cheeks.

"Mrs. Doyle, your sister and I have discovered something very disturbing and we need your assistance in putting the pieces together. Do you mind if we ask a few questions?"

"I'll do whatever I can to remove my husband from suspicion," Constance said.

Walker closed the door behind them and circled the table to the other side. "That's good, ma'am. We appreciate that."

Mercy noticed straightaway how his mannerism changed between Alexander and Constance. With Alex, he was firm, unforgiving, but with Constance he proceeded more gently, and phrased things as if he were on her side and it was all just a misunderstanding.

"Now, I need to warn you. We need you to answer as honestly as you can. If you don't know the answer to my question, please don't guess. Tell me only what you know for sure." As he spoke, Walker set out a notebook and readied a pen.

Constance nodded. "I will do my best," she said between sniffles.

"As I understand it, you are heavily involved in your

husband's business. You assist him and see to certain aspects."

Mercy snorted. "She practically does everything," she said, before she could stop herself. "Sorry."

"Mrs. Doyle, is this true?" Walker asked.

"Yes. I've learned to do many aspects of my husband's work," she said.

"What sort of tasks do you handle?" he asked.

"Well, I meet with potential clients, guide them through the services we offer. I prepare the parlour for viewings and ceremonies. I accept flower delivers and—"

"Do you have anything to do with the handling of the bodies?"

"Oh yes, I am often present when they are brought into the back room. I'll often prepare them and dress them. We apply some makeup and I primp their hair."

"Sounds like you do a fair bit, Mrs. Doyle."

"I do. Well, I should say I did. Since we adopted Maggie I haven't had as much time as I used to," Constance said.

"So now your husband has been overseeing more and more?"

"Yes, I'm just too busy, you see."

Walker nodded as he jotted something down in the notebook. "Mrs. Doyle, last night you went to Ms. Eaton's house. Why did you head out so late?"

"It was Alexander's wish, truthfully. He said he was worried about her."

Mercy snorted. "Sorry."

"Mr. Doyle was worried for Ms. Eaton's well-being. How did he tell you of this worry?"

"I had just put Maggie down to bed when he came up the stairs. He said he had a strange feeling and he wanted to check on her. Make sure everything was all right."

"And was everything all right?"

"No, when we arrived at her house my niece was home alone with a young man—"

"A close family friend," Mercy interjected. "Nothing more."

"Even still, we had no idea what was going on. Edith told us you'd run off with Detective Walker and some lady of the night. What were we supposed to assume?" Constance asked, her attention more on Mercy than Walker.

"You could assume I am a grown woman who is capable of taking care of herself," Mercy said.

"A lady of the night, Mercy. That's what your daughter said."

"What business is it of yours who I associate with, lady of the night or otherwise?"

"Ladies, please, calm down," Walker said. "We are just trying to get to the bottom of this. Ms. Eaton, please allow your sister to speak without interruption."

"She is misrepresenting my character," Mercy said.

"You misrepresent yourself," Constance corrected.

"Connie!"

"You think very little for your reputation, Mercy," Constance said, not even bothering to look at Mercy.

"I couldn't give a damn about my reputation."

"As always." Constance turned slightly in her chair so she could look her sister in the eye, but it wasn't a complete turn. It was more a half turn, as if she were torn between conducting her interview with Detective Walker and correcting her younger sister's behaviour. "The amount of trouble you get yourself into and the mess you leave for others to clean up, it's no wonder you are still unmarried at your age. No one wants the burden—"

"The burden?"

"But someone has to, don't they? Someone has to be there time and again to clean up the messes you make." Constance lifted her chin and reverted her attention back to Walker.

The room was silent for a few seconds, allowing Mercy a few moments to let all her sister had said sink in. Her stomach was in knots and her hands shook slightly. She raised her gaze to Walker, who looked at her apologetically.

"Ms. Eaton, if you'd rather, you can wait outside," he said.

It took a moment for Mercy to answer. "No, I'm fine, thank you," she managed to say. In some ways a part of her did leave the room. She could see herself get up from her seat, make her way to the door, and slip out of the building to the fresh summer air, while another part of her remained seated, frozen, unable to move after what her sister had just said to her.

"Mrs. Doyle, after you found Ms. Eaton, you took her home, yes?"

"Yes."

"And then you and Mr. Doyle went home?"

"Yes... well, not at first."

"No?"

"He said a friend owed him some money. We stopped outside a building on College Street. Some rundown something or other. I couldn't say what the building was used for."

"You stayed with the cart?"

"Yes."

"How long was your husband gone?"

"No more than a few minutes."

"Three minutes? Five Minutes? Ten minutes?"

"We'll call it five minutes, no more."

Walker scribbled something on the paper. "Your husband returns after five minutes. Does he say anything?"

"No. He was quiet most of the way home."

"Once at home, you both went to bed, I presume."

"I did, yes, but Alex said he wasn't tired and he had some paperwork he needed to get done."

Walker raised his eyebrows. "Paperwork?"

"Yes. So you see, my husband couldn't have done what you say. I can account for him the entire time."

Judging by the look on Walker's face, Mercy could tell he wasn't as convinced.

❧ ❧

"If he wasn't involved in some way I'll eat my own hat," Walker said to Mercy as they walked the length of the hallway, having left Constance in the interview room with her tea.

"I agree," Mercy said almost listlessly.

"She can't account for his whereabouts the entire time. The man left her sight at least twice, both of which she cannot guarantee what he did or did not do." He talked over his shoulder, propelled forward by the thrill of the chase, Mercy supposed, a feeling she had partaken in as well and relished until very recently.

"Is something the matter?" he asked, stopping suddenly.

Mercy crossed her arms over her chest. Words failed her.

"Look, I know what she said was not pleasant, but it was just sister-speak, yes? She didn't mean it."

"I wouldn't be so sure about that," she said. "It hard to get excited about finding clues when the evidence leads to your own family."

"Of course." He reached a hand out to touch her arm, then pulled it back when a uniformed officer entered the hall and walked past them. "Why don't you head home? Let MacNeal and me take care of this?"

Mercy rubbed her arm where Walker had touched her, the skin beneath her thin, cream blouse tingling with remembrance. "Perhaps that is best."

Lottie, Constance's maid, appeared at the end of the hall, little Maggie draped over her hip as she walked. Behind her, MacNeal urged her forward, directing her with an outstretched arm. "This way, miss."

Lottie paused at Mercy and passed off the child. "If you don't mind, Ms. Eaton," she said. "This gentleman here wants to ask me some questions."

Mercy kept her gaze as she accepted the child, who fussed and flailed her arms. "Just answer truthfully, Lottie. Nothing is your fault," Mercy said. She so desperately wanted to follow her and MacNeal. She wanted to be in the room with them when the questions were asked. Her curiosity and desire to know the truth, good or bad, was amazingly strong.

Maggie's cries brought Constance to the door of her interview room. Seeing her daughter in Mercy's arms, Constance rushed forward, plucking the child away.

"May I go now, Detective Walker?" Constance asked formally. It was as if all their previous interactions meant nothing, as if Constance had just met him that day and decided she did not like him one bit.

"If it's all right, ma'am, we'll ask you to stay while we interview your maid-of-all-work. You're welcome to be in the room, if you'd like," Walker said.

Maggie fussed, gurgling and then throwing her arms about before letting out whimpering cries. "I really don't know," Constance said over the cries.

"I can take her," Mercy offered. "She can spend the afternoon with me."

Constance didn't acknowledge her sister had said anything. A silence dragged on as she pondered her options. Not once did she look to Mercy. "Lead the way, Detective," she said at last.

Mercy watched as her sister and niece were led to the interview room door where MacNeal stood, Lottie having already been seated inside. Walker gave her one long look down the hall, apologetic but also pleading. Mercy had never wanted to leave a place so fast. Her sister was almost certainly vexed with her, displeased at having brought the investigation to their front door. But how could she have known where the clues would lead? How could she have predicted such a turn of events?

Rejected, Mercy left, marching down the street as quickly as her weary legs would take her. The pavement felt rough and hot beneath her feet, the early summer sun blazing down and penetrating the wispy fabric of her blouse. She could feel sweat beading down her back. A few blocks from the station Mercy felt faint. Her vision blurred and her head throbbed. Each step became a desperate march for home.

The house was empty when she got there, or it should have been. Almost as soon as Mercy walked through her door she could feel the heavy air weighing her down. She went straight for the enamel sink of the kitchen to fetch some water. With the faucet running, she heard a noise from the parlour.

"Hello?"

She turned off the tap to listen. Nothing.

After drinking an entire glass, she grabbed a towel and wet it under the faucet to put along the back of her neck. She wanted to take a seat on the sofa on the other side of the kitchen. After refilling her glass of water, she held the towel to her neck and turned.

"Good day, Ms. Eaton."

Ezekiel stepped forward and Mercy dropped her water. Shards of glass splintered into a hundred pieces and water splashed on the wood floorboards and her skirt.

"He's not here," she said, trying to keep her hand from

shaking.

"I know," Ezekiel answered. "I searched the whole house. I found his things, though." He gestured to a small pile of Maxwell's belongings on one of the chairs in the kitchen. "When is he expected back?"

Mercy didn't answer. She was too busy plotting her escape route.

"Eh? Cat got yer tongue?" Ezekiel raised an eyebrow and stepped closer, a movement that sent Mercy backward into the sink. It felt like her entire body was trembling and the harder she tried to calm herself the shaking only grew worse.

"Don't touch me!" she said, putting her hands up defensively.

"I'm not going to touch you," Ezekiel said, taking another step toward her. "Not unless... you want me too." He was inches from her now, eyeing her like a piece of meat. Mercy dodged to the left, desperate to get away.

She felt his arm encircle her midsection, pulling her toward him as she tried to scurry away. She used her elbows to fight him off and then raised her leg to kick him but only managed to lose her balance. His grip on her was iron tight, bringing him down on top of her. A chair at the table tipped over with their fall. The smile on his face told her he was enjoying this, enjoying their struggle, and he did not fear losing because he had the advantage.

With every ounce of strength she had, Mercy fought, kicking, hitting, pushing him away from her. All the while, images, flashes of Hazel, overtook her senses. Hazel was crying, fighting, beating him with her fists. Mercy cried out against the feelings that engulfed her, the knowledge that he had done this before, that he had forced Hazel into this very same position many times before.

He clapped a hand over her mouth, muffling her cries. "Shut up, you little bitch, or I'll have you sent back there," he growled. He meant Mercer Reformatory. Had he said that to Mercy or was this a memory from Hazel?

Mercy kicked and screamed against his sweaty hand, and tried to bite his flesh even as it cut off her ability to breath. She could feel his free hand on her blouse, unbuttoning her blouse and gracing the rounds of her breasts.

"Mama, are you home?"

Ezekiel and Mercy froze. She felt his hand loosen his grip on her mouth.

"Edith, run!"

He clasped his hand over her mouth and pushed himself off the ground, kicking Mercy once in the side of the stomach before charging down the hall. Mercy scrambled to get to her feet but could only manage to crawl to the door of the kitchen. She saw Edith running down the front steps just as Ezekiel made it to the front door.

"Run!" Mercy cried again.

A frying pan clocked Ezekiel on the top of the head just as he stepped out onto the porch. The man collapsed on the ground. A second later, Mrs. Fanshaw stepped out from her hiding spot on the porch and hit him on the head once more for good measure.

Mercy clamoured to her feet and hastily buttoned her blouse, a relieved smile spreading over her face. "Oh my goodness, thank you, Mrs. Fanshaw," she said limping for the door.

"You sure know how to attract the bad ones, don't you, Ms. Eaton," the neighbour said.

"How I wish I didn't," Mercy answered.

The elderly neighbour stepped over the body of Ezekiel and made her way down the stairs.

"How did you know?" Edith asked, inching back up the walkway cautiously.

"I may be old but I can hear everything at least four houses away," Mrs. Fanshaw said, crossing the front garden. "Remember that."

Mercy closed her eyes and nearly laughed. And thank God for that, she said to herself. When Mercy opened her eyes she found Edith looking over Ezekiel.

"Is he dead?" she asked.

Mercy looked closer. "I don't think so."

Edith looked crestfallen. "Pity."

Mercy reached over the body and grabbed Edith's hand. "Are you all right?" You're not hurt, are you?"

Edith shook her head. "He came for Maxwell, didn't he?"

Mercy nodded. "I need you to fetch Detective Walker.

He's at the station house. Do you know where that is?"

She nodded. "I'll go as fast as I can. What are you going to do with him?"

"Never you mind. I can handle him. Now go!"

Edith tore down the walkway and ran down the street.

With her daughter gone, Mercy took a moment to catch her breath. She grabbed Ezekiel's wrists and dragged his body back into the house, away from the prying eyes of the neighbours.

Chapter 25

Jeremiah closed the door to the interview room where Lottie and Mrs. Doyle were already seated and waiting. Thankfully, little Maggie was enthralled with a broach on Mrs. Doyle's lace collar.

"Thank you for coming down to the station house, Miss Lottie," Jeremiah said, taking a seat next to MacNeal, who sat with his hands folded on the top of the table.

"I don't know anything, Officers," she said. "I stays in the laundry most days." She gave an awkward sideways glance to Mrs. Doyle as if to check if she were answering properly.

"Don't count yourself out," MacNeal said. "Like I said in the carriage, you may know more than you realize."

The young woman was clearly nervous. She kept her gaze on her hands on the table, which she twisted together before Mrs. Doyle tapped her elbow, forcing her to lower her hands to her lap.

"This shouldn't take long. I only have one main concern," Jeremiah said. "Did Mr. Doyle bring you any clothes to be laundered this morning?"

The young woman hesitated and looked to Mrs. Doyle. "Yes, sir," she said, after her employer urged her to answer.

"What did he bring you?"

"Trousers, dress shirt, undershirt, socks... unmentionables."

"A full set of clothing then? In what state were those clothes in?"

"Soiled, sir."

"Soiled with what exactly?"

The maid shrugged. "Dirt... sir."

"Dirt?"

"They looked like he'd been rolling around in dirt, like a child who weren't told no better."

Jeremiah tried hard to hide his smile. Beside the maid, Mrs. Doyle lowered her head, ready to cry.

"When did he present you these clothes?"

"This morning."

"What time this morning?"

"Near five in the morning, sir. The misses weren't up yet."

Jeremiah nodded. "And you washed them straightaway?"

"I had other things to do. I wanted it to be cleared away before the day started."

"It's all right, Miss Lottie, it's all right. No one is blaming you for a thing, understand?"

The young girl nodded, but her face betrayed her concern.

Finally, Mrs. Doyle raised her gaze, revealing tear-stained cheeks. "I didn't know anything about this," she said, her chin trembling. "I should have known but I... I—"

"Mrs. Doyle, we understand," Jeremiah said, trying his best to calm her. "If you and Miss Lottie don't mind waiting here while my partner and I confer in the hallway a moment, yes? Excellent. MacNeal?" Jeremiah gestured for the door and both he and MacNeal filed out, closing it behind them.

"What did you find at the house?" Jeremiah asked.

"Not much. Laundry was already dry and being pressed by the time we arrived."

"You searched the premises?"

"Not entirely, I have a team there now going through everything," MacNeal answered.

"All right, we all but know he did it. Question is, where do you hide a body after you dig it up?" Jeremiah asked.

"Another grave?" MacNeal offered.

"There are no others, nothing recently dug. It's a much more difficult task to dig a new grave. I saw no signs of fresh disturbances." The men stood in silence a few moments, pondering the new direction of the case.

"We can't keep them here indefinitely," MacNeal said, gesturing to the door they had just come through.

Jeremiah nodded. Judging by the way Mr. Doyle refused to cooperate, Walker knew there was nothing they could say to force out a confession. "What if we were to let them all go?"

"The women?"

"And Mr. Doyle. Mrs. Doyle said her husband had gone

197

to a building after they escorted Ms. Eaton home. I imagine he has some connection there, someone advising him what to do. And I have my suspicions who it is."

"Don't hold out on me," MacNeal said, slapping Jeremiah with the back of his hand. "Tell me."

Jeremiah scanned the hallway and leaned in closer to ensure they were alone. "Ezekiel London."

"The alderman?"

"Former alderman. Got caught up in some scandal and lost his seat. You know that kid I arrested at the train station?"

"Yeah, Maxwell. You said you got him released."

"He said his uncle put him up to it. Said Ezekiel sent him and two others to the train station. Didn't tell Maxwell why."

"I bet the other two knew what was up."

"Exactly. I'm also willing to bet that this guy, Mr. Doyle, is under Ezekiel's payroll. Ezekiel's brings him items that need to disappear. Mr. Doyle happily obliges."

"So let's bring in Mr. London."

"Can't prove anything. We've got a bunch of circumstantial and a sixteen-year-old kid who admits he didn't know anything." Jeremiah pressed a finger in MacNeal's chest. "I say, we cut him lose. See where he goes."

"You think Mr. Doyle will return?" MacNeal asked.

"Yes, that man doesn't do anything without someone else's say so. He's not a principal player. He's a goddamn patsy."

"He's not talking at the moment," MacNeal said in agreement. "We'll never get a confession out of him, not even to save his own wife. I saw it in his eyes."

Jeremiah couldn't hide his excitement as they hatched their plan. "We let him go, say it was all a misunderstanding, and we follow him."

"I like this plan," MacNeal said with a smile.

"Let's hope it works the way it already has in my head."

Jeremiah opened the door to the interview room. "Thank you very much, ladies," he said, stepping aside and holding the door open. "Your contribution had been most helpful."

"That's everything?" Lottie asked, looking to her

employer.

"If we need anything else we will let you know," MacNeal said.

The women gathered themselves and stood. At the door Mrs. Doyle paused. "Are you keeping my husband, Detective?"

"At this time, ma'am, the law prevents us from holding him without officially charging him with a crime," Jeremiah lied. He could have held him for another day or so while they completed their investigation, but that would not lead them anywhere.

Mrs. Doyle seemed put off by this. "Well, if you don't mind, would you be able to hold him a tiny bit more so Lottie and I can travel alone? I'm not sure I am ready to see him yet."

Jeremiah nodded. "Yes, ma'am, that can be arranged."

She offered a weak thank you and left alongside her maid.

A few minutes later, Jeremiah popped into his office, startling Mr. Doyle from a snooze. He lifted his head from the desk wearily and wiped some drool that had formed on the side of his mouth.

"Our apologies, Mr. Doyle," Jeremiah said. "It seems we were mistaken."

MacNeal came to the door and looked in. Mr. Doyle was slow to move.

"You are free to go," MacNeal said.

"Am I?"

"Yes, Mr. Doyle, your wife and maid have assured us of your innocence."

Mr. Doyle's eyes grew wide. "They have?" He pushed himself up from the chair.

Jeremiah stepped forward and adjusted Alexander's tie and collar. "No hard feelings, are there?" Jeremiah asked.

"He's got a bit of short fuse," MacNeal said. "Terrible, really."

Mr. Doyle puffed up his chest slightly. "No harm done," he said. "Just be more careful in the future."

"I will," Jeremiah said, nearly choking on his words. "Your wife and maid have already gone on. Shall we hail you a hansom?"

"That's not necessary," Mr. Doyle said, grabbing his suit jacket from the back of the chair and draping it over his arm. "Good day, gentlemen."

"Mr. Doyle."

Jeremiah and MacNeal watched from the open doorway as Mr. Doyle made his way down the hall. The man showed no signs of doubt. He put on his suit jacket before he reached the main lobby and fumbled with a cigar he pulled from his pocket.

"Ready, MacNeal?" Jeremiah asked, reaching for his own jacket.

"Ready and willing."

Chapter 26

Edith ran as fast as she could, sidestepping piles of horse dung on the road. She could not run on the pavement. Too many workers and schoolchildren crowded her out as they made their way home. She was forced, instead, to run in the gutters, dodging carts and carriages that careened toward her. One cart would have surely struck her had she not clamoured up a pile of cabbage leaves and kitchen scraps left at the side of the road.

By the time she ran through the doors of the station house her school uniform was soiled beyond recognition. Her shoes were caked in mud, bits of food, and dung, despite her best efforts to avoid all three. She panted heavily from exertion, her panic-stricken face doing nothing to elicit sympathy from anyone behind the desk.

"My mother—" she said, falling short of breath, "attacked." She leaned in over the counter, touching a uniformed officer on the arm. "I need Detective Walker, please!" she yelled out, her voice loud enough everyone in the room heard her.

"He's just left," the uniformed officer said. "You'll have to sit and wait." He motioned to a bench along the far wall and turned his back to her.

Left? Edith closed her eyes. She should have run faster.

"But my mother! She needs help."

Another officer appeared from behind a door. "What's this?" he asked, coming toward her.

The desk officer waved a dismissive hand.

"Please, sir," Edith said, "my mother has been attacked by Ezekiel London. He's known to us. He's a horrible man. You must come help us!" She stopped short of grabbing his arm and forcing him to follow her. He seemed interested enough in her story, though not necessarily concerned.

"And your mother's name?"

"Mercy Eaton. I'm Edith Eaton."

Edith's eyes were drawn to his lips, where for the smallest moment she saw the edges of his mouth curl into a smile. Her heart sank at the sight of it. A feeling of foreboding washed over her and she felt the urge to back away.

"Let's go then," he said. "Fortunately, the police carriage is right out front."

Edith followed on his heels as he left the station house. She watched as he climbed up to the high bench next to the driver and then glanced to the cab portion of the carriage. She wondered if she should climb in as he hadn't told her so. Realizing he was speaking instructions to the driver she reached for the silver handle of the door and opened the latch.

"Sorry, miss," he said, twisting his body to look at her. Using one hand he pressed back on the door, latching it in place. "You'll have to walk."

"But I don't understand."

"Negroes don't get to ride, not even if they are in handcuffs." He winked at her and smiled as if it were all just a joke. Then the carriage wheels began to roll, narrowly missing Edith's toes. She watched helplessly as the help she'd summoned for her mother was swallowed up in evening traffic. Her throat was dry and her spirits dampened by his remarks. She did not know if she could run the entire way back. She felt her legs go weak and decided to shuffle to a nearby lamppost to keep her upright. Another minute, she told herself. One more minute and then I will go.

"Edith!"

She lifted her gaze at the sound of Maxwell's voice.

"Edith!" His familiar, smiling face came into view through the crowds.

"Oh, thank God," she said.

"What's happened to you?" Maxwell asked, getting close enough to see the state of her dress and shoes.

"My mother's been attacked. I came here for Detective Walker but he just left." Edith grew light-headed as she spoke and the world began spinning faster. She closed her eyes but the spinning sensation did not ease. She felt Maxwell's hand on her back.

"What do you mean 'attacked'?"

"I have to go home," Edith said with closed eyes. "Something bad is going to happen. I just need another minute."

"Edith?... Edith!"

She felt Maxwell's hand on the side of her face. When she opened her eyes she realized she was on the ground, her back leaning up against the base of the lamppost. A small crowd had gathered to look at her, not in sympathy, she soon realized, but for the spectacle.

"Maxwell?"

He was kneeled down in front of her. "We need to get you home," he said.

She felt him lifting her and placing her arm over his shoulders for more support. She leaned into him. "We have to get to my mother," she said, realizing her voice was as weak as her body. "That man," she said. "We need to save her from that man."

~ ~

Constance was three blocks from her home and every clop of the horse's hooves that brought her closer solidified her feelings of dread. Lottie was seated on the cart bench beside her, Maggie held in her arms, shielded from the hot late-afternoon sun. Neither of them had said a word since they left the station house. Too much weighed on their minds.

That morning, Constance had woken without any suspicion against her husband. There hadn't been any inkling of any wrongdoing. She'd been contented with her new baby and new role of mother. Had she not heard the details of her husband's laundry from her own maid she might not ever have believed it.

"Was everything you said in there true?" Constance asked, raising her voice above the din of the city.

Lottie looked taken aback.

"I need to know," Constance said, keeping her eyes on the horse in front of her and the speed of traffic around her. "Was all that about the laundry true?"

"Yes, ma'am. I spoke the truth as I always have."

Constance took in a breath and kept her gaze forward.

"I'm sorry, ma'am," she said.

"Don't apologize," she said. "I should be the one saying sorry."

"Ma'am?"

"I'm sorry I had such blinders on." Constance snapped the reins and pulled the horse to the right, changing their course.

"We were supposed to take a left." Lottie twisted in her seat to look behind them, as if taking better note of their surroundings. "Home was to the left."

Constance shook her head. "We aren't going home, at least not yet."

Chapter 27

Mercy examined herself closely in the hallway mirror. There were red marks on her neck and shoulder where Ezekiel had held her down, red marks that were slowly darkening to purple as time passed. Her cheeks were flushed crimson as well but they were less likely to bruise, thank goodness. The worst injury in the ordeal was the mental image she now had of her good friend Hazel struggling to fight off her own brother. The panic Mercy had felt had doubled the second her friend came to mind with the realization that she had been taken by force at the hands of the same man who had the courts deem her incorrigible.

She heard a muffled groan from the other room and casually went to the doorway to look in. Immediately after dragging his body inside, Mercy had propped Ezekiel up on one of her client chairs and then tied him securely with a bit of rope from the cellar. Not only had she secured his torso to the chair but also fastened his ankles separately and tied his hands behind his back. He had been out for some time, which allowed her to ensure good knots. It hadn't been easy but there was no way he could get out of those bonds until she or Walker removed him.

Mercy tried not to smile as he slowly woke up, confused and groggy from the impact to his head. She crossed her arms over her chest and leaned on the doorframe to watch as he came around slowly. "Welcome back," she said, moving into the room so he could see her.

His gaze lifted, and then his head rolled to one shoulder. "Untie me," he demanded, his voice low.

"You'd love that, wouldn't you?" she said, standing opposite him. Her reading table sat between him and her.

"I won't hurt you, I promise," he said. "I don't know why I did that."

"I do," she said. "You been getting away with that sort of

thing for a long time, haven't you?"

He said nothing.

She pulled out her chair from the table and took a seat opposite him. "Let's play a game, shall we?" She reached for her tarot cards and fanned them out over the table.

"That's complete bunk."

She raised an eyebrow. "Let's see then."

She pulled three cards from the deck, sliding them forward but keeping them face down. In one swoop she brushed the unchosen cards back into a pile and left them to the side.

"I don't believe any of this," he growled, still unable to hold his head up completely.

"You don't have to." She flipped the one in the middle over first. "Oh, the devil, imagine that. This card is a card of warning. There's no escape. Something really bad is going to happen to you. Something you will not be pleased about."

Ezekiel wasn't looking at her, but she could tell he was listening. She continued, flipping over the card on the right. "The Tower," she said, clicking her tongue. "This is not good. Two foreboding cards in a row. Ezekiel, things are not looking good for you right now." She flipped over the last card and smiled. "My apologies, Ezekiel. I usually don't like giving my clients such a negative reading but when you are such a negative soul, what do you expect, really?"

"There's no truth to those cards," he squawked, suddenly interested.

"Oh, then you have nothing to fear," she said. "If you were my client, I'd be warning you to change your ways before it's too late, but in your case, it's already too late. You are finally going to pay for what you did to Hazel."

"You think the universe gives a fuck about that dead bitch?"

"I know I do," Mercy said.

"And who are you? A nobody."

"Unlike you, right? Big powerful man who sends boys and inept funeral directors out to do his dirty work."

Ezekiel smiled. "None of them did anything they didn't want to do."

"Except Maxwell, who had no idea what you'd recruited

him for." Mercy gathered up the cards in single swoop and replaced them into the deck. "Is that anyway to treat your son?"

A muscle on Ezekiel's face twitched as he glared at her.

"Wasn't just the one time, was it?"

"She wanted it."

Mercy shook her head. "Like I wanted it?"

His scowl grew deeper.

"You sent Hazel away to Mercer Reformatory for something you yourself had done to her. You represent the worst of men."

"I assure you, I ain't the worst," Ezekiel said.

"That maybe true, but it still doesn't make it righ—" She was startled by the sound of her front door opening. She stood up from her chair, expecting to see Walker, but was surprised when Constance strode in.

"Connie!" Mercy looked to Ezekiel in the chair and flushed red with embarrassment.

"What's..." Constance's gaze traced the room. Her body stiffened and she recoiled as if she wanted to leave all together. "I don't understand what you are doing," she said.

"It's not what it looks like," Mercy said. "This man attacked me."

Constance scrutinized Mercy closer and must have seen the evidence on her sister's neck and shoulders. "Oh."

"I'm waiting for Walker. Edith's gone to fetch him." Mercy watched as her sister hesitated.

"I'm afraid Edith may not be successful."

"Why do you say that?"

"Because both Walker and Sergeant MacNeal are following my husband." She glanced to Ezekiel in the chair. "Are you sure he is securely tied?"

"Yes, of course," Mercy answered dismissively. "Why are you here?"

Constance stiffened at this question and for a moment it looked as if she would refuse to answer. "I've come to apolog—"

The front door opened again and behind Constance, Mercy could see Lottie backing away toward the kitchen. Once Constance looked, she stepped out of the way as well.

"Walker?" Mercy went to the foyer and found Constable

Green standing just inside her doorway.

"Afraid not," he answered. "Your daughter tells me there was an incident."

"This man attacked me," Mercy said, beckoning for him to come to parlour.

Ezekiel didn't look overly concerned. "Lovers' quarrel."

"Certainly not!" Mercy said. "Constable Green, you mustn't believe anything this man says. He's a liar and swindler. He was the reason Maxwell, my daughter's friend, was arrested a few days ago."

Constable Green raised an eyebrow in surprise but said nothing.

"Where is Edith, by the way?" Constance asked, stepping toward the parlour door. "Officer?"

Green suddenly realized she was addressing him. "Oh, she must be dallying," he said dismissively. "I offered a ride in our carriage but she said she preferred to walk."

Mercy looked at him doubtfully. It was nearly ninety degrees outside.

"I'll take him off your hands, ma'am," Green said, moving toward Ezekiel. He bent down behind the chair and worked on untying the ropes.

"You are taking him to the station house?" Mercy pressed.

"Yes, of course. I'll take him there tonight. You can come in the morning to provide your statement of what you think happened."

Mercy crossed her arms over her chest. "What I *think* happened? I know what happened. He attacked me with the intention to"—she looked to Connie, embarrassed—"to rape me."

"That may be, ma'am, but we presume innocence in this country."

"You sound as if you intend to let him go!" Mercy said.

"I intend to do my job," Green answered. He pulled at the last rope around Ezekiel's ankles and put his hand under Ezekiel's armpit to lift him from the chair. "I will interview both parties and make my decision."

"You can't do that!" Mercy stepped in front of them, barring their way to the front door.

"Step aside, ma'am," Green ordered.

Mercy did not budge.

With one hand on Ezekiel, Green used his free hand to grab Mercy's upper arm and move her. "I said, step aside!" When he released her the pain in her flesh intensified. She rubbed at it as she followed them to the porch.

Once outside Mercy could see Maxwell leading Edith slowly down the opposite side of the street. When Edith realized she was nearly home she picked up her pace and they crossed the street just as Ezekiel was being led into the cab of the police carriage.

It took a moment for Mercy to take in the sight of her daughter, affected by heat and exhaustion, and looking as if she'd spent the night in a refuse heap.

"I ran as fast as I could," Edith said. "Walker wasn't there."

"I know, honey. It's all right." She let Edith slump into her arms. "You should have accepted Officer Green's offer of a ride. You didn't have to walk the entire way back."

"Mama, he refused to let me in the carriage—"

"I know that man," Maxwell said, pointing to the carriage.

"It's your uncle, Max," Mercy said apologetically. "He's done a horribly bad thing."

"No, the officer. I know him."

Mercy shifted her gaze toward Green, snapping the latch of the carriage door and then using the spoke of the wheel to climb aboard the driver's bench.

"He's worked for my uncle for a long time," Maxwell explained.

"But he's a police officer," Mercy said, without taking her eyes from Green. "How could he work for your uncle at the same time?" As she spoke the realization hit her and she couldn't believe how naive she had been. The carriage was pulling away from the curb when Mercy stepped out onto the road to stop them.

"Mercy!" Constance yelled for her sister from the garden but Mercy ignored her. She stood her ground, anticipating the carriage would stop but it kept moving, gaining speed as well. She saw Green smiling from his perch as the two-horse team barrelled toward her.

"Mama!"

Mercy dodged the horses with only seconds to spare and tripped on the hem of her skirt. She fell to the ground in a swirling cloud of dust kicked up by the horses.

"Ms. Eaton!"

Maxwell was at her side first, then Edith appeared. Mercy shirked off their offers of assistance and gathered herself up from the ground. "Constance, I am borrowing your cart," she said, walking for the horse without waiting for permission.

"You can't go after them," Constance said, running to catch up to her sister.

"Connie, that man assaulted me and he's not in police custody. I could never sleep again knowing he was still free," Mercy said, clamouring to the seat of the cart. "You, Lottie, and Maggie can stay here as long as you like, but for now, I have to go."

"Then I am going with you!" Constance climbed up and pushed Mercy aside.

"I can't let you do that," Mercy said. "It's too dangerous."

Constance took a steadying breath. "Mercy, if there's one thing you have taught me, it's doing what you are told isn't always the right thing to do," she said. "And it's not nearly as fun. Besides, Francis can be a little tricky with strangers," she said, indicating the harnessed horse.

Mercy smiled. "Go inside," she said to Edith and Maxwell.

"Be careful," Edith said from the walkway.

Mercy nodded. "As always. Let's go, Connie."

Constance snapped the reins on the horse's back side and the cart jerked into motion.

"Lock the doors," Mercy advised over her sister's shoulder. "Don't trust anyone!"

Maxwell, Edith, and Lottie nodded in agreement. The three of them were headed up to the front door of the house by the time Mercy lost sight of them.

"That's sound advice, little sister," Constance said, keeping her eyes on the road. "Very sound advice indeed."

Chapter 28

Walker and MacNeal walked two astride before branching off, with MacNeal on the opposite side of the street from Walker. They remained in contact, though, through hand signals as they both dodged rush-hour pedestrian traffic, maintaining a good pace behind Mr. Doyle. For a time, it seemed Alexander was heading home and Walker began to question his scheme. But then, unexpectantly, their quarry made a left turn up Yonge Street. Alexander had taken on a harried pace, moving quickly for a man so weighed down in the middle. He seemed to have zero concern for anything around him and did not look back, not even once, which meant Walker could remain close.

When Walker looked to MacNeal, he found him jogging to keep up, his side of the road hosting much more foot traffic. MacNeal struggled to maneuver through the streets and ended up tripping over the edges of carts and sidestepping piles of dung that had been swept out to the gutter. Walker watched with concern as MacNeal pushed past a gaggle of women who walked four abreast without any intention of making room for others walking in either direction. MacNeal made eye contact with Walker and made a motion with his hands toward his eyes.

When Walker looked back to Alexander he was crossing traffic, skipping ahead of a horse-drawn omnibus, which prevented Walker from giving chase. He met MacNeal on the other side, both of them realizing they had let him gain too much distance.

"We can't lose sight of him," Walker said, breaking into a run.

Alexander turned to the right and when Walker finally made it to the corner he realized it was a nearly deserted alleyway. He snapped back into the brick wall of the corner, hiding his body from view should Mr. Doyle look behind him. Unaware, MacNeal stepped out before Walker could grab his shirt and pull him back as well.

They watched in silence as Mr. Doyle quickly made his way down the alley.

"Where's he going?" MacNeal whispered.

Walker strained his eyes against the streaming sunlight and saw him approach a door on the side of one of the buildings. "It's Ezekiel's building. He's going in through the back door."

"He's being cautious."

"Not cautious enough." Walker waved for MacNeal to follow him and they jogged down the alley to the door. Walker waited before entering. He listened, his ear pressed up against the weathered wood. He turned the handle and pushed in the door slowly, readying himself for anything that might be waiting on the other side.

The door opened into a hallway with two steps down and a door to the right. As Jeremiah watched, a woman stepped into the hallway from the door. Ruth.

He pushed his way in. Ruth tried to retreat to the adjoining room but he grabbed her and dragged her from the building.

"Get your hands off of me," she said, batting at his grasp with her one good arm.

Walker brought her to the middle of the alley, and cornered her against a pile of broken crates.

"What are you going to do, Jeremy?" she asked. Her eyes went to MacNeal. "Are you going to shoot me again?"

"I never shot you in the first place and everyone knows it." Jeremiah said, out of breath. "You're a liar, Ruth. A liar and a scoundrel."

Her expression fell at his words, as if caught in a corner she didn't know how to get out of. "If I'm a liar, what does that make you then?" she asked, giving sideways glances to MacNeal. A smirk formed as her confidence returned. "You gonna tell him, Jer?"

Jeremiah's heart raced as Ruth spoke. Nothing pained him more than the knowledge he had been lying to his partner for nearly a week.

"Go on," Ruth prodded. "Tell him."

"Tell me what?" MacNeal asked. "Walker?"

"Tell him about all the lies, the deceit, the sabotage."

"Ruth, quiet!" Jeremiah snapped. He found it difficult to think with her voice ringing in his ears. His anger for her was so pronounced he could hardly believe he had ever done anything for her benefit. "MacNeal, I need to tell you something," he said, without taking his eyes from Ruth He was not proud of what he was about to admit; in fact, he knew he should have come clean long before this. "She's been at my house."

"We know."

"No, not just yesterday... since the night Dubois was killed."

MacNeal shrank back, his features a mixture of shock and disgust. "This entire time? I asked you. I explicitly asked you if you'd heard from her and you said no."

"Yes, I realize this."

"Do you realize what this has done to my investigation— my career? Walker, we can lose our badges over this!" MacNeal grabbed Walker by the lapels and shook him in frustration. Within seconds he pulled himself away as if unable to trust himself. He walked away, his hands on the sides of his head.

"And Ms. Eaton, she was lying too, I suppose."

"Ms. Eaton was only trying to help me."

"Help you? Help you harbour a murderer? I hadn't realized Ms. Eaton was the type."

"She's not. Please, MacNeal, keep her out of this."

MacNeal charged back at him. "You have some nerve asking for favours from me when the prime suspect in *my* murder investigation, my *first* murder investigation, has been under your roof this entire time!" His face was inches from him. Walker could feel the heat of anger radiating from his partner. MacNeal turned away and began pacing the alley.

"I hadn't meant for it to be like this," Walker confessed.

"Oh yeah? What did you intend to accomplish? Your reasoning is completely lost on me," MacNeal said.

Walker fell silent, his mind awash with all the instances his good intentions had collided with reality. "I don't know... I wanted to protect her?"

"Protect her? From what? Herself?" MacNeal pointed to the door. "Because I think the last two years has proven to all of us that she is her own worst enemy. You cannot save her, Walker. You couldn't when you married her and you sure as hell can't now."

Jeremiah's heart sank, not at the realization of it, because this was something he had known for a long time, but at the fact his colleagues as well had witnessed his downfall. He was not upset that his marriage was at an end. He was upset about the shame it caused him.

MacNeal took her under the arm. "Ruth Walker, I am arresting you for filing a false police report *and* for the murder of Edward Dubois."

She struggled against his vice-like grip but MacNeal was determined. He pushed her to her knees in the dry dirt of the alley. She yowled in pain, reaching her good arm across her chest to her wound.

"Jeremy, make him stop," she pleaded, her eyes welling up in tears. "Don't let him arrest me. I didn't do anything. I swore to you."

She writhed against MacNeal's grasp, all the while looking up at Jeremiah pleadingly.

"Jeremiah, please!"

"Please what?" He suddenly felt angry.

"Don't let him do this. You know I didn't do anything."

"Do I?" Walker reached into his pocket and pulled out the pendant Mercy had presented to him that morning. "Where did I find this then?" he asked, bending down low so she could see both what he held and the look of anger on his face.

Her tears vanished almost instantly. "Where did you get that?" she asked.

"Harbouring murderers and withholding evidence—"

"I only received it this morning, MacNeal," Walker said. "This may be the final piece to your puzzle."

MacNeal suddenly showed interest after Walker spoke.

"The chain is broken," Jeremiah said. "There was probably a tussle. He grabbed her and broke the chain seconds before she shot him at close range, probably with the same gun she planted in my house yesterday. She contrived it all. She begged me for help only to set me up for what she had done herself."

Ruth was no longer scared. She was livid. Her face

contorted into a snarl. Like an animal, she glowered, daring either of them to come near her. "It was that bitch, wasn't it? Poking her nose in where it don't belong."

"I knew you had done it the minute this was placed in my hand." He turned over the pendant to reveal lipstick smeared into the backside, a bright red he had known Ruth to wear. "And"—he held it up to his nose—"it smells like gunpowder."

"So what?"

"You pulled the trigger. One shot, right here." He held a finger to his chest. "That was enough to do him in."

Walker watched as Ruth's breathing quickened. She glared at him unblinkingly. "They made me do it."

"Who?"

"London and the others."

Walker waited.

"They said if I didn't do it, they'd find a way to make it look like you did it," she explained. "What happened at the house, that was all them. Don't you see I was protecting you? Isn't that what husbands and wives are supposed to do?"

He stopped himself from laughing. "There are many things husbands and wives do that we don't do."

Once she realized her pleading wouldn't have as much affect as it had in the past, she grew angry once again. Her eyes narrowed and her jaw tightened. "They'll hang me. You know they will."

"Perhaps some society group will take pity on you and plead on your behalf."

"You'll go down with me, both of you. No one will trust you weren't in on this. No one will think you are completely innocent."

"I will atone for my sins; however, I feel like you will never be prepared to admit you were wrong," Walker said. He turned his attention to MacNeal and ignored the rest of her protestations. "Take her in," he said. "Write the report however you'd like. I'll come clean to all of it."

"Walker—"

"All of it. I'm not so proud that I can't admit when I've been manipulated."

MacNeal looked to the door. "What about Alexander

Doyle?"

"I'll take care of him. You go on. Deal with her. I'll not have her getting away again."

After a moment of thought, MacNeal nodded and pulled Ruth to her feet.

"You'll miss me, Walker," she yelled out. "You'll be crying out for me in your sleep!"

Walker turned to the door and placed his hand on the knob. "Don't bet on it."

Chapter 29

"There! Constance, hurry!" Mercy pointed ahead of them at the large police carriage drifting away in the sea of afternoon carriage traffic of St. Andrew's.

"I'm going as fast as I can," Constance said, squinting against the dust the horse kicked up. "I only have one horse while they have two."

Mercy sat at the edge of her seat, waving for people to move out of their way. "Move!" she yelled. "We have to go!"

"Sorry!" Constance called out over her shoulder as they pushed by, narrowly missing a woman holding the hands of her two school-aged children.

"Goodness, Constance, you haven't the fortitude for this sort of work," Mercy said, grabbing the reins and giving the horse one big slap on his rump. The cart lurched forward and picked up speed.

She stood up, reins in hand, and shouted for people to move. "Coming through! Out of the way!" Again, they narrowly missed colliding with another carriage had the other driver not stopped his horse.

Mercy cared little. They were gaining on them. As the city buildings passed, Constance shrunk against the back of her seat and held onto her metal armrest with one hand and pressed down her hat with the other. "Mercy, please slow down!"

"We almost have them!" she yelled back over the clinking of the carriage joints and wheels. What exactly Mercy planned to do once they had them was entirely unknown. When they finally caught up to them, with hardly a carriage length between them, the driver and Green looked back.

"This bitch is mad," Green said.

"What did he say?" Constance asked.

"Nothing important." Mercy didn't let up on her pursuit. In fact, Constable Green's comments made her even more determined not to let them get away.

From her vantage point, Mercy could see Green and the driver talking, though she couldn't make out what was being said. The conversation turned heated and it looked like the carriage was slowing down. Then, unexpectedly, Green pushed the driver from the perch.

Constance screamed and Mercy veered the horse to the right to avoid rolling over him. The cart wheel lifted and rocked the cart to the side. Mercy tried to look over her shoulder to see if they had crushed him, but she couldn't see for all the dust their vehicles kicked up. "Is he all right?" Mercy yelled. "Constance! Is he all right?"

"He's all right!" Constance placed a steadying hand on Mercy's arm. "He's standing. It was just a divot in the road."

"Oh, thank God."

With Green at the reins, the police carriage veered left, making a full ninety-degree turn onto Yonge Street at nearly full speed. Mercy watched as the bulk of the carriage leaned to the right. She pulled back the reins to slow down her horse and watched the left side wheels of the police carriage lift off the ground an inch or so. Mercy winced against the impending topple of the carriage. Then, as if by miracle, the turn was complete. The bulk of the carriage righted itself and Green picked up speed.

"Mercy, stop, we can't make it!"

Mercy had slowed considerably but not nearly enough to take the turn safely. She felt Constance scrambling behind her to get her weight on the opposite side of the bench. The cart wanted to pull to the right and the wheels on the left lifted off the ground.

"Hold on!" Mercy yelled.

Once the turn was over, the wheels snapped back to the ground. Constance's hat bounced from her head.

"My hat!"

"Good Lord, we can get you another hat!"

Mercy snapped the reins to pick up their speed. The police carriage was ahead about thirty yards. She could gain on them, maybe even get ahead of them and force them to stop.

A coal cart from a side street came out onto the road just in front of the police carriage, oblivious to the danger. A young boy stood in front coaxing his donkey forward. Mercy saw the boy look up and then dodge out of the way just as the police carriage hit. Mercy couldn't stop in time. She veered her horse right but couldn't clear the wreckage.

The next few seconds were a tangled mess of horses, carriage parts and cart wheels, splintered wood, and lumps of coal. Mercy was thrown from the cart, catapulted up and over the bulk of the wreckage. She landed next to Constance's horse, her head hitting half horse, half carriage hulk. Something large landed on her and rolled off, then she felt pieces of the cart landing on her feet and legs, ripping her layers of skirt and meeting skin.

Screams and shouts erupted from the crowd as Mercy tried to collect herself. The horse at her side was breathing but barely. She placed her hand on the animal's neck and tried to soothe it as she assessed the damage. On the other side of the rubble, she could see the coal cart boy and his donkey staring at her.

BANG!

Blood splattered Mercy's face. Constable Green, standing in his navy police uniform, unmarred by the collision, had shot the horse dead. Mercy looked on in horror.

"He would have died before long," Green said. "You can call it a mercy." He smiled devilishly as he said her name. He was reloading his pistol as he spoke. Mercy lay frozen, unable to move, partly because of the pieces that had landed on her, partly out of fear. His finger on the trigger, he repositioned his gun, pointing it directly at her. He stood over her like that for seconds that felt like hours. Mercy returned his gaze, silently daring him to be so bold as to shoot her in front of so many witnesses.

"It was you," she said before she could stop herself.

Her words broke his focus.

"You were the shooter at the train station. You killed Mr. Carver."

His mouth twitched at her words.

"It wasn't about the case, was it?" If she was going to die, she might as well know how she had come to it.

"Not entirely." He waved his pistol, directing her to get up.

A moan came from Mercy's right. Constance lifted her head and pushed herself up from the wreckage.

"Oh, thank God!" Mercy scrambled to her and threw her arms around her. Everything in Mercy's body ached, especially her shoulder and lower back, but she didn't care. She and her sister were still alive. Judging by the way Constance moved, she was in pain as well.

"Is anything broken?" Mercy scanned her sister for evidence of blood.

"No," Constance said. "I don't think so. You broke my fall, mostly." A nervous laugh escaped them both.

"Get up, both of you!" Green discharged his gun, this time in the air, to get their attention. "Get up!"

Despite the pain, Mercy and Constance helped each other and got to their feet. Ezekiel was standing beside Green by the time they traversed the wreckage. He had a serious gash to his temple, with blood dripping down the edge of his brow and cheek.

Green got behind Constance and Mercy, and pushed the pistol into Constance's back. "Move," he said.

They followed Ezekiel to a nearby building, limping and going slow. Before they reached the door, Mercy glanced back to the street. Three dead horses and a mass of wreckage lay in the dust. It had all been because of Mercy.

"Let's go." Green gave Mercy a slight shove through the doorway and quickly snapped it closed behind him, fastening the lock.

Mercy's eyes were slow to adjust to the dim light, but once they did she could see they were in a reception area. There was a hall in the middle of a back wall and a set of stairs with intricately carved railings to one side. The walls were painted a deep red with dark-stained chair rails and trim. Each wall had a piece of art or two, oil paintings mostly, each a different pastoral setting from around the world: Holland, the River Thames, the western prairies, and New York City. Mercy's gaze fell on one in particular, a vase with flowers, peonies and roses, set in a dark room. The colours, pastels and soft hues, caught her attention first. The more she looked at it the more the image morphed. Soon she was focused in the movements of the individual brushstrokes and the three-dimensional affect they caused. Within seconds she knew this was the painting missing from the institute.

"Get me out of these fucking things," Ezekiel said, raising his wrists up to Green's face.

"Jesus Christ, Ezekiel, what were you thinking going to that woman's house?" Green asked, slapping his hands down and readying the key.

Ezekiel gave a sideways look to Mercy. "She's a good-looking woman, and I want what I like."

"You didn't expect her to put up a fight then?"

"I like it when they fight." His gaze was menacing enough to make Mercy's blood run cold. She retreated from the painting back to the relative safety nearest her sister.

A floorboard creaked from the hallway and Ezekiel and Green turned to see who was making their way toward them. More to the side of the room, neither Mercy nor Constance could see who stood in the hall.

"What the fuck are you doing here?" Green asked.

"They let me go."

Mercy stiffened at the sound of Alexander's voice.

"They let you go?" Green looked thoroughly confused.

"They have nothing on me."

Green scoffed. "They have enough."

"You shouldn't have come here," Ezekiel said, massaging his wrists. "We've had enough trouble cleaning up your mess."

Mercy looked to Constance, who stood stock-still, staring blankly straight ahead.

"What did you do with the body after all?" Alexander asked.

Ezekiel motioned to Green, who beamed with pride. "Took it on the train to Hamilton. Got a cousin in iron works. He took care of our little problem."

"You took the body on the train?" Mercy asked before she could stop herself.

Green smiled. "In a trunk. A bit of a squeeze but I managed."

Alexander stepped from the hall into the foyer. He must have recognized the sound of his sister-in-law's voice. He blanched the moment he saw Constance standing next to her.

Without saying a word, Constance moved forward, limping from the injury to her foot. Mercy watched as her sister stared unforgivingly at her husband. Alexander remained in place, dumbstruck at discovering her there, worried she might have overheard. Within arm's reach, Constance stopped and kept his gaze.

"Constance, I—"

She slapped him hard across the cheek. He pulled away but she didn't relent. She delivered hit after hit with closed fists and a fierce determination Mercy had never seen her sister display. "How could you?" she yelled at him, growling through gritted teeth. "How could you ruin everything like this? After everything I've done to build you up!"

The sound of her fists hitting him filled the room. Both Green and Ezekiel looked entertained and did nothing to save their partner in crime. Mercy stepped forward, more so out of mercy for her sister than for her brother-in-law, but she couldn't get close enough with Constance's arms flailing about each side of her.

"Constance... Constance!" Mercy was able to grab her wrist and held fast. Constance looked to Mercy, revealing red eyes filled with tears.

Alexander took her distraction as an opportunity. No longer defending himself from blows, he drew back a hand and delivered a hardy smack to his wife's face. Mercy immediately dropped her sister's hand and stepped between them. Her attack came as such a surprise Alexander fumbled back, falling to the floor. "Don't you dare lay another hand on my sister!" she yelled as she leaned in to strike him as many times as she could. Her hands hurt by the time Constance pulled her away.

"Enough!" Ezekiel yelled. "Clearly, gentlemen, we have a problem... we have two very clear problems."

Mercy and Constance clung to each other and backed away. The looks on Ezekiel's and Green's faces were menacing. Mercy already knew neither of them had any scruples with regards to human life.

"My cousin at the iron works offered his assistance any time," Green said, with a smirk.

Mercy huffed. "Good luck getting me in a truck quietly."

"You won't be alive enough to scream, darling," Ezekiel said.

Mercy felt her sister's hands tighten. "Take heart,

Connie, they won't get away with it. Everyone saw them bring us in here," Mercy said.

"A minor problem," Green said. "Witnesses are notoriously unreliable."

"You expect everyone to believe all those people are mistaken?" Constance asked.

"We have a gift of persuasion," Ezekiel said, "especially in this neighbourhood."

A flash of movement down the hall, behind Ezekiel, caught Mercy's attention. It took a moment for her to realize Walker was hiding in a doorway. He placed a finger to his lips. She swallowed nervously and looked to her sister, who looked genuinely scared.

Green grabbed his gun from the tabletop and casually waved it toward Mercy and Constance. "Let's go," he said, pointing between them and the hallway.

"What are you going to do with them?" Alexander asked.

"What does it matter?" Green asked.

"You told us your wife wouldn't be any trouble," Ezekiel said.

"She isn't. It's that bitch of a sister she has who gets her in all the trouble," Alexander said.

Mercy felt herself tensing up and took a steadying breath to calm down.

"She knows too much. She has to go," Green said unapologetically. "That's how this works."

"You can't take her..." Alexander's words dissolved into a mumble. "I won't let you."

Ezekiel raised an eyebrow, amused by Alexander's sudden sentiment for his wife.

"Won't let me?" Ezekiel laughed. "All right, let's see how you won't let me."

After a moment's hesitation Alexander stepped forward. BANG! He fell back, trying to catch himself on a nearby armchair. A splotch of blood spread on from a central point in the middle of his stomach.

"Alex!" Constance rushed to her husband's side. Mercy would have gone too had the gun not been immediately pointed at her. She raised her hands in submission and took a step back.

Constance's wails filled the empty space. Alexander lay

flat on his back, the blood spot on his chest widening.

"Why did you do this? Why?" Constance's tearful crying turned to growling anguish as she beat his chest, not as hard as she had before. Soon her hands were covered in blood.

"Constance." Mercy tried to go to comfort her.

"Don't move!"

Mercy recoiled.

Alexander's breathing became rapid and disconnected. He'd barely pulled in a breath before he exhaled. The blood from his wound slowed and then there was nothing. Alexander was gone.

Chapter 30

"All right, enough of this," Ezekiel said.

Green stepped forward to pull Constance from the ground. Mercy could see Alex's blood had stained the front of her dress and was spread over all her hands. Constance cried even as she was lifted from the ground.

"Both of you, move."

Mercy and Constance were pushed together. Constance practically fell into Mercy's arms and it was Mercy who kept her upright and walking until the weight of her sister became too much and Constance collapsed to the ground.

"Constance, get up," Mercy said, hunched over, desperately trying to get her sister to her feet. She could feel the pressure of the men behind them, their gun pointed at their backs. "You need to get up." Out of the corner of her eye, Mercy saw movement ahead of them and realized Walker was telling her to get down.

Mercy collapsed onto her sister, shielding her.

The first shot rang out over their heads. Ezekiel returned fire and Mercy realized she and Constance had to move. Walker was standing in a dark doorway not a foot from them. Mercy crawled and then began pulling Constance to the room. A shot from Ezekiel lodged in the doorframe next to Mercy's head. After that Constance moved quickly and soon they were out of the direct line of fire with their backs against the wall. Constance was hiding her face in her hands.

Mercy saw a window on the far wall, covered by a sheet of fabric. Crawling, she made her way over and pulled the fabric down. Light streamed in, illuminating the space, revealing painted canvases, large and small, leaning against each other and propped up against the walls. Some paintings she recognized, others she did not.

The window was too high for Mercy and Constance to crawl out of. And there was nothing in the room to create a platform, nothing but canvases and some raw wooden boards behind the door.

The shooting stopped and Mercy realized Walker had disappeared from the door. When she peered around the doorframe, she saw Walker bear-wrestling Green. Their guns out of ammunition, they had resorted to fisticuffs. Ezekiel was on the ground, moaning and holding a wound to his shoulder.

Walker landed a decent blow to Green's face and then worked to set him off balance. Green, however, was stronger than he looked and fought off Walker's attack. Green pushed Walker backward, sending him into the wall, which rocked the walls of the room Mercy and Constance were in. The wooden boards behind the door jolted and started to slide. They hit the back of the door, forcing it to close, with Mercy on one side, Constance on the other.

Frantically Mercy began to hit the door. "Constance! Constance!" She didn't trust her sister to respond. She was in no state to save herself. Mercy saw Walker and Green coming toward her and she pressed herself against the door to stay out of their way. She watched the fighting, desperate to find anything she could do to help.

Green's hands were at Walker's throat but he was unable to get a good enough grip to be effective. Walker pounded him into the wall, dislodging a lit wall sconce and sending the oil and flame down the wall to the floorboard. Smoke gathered quickly and the flames spread wantonly.

Mercy hit the door to the room where Constance was and then started throwing her body weight into it. "Constance!" The hallway grew warm as the flames spread. Mercy felt the door give slightly.

When she looked to Walker she found he had Green on the ground, and was putting him in manacles. The flames were creeping along both sides of the hall now, reaching for the ceiling. Mercy slapped the door with her open palm. "Constance!"

The door opened and Constance stood, weary but alive. Mercy flung her arms around her briefly before pulling her out of the room. "Go with Walker, go, go!" She veered Constance down the hall, ensuring she was clear of the worst of the flames before heading back to the room.

Without thinking Mercy used one of the boards to break the window and systematically began feeding canvases through the opening.

"We have to go," Walker said, pulling at her from the door.

"But the paintings! These are the missing paintings!"

She pushed past him and ran to the front where the flower vase painting was. She turned the corner and then sank back from the flames. The paintings were engulfed Their oil sizzled and charred with the heat.

Walker appeared behind her and pulled her toward the door. "We have to go now!"

"The paintings!"

"They're fakes!" he said against the roar of the flames He wrapped his arm around her waist and guided her from the room. Ezekiel moaned and reached for them from the floor. Without a word, Mercy and Walker each grabbed an arm and pulled Ezekiel down the hall to the side door of the building. Mercy could hear the bells of the fire brigade as soon as she entered the alley. The coughing started immediately. Mercy hunched over, unable to keep herself upright.

Constance was against the furthest wall, MacNeal holding her back, preventing her from going inside. When Constance's gaze fell on Mercy she pushed the officer to the side and wrapped her arms around her sister.

"I thought you were dead," she said, her voice muffled against Mercy's shoulder and neck.

"I thought *you* were dead," Mercy said, closing her eyes and enjoying the embrace.

Constance pulled back. "Don't you ever do anything like this again!"

Mercy smiled.

"I meant it, Mercy," her sister continued to scold.

Beside them, MacNeal placed handcuffs on Ezekiel, who moaned and coughed and begged for help.

"He's shot," MacNeal said.

Walker shrugged. "I should have aimed better."

Once Green and Ezekiel were loaded into the police carriage, Mercy walked over to the half dozen paintings she had pushed out of the window. She picked up one, a well-clothed man standing next to a horse, and looked it over. Walker came alongside her. "How do you know they are fakes?" she asked.

He took the canvas from her and studied it more closely before pointing a finger at the shadowing of one of the horse's legs. "See? There."

Mercy squinted in for a closer look.

"It's the painter's mark."

Mercy looked to the bottom right and pointed to the artist's signature. Gros.

"That's a fake too," Walker explained. "This is the real artist. They can't resist making their mark even when copying others."

MacNeal came alongside them for a look of his own.

"How did Ezekiel come into possession of so many forgeries?" Mercy asked, picking up another canvas to search for the mark on that one.

"Mr. Carver sold them to him."

"But we couldn't find any connection between Ezekiel and Mr. Carver," MacNeal offered.

"Except Mr. Dubois," Walker said. "He was the intermediary. He made all the arrangements between Mr. Carver and Ezekiel."

"Ezekiel must have found out he'd been swindled, that they weren't the authentic paintings," MacNeal said.

"Constable Green was the one who killed Mr. Carver at the train station," Mercy put in. "Ezekiel was probably behind that too."

"But if these are forgeries, where are the originals?" MacNeal asked. "Nothing's ever been recovered."

Mercy smiled. "I have an inkling."

Chapter 31

The sound of the brass knocker broke the tranquility of an otherwise silent residential street. Unlike their last visit, Mrs. Carver was quick to answer the door but her heart sank the minute she took in the faces of her visitors.

"Good morning, Mrs. Carver," Walker said. "A moment, if you please." He pushed in without waiting for her to step aside.

Mercy smiled when she saw little had changed since their last visit. "Everything is as it was," Mercy said.

Mrs. Carver looked around, as if looking for the appropriate words but also looking for anything that would draw the unwanted attention of her visitors. "A tribute," she said after a moment, "to my husband." She forced a smile in return, awkward and contrived.

"That's not entirely truthful, is it?" Walker asked.

"I'm sorry?"

"We know Mr. Carver was not the artist in this house," Mercy said. "It was you."

Mrs. Carver's features froze, unable to utter a defense or denial.

"Your husband was a thief. He didn't travel for inspiration, he travelled for paintings," Walker explained.

She swallowed hard but remained silent.

"Is it true your husband would steal works of art, bring them here for you to copy?" Walker asked.

"I... I don't know what..." Her voice was shaky. "I don't know what... you are talking about." Her brow glistened with sweat and her eyes dropped to the floor.

"Were you denied entry into art school?" Walker asked. "That must have hurt your pride."

"They accept more men than women," Mrs. Carver said in defense. She looked to Mercy. "It's a fact."

"So what did you do?" Mercy asked. "You'd copy the works of great artists, sell them as if they were authentic and stash the real ones. It's a double investment," Mercy explained. "One sale now, one sale down the road." As Mercy paced she sauntered up to a canvas fastened to the easel. Something new which hadn't even been started the last time they were there. "It's quite good," Mercy confessed. "You have me fooled, but I'm not an artist or an art dealer."

"Where'd you stash the originals, Mrs. Carver?" Walker asked.

She said nothing.

"There are half a dozen galleries scattered over Canada and the United States that would love their artwork back," he said.

Mercy looked to Walker. "Imagine the amount of arrogance needed to convince yourself your paintings are as good as the great artists of our time. Think of how you'd have to lie to yourself—"

"I never lied to myself!" Mrs. Carver snapped. "I knew I would never be as good. I could never dream up my own original compositions." She took a steadying breath. "I never intended to keep them. It was only for practice, at first. James would bring a painting home and I'd make a copy or two and he was supposed to take them back, leave them at the back door or something, some place safe."

Walker lifted his chin. "The early days..."

Mrs. Carver nodded. "Yes, but then he gifted one of my paintings to a business associate. One day he showed up wanting more and we realized we could finally see that our bills were paid. There was so much debt at this time, you see." She lifted her gaze, revealing tears pooling in her lower eyelids. "We never had the chance to take them back. It was too risky as well. He wanted to wait until things died down. We were going to return them, honest."

"But then Mr. London found out he'd been sold fakes," Mercy said. "How much had you and your husband taken him for?" She waited. "One thousand?... Two thousand. No... a man like that doesn't lose his head for so little an amount. You took him for tens of thousands, didn't you? And your husband paid the ultimate price for your greed."

"His greed!" Mrs. Carver snapped. "He wanted me to make more. He wanted more copies even though I begged him to let me do my own work. He died because he just couldn't stop!" Mrs. Carver fell into a chair and put her hands to her face, crying. "He left me here alone and I don't know how to do it."

Mercy and Walker exchanged glances.

"Where are they, Mrs. Carver?" Walker pressed.

She closed her eyes, defeated. "The attic," she said after a long pause. "I kept them safe in the attic."

Mercy saw Walker's face alight at the revelation. "Thank you," Mercy said. "We appreciate your honesty."

Walker was already at the door, waving the uniformed officers inside. "They're in the attic, boys," he said.

Mercy knelt down in front of Mrs. Carver and offered her a clean handkerchief. "Mrs. Carver?" she said, reaching over and placing a hand on Mrs. Carver's knee. "You aren't the only one taken in by the man in your life," she said sympathetically. "I don't know what is going to happen to you after this, but I do know that you'll do the best you can."

Mrs. Carver lifted her gaze, amazed by Mercy's confidence. "How do you know?"

"We women can handle more than we think. It's only when we are challenged that we truly learn how strong we really are."

MacNeal appeared then, handcuffs at the ready.

Mrs. Carver nodded her gratitude to Mercy and raised her wrists so MacNeal could place her in handcuffs.

"Maybe you could come visit me in jail. You could do another tarot reading for me," she said as MacNeal pulled her up from the chair.

Mercy stood up and nodded. "My pleasure."

Chapter 32

"Are you going to see Detective Walker again?" Edith asked, twisting the mound of dough over the pastry board.

Mercy was cutting apples on the other side of the table and stopped the minute Walker's name was brought up. She said nothing and after a few minutes Edith spoke again.

"Did he get in a lot of trouble?"

Mercy raised an eyebrow.

"Maxwell told me he could lose his job for harbouring a murderess."

"He didn't know she was a murderess, not at the time," Mercy said. She took a breath and started peeling her apple once more. "Honestly, I don't know, but I don't think so. Walker's too valuable as a detective," she said, after taking a moment to compose herself.

"Why hasn't he come to visit us?" Edith asked.

"Ruth's trial only ended last week."

Edith's expression soured at the mention of Ruth's name.

"She's his wife, Edith," Mercy said. "Nothing can be done for that."

"He can divorce her—"

"Edith!"

"I was reading up about it. A man can divorce a wife on the grounds of insanity. I believe this situation applies," Edith said evenly.

Mercy shook her head. "I won't get between a man and his wife," she said, "no matter how much I think she doesn't deserve him."

"She doesn't," Edith said. "We deserve him."

Mercy lowered the apple and knife in her hands. "We?"

Edith gave a weak nod and looked as if she could cry.

"Oh, darling," Mercy said, rubbing her forehead. "Only providence knows what's in store for us. I can't... I've never made any promises to you. It's you and me, that's what I know for sure." She rounded the table and pulled her daughter into her. "It will always be you and me, no matter what."

Mercy felt Edith nod into her shoulder.

A knock sounded from the front door. Edith pulled away, a look of anticipation on her face. "It's him," she said.

Mercy shook her head. "Edith."

Edith dashed down the hallway and through open the door. Lottie stood on the porch.

"Come quick, Ms. Eaton," she said. "Mrs. Doyle is having another fit."

Mercy went to the hall table to grab her shawl and hat. "It's been weeks since she's had one," she said. "I thought she was doing better."

"This one is bad," Lottie said. "Worse than the others, I dare say."

გ ა

Mercy entered the funeral home and found it quiet and empty. Since Alexander's death the business had been closed. At first, Constance said it was temporary, a week, two at the most, but then weeks turned into months and now it was autumn and still the lower level of the home remained untouched.

Mercy climbed the main set of stairs, pulling at her hatpin as she went. The farther up she went the louder Constance's cries became.

"Connie?" Mercy put her hat on a stool on the top of the stairs and removed her shawl. "Honey?"

She found her sister crouched up in a corner, her arms circling her bent knees, crying despondently. Maggie slept soundly in a nearby cot, oblivious to the plight of her adoptive mother.

"Constance?" Mercy moved closer and then knelt in front of her, but Constance did not move or acknowledge her sister's presence. "Can I do something to help you?" Mercy asked. "A cup of tea, perhaps." Minutes passed without a response. "You really aught to stop this," Mercy said. "He doesn't deserve so many tears."

Constance shook her head. "I can't do it," she said. "I can't do anything on my own. How am I supposed to do this on my own?"

Mercy placed her hands on top of Constance's and gave a gentle squeeze. "Oh, but Connie, you have been doing it on your own for years. All this time, you've taken care of everything."

Constance shook her head in protest.

"Yes, you have!" Lottie said from behind Mercy. "I've seen you, ma'am. You'd run circles around Mr. Doyle. He weren't nearly as capable as you are."

"See?" Mercy said. "We all see how good you are. We know how independent you can be. Constance, you have to believe us!"

"I can't do it," she said through a fresh round of tears.

"Yes, yes you can." Mercy stood and grabbed her sister's hands to pull her to her feet. "Now, that's enough of that. Let's get up and make an apple pie."

"Mercy, you're being cruel," Constance whined. Mercy yanked her to her feet.

"I am not," she protested. "I am doing the very best for that little girl over there and I expect the same from you. Do you think raising Edith on my own was a picnic? Absolutely not. It was difficult, but I did it."

"But I'm not you," Constance said. "I'm not strong like you. I'll never be as strong as you."

"Oh yes you are. You've just been under Alexander's shadow this entire time and I say it's time to shine. Let's go..." She guided Constance to the kitchen. "You interrupted my pie baking, so now you are going to make it up to me. Besides, your pies are so much better than mine anyway."

"It's the pastry," Constance said, wiping away a few last tears. "You have to make a good pastry."

"Then show me," Mercy said, handing her sister an apron. "Tell me what to do and let's see if I can't copy you."

Constance nodded and tied the apron around her waist. "You can't come over here every day and coax me into teaching you how to make pies."

"Of course not, there's cakes and puddings and—"

"Mercy."

"I need you, Constance. Maggie needs you. Edith needs you. You can't give up that easily."

A moment passed, a quiet moment of understanding and realization. "All right," Constance said, with a determined nod. "Grab the apples."

ॐ   ॐ

Mercy returned home later that afternoon, a cooled pie tucked in a basket she borrowed from Constance. She wondered if Edith had taken it upon herself to finish what they had started earlier in the day. She walked through the front door and placed the basket on the floor so she could remove her hat and shawl.

"Edith... Edith, I'm back," Mercy called out. "Don't worry about Aunt Connie, she'll be—" Mercy stopped at the sight of Walker in the doorway to her kitchen. "Oh."

"Good afternoon, Ms. Eaton," he said, rather formally.

"Hello, Detective Walker." She smoothed out the fold of her skirt and checked the bottom of her blouse.

"Edith let me in. We hope that's all right," he said.

"Yes," Mercy said, stammering slightly. "Of course. You are always welcome here."

He moved into the hall. "I want to apologize for not coming sooner."

She waved off his apology. "Don't fuss," she said. "I know how busy you've been with the trial and everything."

"She was found guilty."

"I know. I read it in the papers."

According to Alistair George and the other newspapermen, Ruth had been promised a position within Ezekiel London's new enterprise as madam. "She had begun to erroneously envision herself as akin to other well-known madams of the region," George wrote in his less-than-flattering report about her. The offer of employment, however, was under condition that she kill Edward Dubois, the man who had facilitated the sales of the forgery artwork, and then set Detective Inspector Jeremiah Walker up for his murder. The plan was to effectively kill two birds with one stone.

"I've decided to petition the judge to rule out the death penalty. She'll spend life in jail but..."

"No, of course... it's better than the alternative." Mercy met his gaze and quickly looked away. She could not handle his intensity, not anymore. "Did you get in much trouble?" she asked, trying to sound light and unaffected.

"A little, but nothing I can't handle."

"Good. This city needs officers like you." Mercy smiled awkwardly and tried to pass him to the kitchen.

"I'm seeking a divorce," he said before she made it to the door.

Mercy turned to look at him. "Oh?"

"I filed the paperwork months ago, before the trial even started," he said. "I bet you didn't read that in the papers."

Mercy shook her head. "No, they left out that part."

"Not salacious enough, I guess, as the 'devoted police officer husband of a convicted murderess.'"

"No, I guess not." Mercy smiled.

"I... I just wanted you to know," he said. "I wanted you to know that I don't love her anymore. I haven't for a long time. Maybe I never did."

Mercy shifted her weight from one leg to the other. She couldn't bring herself to look at him, not while everything was so unsure between them. Coming to terms with the fact he no longer loved his wife was entirely different from confessing his love for Mercy.

"It's always good to know where you stand," she said, and immediately regretted it.

"Exactly," he said. "I guess I also wanted to stop in to thank you for all your work... on the case."

Mercy nodded. "Don't think of it."

"No, Ms. Eaton, you've been a great asset."

She raised an eyebrow. "An asset?"

"Yes, a real benefit."

She offered a closed-mouth smile. This wasn't quite how she'd hoped the conversation would unfold.

"I guess I should be on my way then," he said, moving for the door. "Thanks for all your assistance, Ms. Eaton." He paused briefly before turning to the door.

"Walker..."

"Yes?"

"When are you going to start calling me Mercy?"

His gaze went to the floor and he pressed his lips together.

"You can call me Mercy, you know," she said. "I don't mind."

"No, ma'am," he said.

Mercy's heart sank.

"If it's all the same, I'd prefer not to call you Mercy until I have the privilege of calling you wife."

About Tracy L. Ward

A former journalist and graduate from Humber College's School for Writers, Tracy L. Ward is the author behind the best-selling Marshall House Mysteries which tells the story of morgue surgeon, Dr. Peter Ainsley, and his highborn sister, Margaret Marshall, as they solve crimes using early forensic science. Mercy Me is the first book in a new series set in 19th century Toronto. Currently, Tracy lives on a rural property outside Barrie, Ontario with her husband and their two teenagers.

To find out more about Tracy's books follow her on www.facebook.com/TracyWard.Author or visit her website at www.gothicmysterywriter.blogspot.com

www.ingramcontent.com/pod-product-compliance
Lightning Source LLC
Chambersburg PA
CBHW051105030726
47504CB00006B/1796